THE LAST STAR STANDING

A Psychological Thriller

C.G. TWILES

HURACAN
PUBLISHING

Ebook cover design by Mary Cain

Paperback cover design by Cathy's Covers

More about the author: CGTwiles.com

Prologue

*I*n three minutes, I'll be a murderer.

A famous one. Because the man I'm about to kill is very famous. Me, much less so. He's recognized regularly on the streets. Me, not anymore, especially not in my "condition."

But my semi-fame combined with his worldwide fame means I'll be known more for a murder than for anything else I've done thus far in my life. Even my win.

I never wanted to be famous for murder.

I shouldn't say "murder." In law circles, that would mean the murder was planned, premeditated. And no one but me will know that was the case. Well, my "friend" will know. But my "friend" will never tell.

With any luck, my act of taking a human life will fade into obscurity, much as it has with other celebrities who have killed. You don't think that's happened? Put "celebrity manslaughter" into a search engine. You'll be shocked. Some of your favorites are there. Drunk driving accidents, hit-and-runs, fights, shootings. The majority of these celebrities served a few months in prison, if that, and went on with their lives. For all I know, this might boost my career.

That's a terrible, dark joke, a coping mechanism. The inside of my mouth is filled with cold, coppery adrenaline, long streams of clammy sweat are rolling down my neck and back, and my hands are trembling powerfully.

According to the timetable above, it's two minutes until I need to do something that I was not born to do. This is not who I am, not on any level. I'm going to cross a line that shouldn't be crossed. One I can never come back from. My body is trying to overrule the determination of my brain. But the very real sweating and shaking, it's all helping my performance.

I've already put my hand to my forehead a few times, as if dizzy. I've looked down at the dirty tiled floor, shook my head, confused, and swayed slightly like a newborn giraffe. Several times, I've reached my hands protectively around my swollen stomach.

Two minutes.

Now I act like I've just seen him. I'm squinting at him, craning my neck around some commuters, opening my lips slightly, trying to decipher if the man in the baseball cap is who I think he is. Yes, yes, it *is* he standing over there. Surveillance cameras will pick it all up, and each move will be blasted throughout every media outlet. I have to play it right.

I'm walking towards him—unsteadily, hands cupped around my stomach, determined to say hello to him despite my quickly weakening state. It wouldn't be out of the question for a pregnant woman to faint, especially as I'd nearly fainted last week. Conveniently, this was documented at the hospital.

I have a bottle of water in my hands. When I'm about ten feet from him, I'll suddenly stop, let the bottle tumble from my fingers, and lurch towards him. I'll plunge directly into his back as I fall, making sure I remain on the platform. That will be the most difficult part, not going over with him.

Closer, get closer. Closer. Remember to turn to the side so that when you fall you can come down with your arms outstretched and not land on your stomach.

One minute, according to the timetable. I hear the distant rumble of the train and feel its soft, quaking approach under my feet. He's looking towards the train gulley.

He has less than a minute to live.

Chapter One

"*I*t's Amy Baldash of *Entertainment Daily*," said the woman on the phone. "You probably don't remember me."

"Amy!" said Piper, not remembering. "Sure I do."

Entertainment Daily she did remember, of course. She'd been on three covers. One with the *American Star* top ten finalists and two on her own: one right after her win, one when her first album debuted. She vaguely remembered a perky, brunette twenty-something reporter who'd profiled her for both solo covers. She supposed Amy was the reporter in question.

It was Piper's job—or *used* to be her job—to remember people in the business, their names and faces, and she'd been good at it. But the pregnancy seemed to have softened her brain, dulled the edges of her recall.

"Am I bothering you?" Amy asked. "I didn't think you'd pick up and was going to leave a message."

"Not bothering me at all. To what do I owe the pleasure?" she asked, though she pretty much knew to what she owed the pleasure. There would be no other reason an entertainment reporter would be calling her these days.

Piper turned from the sink, where she'd been washing dishes before picking up the phone, and sat down at the dark mahogany antique dining table she'd been excited to find at a flea market. Only five hundred dollars and the sturdy, monstrous thing sat eight people.

She also pressed "stop" on the song list she'd made on her laptop. She liked to listen to her favorites while doing chores. Her tastes were eclectic: Elliott Smith, Tori Amos, Johnnie Taylor, Crosby Stills & Nash, Janis Joplin, Carole King, Stevie Wonder, Patsy Cline.

Her mother had loved music, and so had her grandmother, an organ and piano teacher who'd introduced her to Frank Sinatra, Billie Holiday, and Rosa Rio. Her mother used to tell Piper that she'd come out of the womb singing, insisting that her cries were melodious.

In the past, she would have belted out to any song she liked that happened to play anywhere, but now she only listened. Ever since the paralyzed vocal cord, her singing voice occasionally sounded strange and dissonant to her, and after her indie albums failed, she became convinced this wasn't her imagination.

"I'm not sure if you're aware," Amy said, "you probably are, but next month is the tenth anniversary of Season 7."

"Is it?" Piper asked, convincingly. She hadn't been sure that the ten-year anniversary would inspire an actual interview rather than a bunch of round-ups with no primary sourcing, but apparently, it would.

Ten years. It seemed much, much longer, a lifetime ago, that she'd stood on that stage and heard the most outrageous words she could ever imagine: "And the winner, last Star standing, and new *American Star* izzzzzzzz… Piper Dunner!"

Pronounced with manic enthusiasm by host Mitch McCabe, the words momentarily echoed in her mind, clear as anything.

"We're doing a round-up, a where-are-they-now kind of thing, on the top ten," Amy continued. "Of course, we want the first person to be you. You've had so much post-*Star* success. I'd love some more details."

Piper cradled her bowling ball-sized belly and hiked her feet up on a chair. Amy was a good reporter—acting like she didn't know Piper's post-*Star* success had long since faded. If Amy didn't know, the fact that she hadn't spoken to Piper in at least eight years should have clued her in.

As far as the music business went, a person could be busy finding the cure for cancer, yet considered a pathetic failure if not topping charts, releasing albums or singles, and selling out venues. And Piper was far from finding a cure for cancer. But she was proud of the strides she'd made within the past year in getting a new career going, and those she'd made in her personal life.

"Well, I got married and my first child is due in December. There's your exclusive on that."

"Oh, congratulations!" Amy enthused. "Can I use your spouse's name? And what does your partner do?"

"Sure, Porfirio Romano." She spelled it before Amy

would have to ask. "I call him Firio. He's a wonderful man and in finance."

"That's great," Amy said, though Piper knew it must be fairly boring news. Still, Amy was doing an excellent job at sounding interested. "Any projects you'd like to let us know about?" she prodded, then added, "Besides motherhood?"

Piper knew this was code for, "Are you still working in the business? Or have you slunk back to obscurity because—let's face it—you didn't make it."

"I do a lot of audiobook narrating," Piper said. "I read *The Nantucket Wives*, which was number one on the *New York Times* bestseller list."

"Did you?" Amy asked, still doing a fair job of sounding impressed. "That's fascinating. I love those audible books. I'll have to get that one." She paused, and Piper let her twist in the wind, curious as to how she'd phrase her next question.

"And... any singing?"

Piper pondered how honest she should be, whether she should allow a smidge of bitterness to sour her tone. Whether she should even go so far as to say something like, "I would have loved for it all to work out, to be Beyoncé-famous right now. But that didn't happen and it took me a long time not to be irritated every day about it."

But that was a fantasy. No one could say something like that and live it down. It would be on her gravestone. So she said, "Nope, no singing. You probably know that only the very top make decent money releasing music these days. The money is in touring and live events. I didn't have the stamina for that anymore, and I'm enjoying my new life, and I'm pregnant, so…" She shrugged into the phone.

"Of course. Hard to go on the road with a baby on the way."

"That's for sure."

Not that she would have had a choice anyway. Amy must know that Piper had been dropped by her label seven years ago and had only released two indie albums in the meantime, and neither had sold well. Amy had refrained from mentioning all this, but Piper had no doubt it would all be in the story.

No matter how positively the article was slanted, Piper would still come across as having squandered the massive opportunity winning *American Star* had lain at her feet. People online constantly said things like, "What happened to her? She was so talented. Why isn't she still famous?" and "The runner-up is more famous. Hayden should have won! He was robbed! The show was rigged!"

She waited because she was sure it was coming, could tell by the way Amy was silent with only the very faint sound of her breathing.

"Do you still keep in touch with any of the group?" she asked, cautiously.

"A few months ago, I saw Ben Gables when he played at the Soul Café. I saw Bailie Slinger when she came to Carnegie Hall. Jojo Barr and I are still friends." She knew that wasn't what Amy wanted to know, but damned if she was going to voluntarily bring him up. Let Amy earn her salary.

"That's amazing." Amy paused. Here it comes. "Ever speak to Hayden?"

"I haven't spoken to Hayden in years," Piper said, joyfully, as if the name had opened up a treasure trove of precious memories. "But I saw *Ghosts of Time* and I'm so glad he won the Oscar. He deserved it."

So there it was, put to words. The *American Star* runner-up was enormously successful. And the winner wasn't. Feed those wolves and trolls, Amy. Enjoy!

"He was very good," Amy agreed. "Have you had a chance to see *Loverly* yet?"

Loverly was Hayden's big Broadway hit. He'd been nominated for a Tony Award, which Piper remembered with some small degree of satisfaction, he hadn't won.

"No, I haven't. But if you speak with him, be sure to tell him I'd love a couple of tickets," Piper laughed. "It's easier to get into Area 51."

"I'll pass that along," Amy laughed back. "I wanted to call you first, but hopefully I'll reach him soon."

This was code for, "He's much more famous than you are. I can't call his cell phone as I could for you. I'll have to go through his publicist."

"Tell him I said hello and I'm so proud of him," Piper said. Let Amy print *that*.

"I will. Do you have any recent photos you can send me for the piece? One with your husband would be great."

"Oh, I don't think he wants that kind of attention, but I can send you a few of me. The last good ones I have are from before the pregnancy."

"That's fine. Whichever you prefer." Amy gave her

email address so Piper could send the photos. Then she said, "None of us will ever forget the battle of the Glory Notes."

"The Glory Notes" was what Piper and Hayden had been nicknamed, for the obvious reason that both of them could hold inordinately long notes. When the finale came down to the two of them, the press had labeled it "The Epic Battle of the Glory Notes."

"I won't forget it either," Piper said. "Such a great time in my life."

They spoke for about ten more minutes, and Amy, seeming to realize that the question would go nowhere, didn't bother to ask about the "love/hate relationship" the press and much of the public had invented for Piper and Hayden.

This supposed attraction between the pair contributed as much as the rivals' powerful long notes to drawing a record number of viewers to the finale. The ratings had been on a slow downward slide, thanks to cable and large blocks of viewers who'd vow to never watch again once a favorite had been voted off—and who apparently meant it.

But more viewers tuned in for the seventh season finale than any since the show's inception, and up until Season 10, when *American Star* went off the air. The show's star judge, the cranky and no-nonsense but still somehow charming music executive Nolan Ferrari, left for greener pastures, and the network had decided to pull the plug.

The show had been a ratings juggernaut, with a combined eighty million people tuning in twice each week for the performance and elimination shows, almost a quarter of the country's population, second only to the Super Bowl. You could take the next three most popular shows, add up their ratings, and it still wouldn't equal the number of people who'd faithfully watched *American Star*.

It was all the more impressive because, at the time, talent competitions had been considered tawdry and passé, a leftover from another era. But this one had a few special ingredients—Nolan Ferrari's scathing wit, a willingness to humiliate sincere but off-key singers on air, and to everyone's great surprise, it immediately began launching superstars who not only sold millions but also won prestigious awards.

Network television would never see anything like it again.

After hanging up with Amy, Piper felt a deep heaviness creeping into her chest, the kind of heaviness that always seeped in when she thought too much about her career, all she'd had, and all she'd lost. But it wasn't the brutal heaviness she'd had when her career started to go downhill only a year after her *American Star* win.

The thick melancholy in her chest ebbed away as she rubbed her belly and looked around her pretty, sunlit kitchen. Even a year ago, the phone call she'd had with Amy would have sent her into a depressive tailspin.

But now, that wasn't going to happen. She felt pretty good about the interview, and to hell with people who would make snide comments about her failed shot at long-term stardom.

Pop stardom had a short window of opportunity

before one was considered too old to break out. She'd had that opportunity at the perfect age—twenty-four—but by the time she'd recovered from the paralyzed vocal cord, an apartment fire that destroyed years' worth of demos, and helping her mother as she succumbed to cancer, Piper was pressing up against thirty.

For most industries, this would be considered young. The music business wasn't most industries.

But Piper was happy again. She had a kind-hearted, hard-working, handsome husband, and a baby on the way. And the new narration career was giving her deep enjoyment. Not the kind of sky-touching elation that singing used to give her, but still a sense of pride and accomplishment.

Let Hayden have the Oscar, the multi-platinum albums, the world tours, and the Broadway hit. Let him have the *Entertainment Daily* cover, for no doubt he would get it, while Piper and the rest of the top ten finalists would be buried on the inside pages.

It was here in her new kitchen that Piper had an epiphany. Memories of *American Star* and the blinding burst of short-lived fame that followed it now settled on her with wistfulness and pride instead of mental torture and heartbreak.

Caressing her rotund belly, she looked down and said, "What do you think about that? Your mommy was famous once, but now I have a better job—cooking up your existence."

Chapter Two

"*N*ow girl, come on! It's been ten years. Let's watch it!"

Jojo was grinning at her from across the slick, dark-gray granite kitchen island in her beautiful Chelsea apartment, a glass of red wine in hand. Piper had her own glass, as her doctor had told her it was fine to drink alcohol in small amounts, but she was only taking baby sips as the smell of wine could bring on small waves of nausea. The sips were so insignificant they were more for psychological effect, like placebo drinking.

Jojo was back in town, and the two had agreed to get together to have their own little tenth-anniversary cele-bration. A copy of *Entertainment Daily* lay near a plate of Chinese dumplings, and they'd already read the article together.

It was a nice story, with each top ten finalist, listed in order of where they placed in the contest, having half a page about them. Piper and Hayden each had one page to themselves. This was gracious of the magazine, as

Hayden—with his impressive career—certainly deserved more coverage than Piper did.

In fact, she wished the magazine had given her less coverage. Her talk of her marriage, book narration job, and pregnancy ("I've been craving watermelon and okra!") was hardly riveting material and would only leave her open to being mocked. At least her failed indie albums hadn't been mentioned.

As expected, Hayden had the cover to himself. He either hadn't aged in the slightest or had been Photo-shopped to a waxy sheen. His sleepy hazel eyes were greener than Piper remembered, or had been digitally enhanced.

He had on his famous "crooked grin" with the right side of his mouth sloping up towards his cheek. The dark brown hair was expertly tousled. Piper remem-bered how the *Star* hairstylists had spent almost as much time on his hair as they had on hers, fluttering around him with an array of acidic-smelling gels and ozone-depleting sprays.

"Humph," Jojo scoffed when she saw the cover. "*You* won, not him."

Piper had waved her off. It was painfully obvious who the "real winner" was. Now Jojo was insisting they watch a video of the crowning moment on YouTube.

Piper hadn't seen this seminal event in her life since she'd watched it on TiVo a week after the finale. There had been no watching it on the night in question, as the show aired live and, afterward, she'd been busy with back-to-back media and desperately trying to snatch catch-up sleep. Through the years, she'd had no real desire to watch it again, much as a divorcée might not wish to watch her wedding again.

But Jojo wouldn't be dissuaded. "Ready?" she asked, cursor poised on the "play" button.

Piper took a larger sip of wine than intended and nodded, saying, "Do it before I change my mind."

Jojo hit the button and the familiar *American Star* graphics—a red star flipping within a golden moon—swirled into the frame over the catchy, hard-beating theme music.

On screen, Piper and Hayden were standing next to each other on the stage of the Hollywood Theater in Los Angeles, with host Mitch McCabe on the far right side.

Piper was struck by how young and skinny both she and Hayden appeared. What people didn't realize was how exhaustively taxing the show was. By the end of it, most of the finalists had lost at least ten pounds.

There was a jump-cut to the darkened audience and the back of the judges' table, at which sat acerbic British talent scout Nolan Ferrari, record producer Miles Bennett, and singer Crystal Pell who, at the time, was still selling a decent amount of records. (Biggest hit: "He's Lying, You're Crying.")

As the audience whooped and cheered, the camera swooshed down from an upper balcony to the three slight figures on the stage. Piper regretted her choice of a pale pink one-shoulder gown that, at the time, had seemed glamorous in a Princess Diana kind of way.

Hayden looked scruffily attractive with his dark

bedhead-gelled hair, three-day stubble, and tuxedo jacket over black jeans and a long-sleeved white shirt.

Mitch, Ken-doll handsome with blonde curly hair and a golden tan, began his hyper-patter: "We're live from downtown Los Angeles with the results. In a few minutes, America will have a new American Star, picked by *your* votes!"

He went on to say that ninety-eight million votes had been cast, the most in the show's history, and had created a new world record for number of calls made at the same time.

"Ninety-eight million!" Jojo cooed at Piper.

A stiff-looking man from some kind of "vote management company" walked out on stage and handed Mitch an envelope.

Piper's heartbeat kicked up a notch and she found herself tightly clasping the stem of her wine glass, as if she didn't know who the winner would be. It was bizarre how much of this defining moment of her life she didn't remember, not even the man coming out with the envelope.

Everything had been a wash, a noisy blur in her mind, too much stimuli for her brain to process. She'd gone numb, checked out. Yet looking at the vision of her younger self, with chestnut hair glossily coiled on her shoulders and a pearly smile, twenty-four-year-old Piper appeared serene and composed.

More stuff happened that she barely had any recollection of. The judges gave their "final comments," congratulating them both and refusing to call a winner when Mitch pressed. This was unheard of. It was expected that at least Nolan, who never minced words, would call a winner. But he'd said, "For the first time in all my years of judging talent, it's too close for me to call."

Then Mitch, microphone up to his mouth, leaned towards them, punching out the words: "This has been one of the most exciting shows I can remember and you're both winners."

Hayden, who looked his usual unconcerned self, put his arm around her. Piper watched as her younger self smiled even wider, and laid her head on his shoulder. The audience's cheers rose to a deafening crescendo as Mitch raised his eyebrows at the camera as if to say, "See? We knew they liked each other."

"Best of luck to you both, Glory Notes," he said, and opened the envelope.

"Here we go," Jojo said, giddily.

"Ladies and gentlemen, by the tightest margin yet, only one million votes, the winner, last Star standing, and new American Star iiiiiiiiiiizzzzzzzz...." Mitch drew out the suspense while the audience's cheers roiled like an angry ocean.

Piper saw her younger self rest her chin on Hayden's chest. The pair then stared into each other's eyes. Hayden bit his lower lip and looked out over the crowd. Young Piper closed her eyes, her smile disintegrating into a tense line. Someone in the audience screamed a stream of gibberish, and all at once the audience grew hushed.

"Piper Dunner!"

The audience roared. This, Piper remembered. The

roar had been so strong it was like a physical slap of gale-force wind at her face.

On stage, her eyes popped open and her hand flew to her mouth. Hayden turned and was hugging her. This, she remembered too, sort of. The pair rocked back and forth in each other's arms, and Hayden clasped her by the cheeks and was talking into her face. Whatever he'd said, she would never know, because the thunder of the crowd was too overpowering.

Piper watched as her younger self finally withdrew from the hug, looking like she might fall down. The camera panned to the cheering, standing audience. And to her parents, who had their mouths open in screams. And to Hayden's parents, who were politely clapping.

"Tell us how you're feeling, Piper," Mitch directed.

"I—I—I'm so—so grateful, and humbled, and—and —thank you—thank youuuuu—and—oh my gosh, I didn't expect this—I—oh my gosh—"

"This is cringey," Piper mumbled, as Jojo rubbed her on the shoulder.

Hayden had moved away from center stage, leaving young Piper in the wide, white spotlight. The music swelled up and she began singing the coronation song that would be her first single, "There's Nothing Between Me and My Dream."

As was typical for *American Star* coronation songs, Piper's tune had topped the iTunes chart at number one an hour after the finale aired. Even in her youthful, almost religious-like fervor for *American Star*, she knew her winning song had a facile melody and every bald-faced cliché imaginable for lyrics, the most notoriously laughable being, "I'm mellow like Jell-O; I'm sweet as marshmallow."

But having her talent validated after so many years of struggle allowed her to sing the lines with authentic tears in her eyes.

Music wasn't about entertainment so much as human connection. The lyrics weren't as important as the message. Everyone had a dream, after all.

Confetti flurried around the theater as if it was in a giant snow globe that had been shaken. Sparkle-showers of white light rained down above the amethyst-lit, special-built space-age stage. The show was awash in hundreds of millions in advertising dollars and no expense had been spared.

The scene ended as Piper, surrounded by the other top ten finalists, cry-sang her last note. The camera practically fondled her teary face as she unfurled one of her signature glory notes, a seventeen-second hold, in a sustained, resonate B4.

Jojo closed her laptop. "Not so bad, eh? Do you remember what Hayden said to you?"

"No. I don't even think I heard him. I was in complete shock. I'd assumed he had it in the bag."

"He looked happy that you won."

Piper only took another baby-sip of wine and tore apart a dumpling.

"Maybe he wasn't as much of a dick as we thought," Jojo continued. "We were so young. You and I had some experience, a lot of us did, but Hayden... he came from a bar in the middle of the cornfields. Where was it?"

"Iowa."

"I don't know...." Jojo shrugged. "He could have been intimidated and it came out as an attitude problem."

"So you don't hate him anymore for stealing your song?" Piper asked, teasingly.

"I did kind of hate him for awhile, didn't I?"

"*Kind* of?" Piper laughed.

Hayden's peak had come with an unpredictable performance of Aretha Franklin's "I Say A Little Prayer." He'd arranged the boppy R&B song into an alt-rock tune with a slightly sneering edge. In his hands, the lyrics about a prayer sounded more like a threat than a sweet blessing. The audience and judges had loved it. Nolan had used his highest praise, terming the song choice "brave."

But Hayden's song choice kicked off the end of Jojo's run. Everyone else had stayed away from the song, knowing it most suited Jojo. But the day of song selections, Jojo had been in her hotel room trying to sleep off the flu.

By the time she'd recovered enough to claim a song, she'd been left with a small batch to choose from and stumbled for the first time with Nancy Sinatra's "These Boots Are Made for Walking." The cynical, talky tune didn't match her big, emotional voice.

The next night, she'd been eliminated in sixth place. It was considered the most shocking boot of the season, perhaps of every season. The press had called her "the next Adele" and she'd always topped polls of who was expected to take the crown.

When she was prematurely booted, the public, and

even some of the press, blamed Nolan, saying he'd rigged the votes so that a nearly three-hundred-pound woman wouldn't win.

But both Jojo and Piper doubted Nolan had vote-rigging powers. If he had, surely Hayden would have been dispatched earlier.

The two men, both alpha-male to the core, had clashed a few times, Hayden unwilling to take Nolan's insults without a few words in his own defense. It was a gutsy but foolhardy thing to do as the audience usually voted off anyone who back-talked Nolan. But Hayden had miraculously gotten away with it.

Piper even somewhat credited his taking Jojo's song with her win, as his unorthodox performance made her realize she needed to step up her game. The next week she'd done a piano ballad arrangement of Radiohead's "Karma Police," a risk with an audience not known for appreciating alternative music. But it had been a success, finally cementing her position as a frontrunner.

"It all worked out," Jojo said, helping herself to a dumpling. It was the first one Piper had seen her eat; she hoped Jojo wasn't back to dieting.

Jojo had said she'd come to *American Star* happy with her body, but when Nolan had made a nasty crack on camera about her weight during her audition ("How big is our stage this year?"), it had triggered the beginnings of her being self-conscious.

When she saw how thin everyone else was getting thanks to the show's punishing schedule, she'd felt even more out of place. That had sent her into a long stretch of yo-yo dieting. But for the past few years, Jojo was again at peace with her body.

"I admit that for a long time I didn't like him for taking my song, but I'm happy with where I'm at," Jojo said, finishing off her dumpling.

Jojo had worked nonstop since the show, mostly in musical theater, but she was also in heavy demand at private events, for which she charged good money. She'd been able to buy a luxury two-bedroom condo overlooking the Hudson River, and her mom a house.

"What about you, hun?" Jojo asked. "You doing all right these days?"

"I am," Piper said, emphatically. "Narration is fun. The money is small but steady." She rubbed her stomach. "I need to not be stressed right now."

"Still don't know the gender?"

"No, Firio and I want it to be a surprise."

They were quiet. Then Jojo said, "It's all good. I wouldn't have predicted Hayden to be the one to go all the way, but it makes sense. He has that ruthless gene you need to get ahead in this business."

"He sure does."

Jojo placed her wine glass directly over Hayden's uptilted grin and unnaturally smooth face on the *Entertainment Daily* cover, and the pair laughed.

Chapter Three

*a*t home, Piper and her husband lay on the couch as he rubbed her feet with Shea butter. The city was suffering through an unseasonal mid-September heat spell, with crushing, furnace-like gales of heat. Although the walk from the subway to her front door was only a few blocks, her ankles had swollen into thick, pink skin-bands. She kept her feet hoisted up on a pillow on Firio's legs as a movie played in the background.

"How did it go?" he asked. "Did you manage to watch it?"

"I did. I had such mixed-up feelings about the show for so long, but I seem to have gotten over it. People would kill for a moment like that and I had one. I think I'm coming to a place of nostalgia about it."

"I didn't want to tell you this, but I've watched it a few times. You looked cute as a button. Even in that pink dress."

"Ugh," she said as he lifted one foot and playfully

kissed it. "That dress. Now *that* I would change if I could."

She remembered how she'd been stuck in the dress for twenty-four hours as she'd hurtled along from media event to media event. She'd gotten Jojo to go back to the hotel and meet her out with flats so she could dispose of her pinching high heels. All through the show, she'd felt the men had an unfair advantage being able to stalk around the stage in regular shoes.

"It's a great achievement," Firio said, dark eyes twinkling at her. Then he added, "Not the dress."

She smiled at him. "It's just hard to see it and know what comes after it."

"You had a big album. Not many people ever get that."

"Yeah, and Diamond Entertainment and my manager took most of the money. Then the vocal cord, and the fire, and my mom's death. It's like the damn thing cursed me." She grimaced and rubbed her throat. "I still can't sing properly. Sometimes I think I would have been better off not winning, like Jojo. I could have worked at my own pace. Sorry, I know you've heard all of this a million times."

"I'm sorry it still pains you so much, Bella," he said, using his pet name for her.

"Honestly, it doesn't. Not as much. I've got you, I've got *this*…" She patted her stomach. "I like my new job. I guess I'm scared. Things are too good. Something bad is going to happen."

"Don't think like that and it won't. Besides," he grinned. "I'll protect you."

He flopped her feet to one side. "Oh!" he said, standing. He walked to his briefcase, opened it, and took out an envelope. He handed the envelope to her and she saw it had already been slit open. She slipped out a folded sheet of paper. Inside were two tickets for *Loverly*.

"How did you…" She gaped questioningly at him.

"I didn't. Read the note."

Handwritten on the sheet of paper was:

Pip!

Long time, no see. That reporter said you wanted tix to the show, so here you go. I couldn't find you on social media!

There was literally only one Porfirio Romano in New York, and the story said he was in finance, so I figured this had to be his company address. Hope you can come! And if I got the wrong Porfirio Romano, then, hey man, if you want to come to the show, that's cool.

Hayden

PIP. THE ONLY PERSON in the world to call her Pip.

"Wow," Piper said, staring at the tickets. Hayden Tower had gone to the trouble of tracking down Firio to give them tickets. And no, he couldn't find her on social media, because a year ago when she'd decided to give up the ghost of a singing career, she'd deleted it all.

She had a small core of diehard fans, "Pipermints" they'd christened themselves on the show's forums. She felt guilty abandoning them but couldn't take their questions anymore about when she would tour again, when she'd make another album. It was impossible to tell fans, "There's not enough of you to make it financially viable for anyone."

Besides, her last series of events had been depressing. Held at beer halls and carnivals, people chattered through her new songs, a wall of painful and loud disinterest. All the more embarrassing as this was about the time she'd read that Hayden had been nominated for an Academy Award.

Speaking of Hayden, it was odd that he hadn't asked Amy Baldash for Piper's number and contacted her directly to ask if she wanted tickets, but she supposed this way would avoid awkwardness. Their relationship had never been wonderful but had deteriorated even more on the *American Star* tour, during which they'd hardly spoken to each other.

"You want to go?" Firio asked.

"I—sure."

She pasted a smile on her face as he turned his attention back to the movie.

Truth was, her ego was at stake. Watching Hayden shine in his Tony-nominated role while she trudged to a small recording studio three times a week, and otherwise puttered around her new house, setting up the baby room, and tending her small garden out back, could bring on a bout of fierce envy.

But she had gone to Jojo's shows. Those hadn't

made her envious—because she liked Jojo, and she wished only the best for her.

It was all about her dislike for Hayden, how he'd grabbed the song Jojo should have had. How he was always so icy and sneering towards her off air. How every time she came backstage after a performance, while the others congratulated her with enthusiasm, he'd say something like, "Little flat at the top, Pip" or "Not sure about those runs." As if he had the right to critique her! He fronted a bar band and not a very good one!

Then there was the worst incident. Nolan had been rapturous about her performance of Whitney Houston's version of "I Will Always Love You." The sharp-tongued judge had a reputation for mocking anyone who dared to take on Whitney, inevitably saying it sounded like "bad karaoke."

But the competitors were only given a small number of song choices for each show—ones that had been cleared for rights—and it was the only song left that Piper felt she could do justice. Nolan had loved her plain, heartfelt interpretation, and the bit of jazziness she'd put into it. He'd praised her performance, telling her it was the best version he could remember in the history of the show, and had even thanked her for "not trying to do Whitney."

When she'd come offstage, so high with euphoria she couldn't feel her feet, Hayden had been in the wings. When she'd passed him, he'd drawled, "You and Nolan wanna get a room?"

Piper had been so shocked that she'd laughed even

though she was irritated. By now, Hayden was known for his off-putting sense of humor.

But after the filming, Nolan had sought her out backstage to again tell her how much he'd liked her version. She was staring up at him with awe and gratitude because it was highly unusual for any of the judges to seek the contestants out privately. Especially Nolan. She had thanked him and, being young and extremely nervous, perhaps thanked him too profusely. After he'd left, she'd turned and saw Hayden watching her with that infuriating smirk on his face.

It was a few days later that Jojo, who was her roommate at the hotel, told her a rumor that was going around the cast—that Nolan and Piper were having an affair.

"Affair?!" Piper had screeched. "Because he liked my song? He barely acknowledges me off air! And isn't he gay?"

"I'm only telling you what I heard," Jojo said. "I didn't say it was true."

"And who did you hear this from? Hayden?"

"No, it wasn't him, and I don't want to say who and have you confront the person because I'll be the bad guy. I'll stamp it out for you."

"It had to be Hayden behind it," Piper growled. "I'm going to rip him a new one."

"No, girl, don't do that," Jojo warned. "Someone could squeal to the press. Then you're a diva. You know how this show is. They like their winners humble."

"Hayden's not humble!"

Every day Piper was busting her ass on the show.

They were all up at daybreak, learning and rehearsing their performance songs, recording full-length versions for iTunes, learning a group song and its choreography, and a song and its choreography for their sponsor's commercials. They often didn't get to bed until midnight.

It felt like months since she'd been in the sun. Piper had turned a shade so white her veins were practically visible. Sometimes she thought the winner would simply be the contestant who didn't drop dead from exhaustion.

The press and public constantly traded grassy-knoll conspiracy theories that producers and Nolan could somehow rig the votes to favor pet contestants. The last thing Piper wanted was the idea out there that voting had been tampered with to favor her because of the preposterous notion that she could sneak ten minutes into her jam-packed schedule to have sex with a judge.

It was even more provoking because, as she could see on the *American Star* website forums, viewers had started to rumormonger that Hayden and Piper had a "thing" going too.

As proof of their "love/hate" relationship, the fans screen-shotted any time the pair glanced at or touched each other during choreographed group numbers, and mused under threads about "Hayder," which included links to fan fiction. The cast had been warned not to read online commentary, as it might affect their performances.

"You don't know how seriously people take this show," the head producer, Oliver Corbyn, had told them. "You may think you know, but you don't. You'll see things written about yourself that you could never imagine. You'll never be able to unsee them."

But they were all young and giddy with the first taste of fame and basically held captive. And they were allowed to keep their laptops. So, of course, most of them sought out any mentions of themselves.

The "hate" portion of the alleged romance between Piper and Hayden stemmed mostly from one incident that embarrassingly took place live on air. Mitch had been taking call-in questions from the public, and one young woman asked if she could go on a date with Hayden.

As the audience roared and Hayden looked stumped as to how to answer, an eagle-eyed cameraman had caught Piper's reaction as she mouthed "Nooooo" to Jojo. Half the viewers thought this meant Piper herself was dating Hayden and he was off-limits to female fans; half thought Piper was expressing her distaste for Hayden. The two theories merged, and viewers decided the rivals had a "love/hate" dynamic.

(For the record, Piper hadn't mouthed "Nooooo" but "Oooohhhh myyyy" and the camera had "conveniently" cut away from the "myyyy." On such misinterpretations are kingdoms toppled and, in this case, thousands of fan fictions born.)

But all of that was ten years ago when they were practically kids. Presumably, everyone had matured. Perhaps, as Jojo had said, Hayden had been intimidated by the others' experience and hadn't just been a jerk.

Yes, she would go see *Loverly*. And she would even enjoy it, damn it.

Chapter Four

overly was good, really good. Hayden was excellent. His voice had always sounded like velvet spread with a thin layer of gravel, but now it had emotional nuances and vulnerability that Piper didn't remember from *American Star*.

He was a dynamic tenor with a ringing, dark timbre, who could transition flawlessly from raspy baritone to clarion falsetto. He was a little thicker in the waist (who wasn't?) and had a smattering of gray at the temples. But at thirty-three, he was a ruggedly attractive man.

His performance was thrilling, Piper admitted as she stood wildly clapping at the show's curtain call. And yes, she did feel several stabs of envy during the show, because if the vocal cord paralysis and everything that came after it hadn't happened, perhaps she too would be up there on a Broadway stage.

But then she wouldn't have met Firio and very likely wouldn't be pregnant now.

Besides, much worse could have happened to her.

Poor Dylan Lopez had died of cardiac arrest a year after coming in fifth place. Piper remembered that he'd just scored a big label deal too, and he'd had a wife and baby. His death was horrible and tragic, sending shockwaves throughout the top ten, all of whom had immediately contacted each other in shared grief.

Except Hayden. No one in the top ten could seem to reach him. As Dylan had been Hayden's roommate during the show, and the two had seemed close, Piper figured that he was too devastated to talk at the time.

Hayden and the cast took their bows, and as he came up front to take his solo bow, he blew a kiss where she and Firio sat in the second row, then called out, "My fellow Glory Note, Piper Dunner, everyone!"

The front row turned to stare and recognizing her, or at least pretending to, clapped in her direction. Her cheeks flamed with embarrassment though a part of her was quite pleased for the acknowledgment.

As she and Firio were getting ready to leave, a young woman in a black dress suit with a white tag around her neck that read "*Loverly* Backstage" came over to them. "Miss Dunner?" she officiously asked.

Piper nodded.

"Mr. Tower would like to meet both of you in his dressing room if you're available. I can escort you."

After following the young woman through a maze of hallways, the three of them arrived at a white door with "Hayden Tower" etched in a star plaque. The woman opened it and stood aside.

The room was fairly large, with mellow lighting, a long theater mirror, a white couch, a table with foodstuffs, and the richly sweet aroma of burning vanilla candles. About a dozen people milled inside the room. Piper didn't see Hayden until she heard, "Pip!"

He had changed into streetwear—jeans and a T-shirt with "Broadway Rocks" spelled out in light bulbs across his chest. He also had on glasses, the first time she'd ever seen him in them. Behind his blocky, rectangular frames, the sleepy hazel eyes that the female *Star* viewers had fallen in love with looked at her warmly, without any trace of the smug arrogance she remembered.

They hugged awkwardly—hugs were awkward with her third-trimester belly—and she heard herself gushing, "Hayden, you were so great. So, so great," and he was thanking her and shaking hands with Firio.

"Congratulations," Hayden said, in his soothing, slightly husky voice, indicating her stomach.

"Thank you, and thanks so much for the tickets."

A woman carrying a clipboard came over and murmured in Hayden's ear as he nodded pensively. "Okay, a few minutes," he told her, turning his attention to a tall, willowy woman with ice-blonde hair who'd sidled up to him. He put his arm around the blonde's waist. Piper thought he was about to introduce his wife or girlfriend, but he said, "Piper, Porfirio, this is Ava Smythson, my business manager. Anything good that's happened to me, it's because of her."

The woman smiled and shook their hands. "He's being modest," she said. Ava had a porcelain-skinned, old-Hollywood kind of face, and penetratingly dark blue—almost violet—eyes.

"Ava used to manage DJ Gold and Breaktown and The Rush Boys," Hayden said, puffed up with pride.

"Shh." Ava put one finger to her lips. "You're aging me."

"Oh, sorry," Hayden said, abashed.

"I'm kidding, darling." She looked at Piper. "Forty and proud of it. Every year gets better and better." She glanced meaningfully at Hayden and the look that passed between them made Piper feel they were more than business partners.

Piper doubted that Hayden's success was because of Ava, but his words brought to mind her former manager, Tony Cabera. Moxie Management had assigned him, and given that he'd helped usher other *American Star* winners to success, she'd thought he was a fitting choice.

But by the time he'd got to Piper, he seemed burned out and disinterested in her career, other than to suggest that she dye her chestnut hair blonde and shed ten pounds. Coming off the weight-melter that was *American Star*, she was 110 pounds on a five-five frame and had no intention of losing more. And forget dyeing her hair.

Nor had Tony backed her up when she'd begged the label to release "H-E-Double-L-No" as her third single. It was a song she'd written in a white heat after a fight with Marco, her sexy but moody drummer ex-boyfriend. But the label executives said the song was "too angry" for an *American Star* winner. They buried it as a bonus track that only appeared on preorders. Sure enough, the song ended up being quite popular—on YouTube, where she didn't see a dime from pirated uploads.

She wondered how differently things might have gone if she'd had someone like Ava to guide her career, someone who actually cared.

"He's lucky to have you," Piper told her.

"I'm lucky to have him," Ava responded, and there was a momentary snap, a steely spark, in her violet-blue eyes, leaving Piper with the fleeting sensation that Ava didn't like her. As Ava beamed a personable smile, the feeling floated away.

"Pip, I have to get outside and greet the masses," Hayden said. "But it's good to see you. Ten years is too long. And, hey, you remember this guy?" He turned and called, "Ferrari! Come greet someone!"

Piper saw Nolan Ferrari emerge from a small group of people near the back of the room and make his way over. He looked older but was doing an admirable job of trying to stave it off, and his face had the slightly stiff, unnaturally preserved look of one who regularly had Botox injections. His black hair was still thick but now flecked with silver. His teeth retained their glowing whiteness.

"Piper Dunner," he pronounced in his smooth British lilt. "Just the person I wanted to see."

"It's so good to see you. You haven't changed a bit," she said, hoping that didn't come across as an underhanded dig at his Botoxed face.

Hayden clapped Nolan on the shoulder. "Hey, man, I better get outside before they riot."

"Or leave," Nolan drawled. He hadn't lost his biting sense of humor.

Hayden grinned good-naturedly at him. "Let's talk more this week."

"If you don't call me, I'm calling you," Nolan said, flexing a bejeweled finger at him.

There was a round of goodbyes, and Hayden and Ava left, trailed by the woman with the clipboard.

Nolan looked straight at Piper in that supremely confident way he had, as if life had never given him one ounce of trouble or disappointment.

"Piper, I'd like to discuss something with you. My staff was going to track you down, but since you're here..." He looked at Firio, then back to her. "Can I bring you both for a nightcap, non-alcoholic for the expectant mother I presume, across the street at Shelby's?"

* * *

"Hayden was so good, don't you think?" Piper asked Nolan, almost expecting him to give one of his critiques.

"Absolutely," he said, nonchalantly, and ordered a Scotch on the rocks as the waitress arrived. Firio ordered a beer and Piper soda water with lime.

The trio sat a dark wood table in a back room at Shelby's. Gas lamps flickered on its scarlet walls, which were checkered with framed headshots of various celebrities. Shelby's was famous for attracting a Broadway crowd.

Piper could hardly believe Nolan Ferrari was sitting across from her. While her star had peaked, then crashed, after *American Star*, his had only kept rising. After the tenth season, he'd returned to London and headed up another talent show. This one had produced several bonafide stars, including a grandmotherly-looking fifty-year-old woman named Pearl Porter, whose audition showcasing her surreally angelic voice had become the most famous audition on the planet. She'd since sold millions of records.

Nolan had also founded one of the most successful girl bands in the world, Five Alive. Inviting Piper and Firio for a drink was unexpected, to say the least.

"He was very good," Firio nodded. "I'm not much of a theater guy, but I'd see this twice."

Piper was pleased that Firio had enjoyed *Loverly* so much, given that he'd never seemed interested in show business, part of what drew her to him. Though she had to admit it, deep down she was a little peeved that her husband would never get to see her shining on stage, unless he looked up her videos online, which was hardly the same thing.

"*American Star* has only launched a few superstars, to be honest," Nolan said, in that frank fashion that went a long way towards making him tolerable. Anyone else would have insisted the show had produced more stars than are in the universe. "Hayden's one of them. I admit that's one I didn't see coming. Talented? Yes. Superstar material? I didn't think so." He leaned towards Piper and spoke in his clipped, confident tone. "*You're* the one I'd thought would be where he is right now. When I heard you sing at your first audition, I thought, *a star is born*."

Piper squirmed uncomfortably. Nolan was a partner

in Diamond Entertainment, the label that had released her debut album. It had gone platinum, thanks to her *American Star* coronation song "There's Nothing Between Me and My Dream," and a single written by judge Crystal Pell, "You Were My Forever, Now You're My Never."

Three years later, after her series of disasters that kept her from recording a label follow-up, it had dropped her. Tony hadn't even bothered to call with the news. Piper had heard it on the radio, then had to call him to get confirmation. That was the music business for you. For every one true visionary, there were a dozen cowards and snakes.

"Thank you, Nolan, but there wasn't much I could do about a paralyzed vocal cord. By the time that healed, I lost years of work in the fire. And my mom…"

It was shortly after her apartment burned down that her mother had been diagnosed with uterine cancer and died six months later. There was no way Piper would have abandoned her mother to do a support tour for her indie album.

By the time she'd managed to get her life together and released a second indie record, music tastes had changed dramatically. Hip-hop and country were still huge, but Piper wasn't versed in either. Her brand of girl-power rock wasn't in demand anymore, except from the precious few stars that already had large fan bases.

Their drinks were delivered. Nolan took a sip of his Scotch and pointed at her over the lip of his glass. He still loved to point at people.

"I'm very sorry about your mother, Piper. You had a

string of bad luck. But you're still young, you look great, and I'm willing to bet you'd still connect with an audience."

She froze with her soda water halfway to her mouth. "Connect with an audience? Oh, I've given up touring. I can't with—"

"I'm not talking about touring. I'm talking about television." He took another sip of Scotch and canvassed the area behind him, as if searching for eavesdroppers.

Piper noticed that people at a table nearby had their heads tilted, casting "Is that really him?" glances at Nolan. A man at the table was staring into his phone, but Piper had the feeling he was surreptitiously filming Nolan. They didn't appear to be tourists. A Nolan Ferrari sighting was impressive even for locals, apparently.

"This is all confidential," he said, looking back at her, "but we're rebooting *American Star* on another network."

"Really?" Piper gasped.

"They made me an offer I couldn't refuse," he said, patting at his V-neck. His penchant for V-necks had become a joke on the show. "I realize times have changed, people whinge about everything now, and I can't be quite the ass I was on the old show," he said, sounding disappointed. "I've been asked by the press if I'll ever issue an apology for all my past transgressions. And the answer… is… NO."

"I'm sure you'll do a fine job," Firio said, making a valiant attempt to be engaged in the conversation.

Nolan flashed his glowing white teeth at him. "I like this fella," he said to Piper. Then, "Let me get to the point. We'll need three judges. I'm one and Crystal is the other. But Miles isn't interested in returning, he's retired in St. Bart's. So we need a third judge."

Piper listened, confused. Was he going to ask her for suggestions? Her brain could not take in the obvious.

"I think you could be that third judge," he added.

Piper sat utterly still, her mouth half-open, and her baby turned inside of her, a long, fluttering feeling, like rotating bubbles of gas. She couldn't seem to close her mouth.

"Of course, the network wanted Alyssa or Mindy," Nolan said, naming the two most famous singers to come out of the show, from different seasons. "But inquiries went out and either one would bust our budget. Besides—" He rubbed his V-neck. "*I'm* the star."

"Piper would be amazing," Firio couldn't stop from injecting.

"Now, hold on," Nolan said, putting up his hand. "I said I thought she *could* be the third judge. Not that she *was*. Season 7 was our highest rated, and the network agrees if it can't be Alyssa or Mindy, it should be someone from that season. But they're pushing for Hayden."

"Sure," Piper nodded, a throb of disappointment in her throat. "That makes sense."

"But I think having Hayden and me at the same table is like having two lions in a cage. That's not how it should work. There should be two tigers and *one* lion."

The lion grinned. "So I made sure to get your name on the shortlist. Oliver Corbyn also suggested Jojo Barr, and I agreed. I saw all those stories that I had her voted off. What tosh. What am I, the God of phones? I can't control how people vote."

"Jojo," Piper breathed. "She'd be perfect."

Firio bumped her with his thigh and she was pretty sure he'd done so purposefully.

Nolan sipped more Scotch, then leaned back and crossed his arms. "It's between the three of you," he said. "I'll push for you or Jojo, and the network is going to push for Hayden, but we shall see. We'd like the three of you to do a little audition, make sure you're comfortable with critiquing, and test everyone's chemistry. Are you interested?"

The reality of what the job would entail crashed over her. Critiquing young, hopeful, nervous contestants —could she even do that? Was she capable of crushing a young singer on national television? As a performer, she knew that even a politely tepid response when you've sung your heart out could be crushing. But she shouldn't lie either, as that wouldn't help anyone improve.

"Nolan," she said. "I'm honored. But… you can see I'm pregnant. I'm not sure I should commit to a show right now."

She felt the heat of Firio's eyes boring into her side. He clearly wanted her to go for it.

"I understand that. When is the baby due?"

"Mid-December."

"Christmas baby," he smiled, and began rapid-firing at her: "Out-of-town preliminary auditions start in June.

Six cities. Live shows start in September. You won't have to move, we're filming here this time. Then it's only two days a week, three hours a day. We'd have to make concessions for you in terms of bringing the baby. Hire a nanny. You'll earn enough for it. I don't want to be coy. Salary is two mill per season, non-negotiable for the first three. If you don't have an agent anymore and feel you need one, there are a few people I can recommend."

Piper hardly took in the specifics of what he was saying, but one bit of information leaped out from the rest: Two million dollars a year. While hardly a blip for Nolan, this would be more money than Piper had ever earned, even when her debut album topped the charts.

Because only one song she'd authored had made the album, and that hadn't been released as a single, she'd come off the album without much of a nest egg. That had since dwindled to almost nothing after putting what savings she had left into the new home's down payment.

She'd long suspected her old label wasn't giving her all the royalties she was entitled to receive, but one didn't take on the labyrinth of a record label's accounting system without spending huge amounts on lawyers and risk getting blackballed from the industry. She still didn't feel she had the clout or money to go after it.

She'd also made some classic financial mistakes over the years: Paying out-of-pocket for two indie albums that went nowhere; buying a house in the Santa Ana mountains as the real estate downturn hit; paying the bills of friends and distant relatives who'd come out of the woodwork after her win with various hard-luck stories.

The one thing she didn't regret was paying for

experimental therapy for her mom's cancer—but that too hadn't worked out.

A steady two-million-dollars-a-year paycheck—even if it only lasted a few years—would be for her, as it would be for most people on the planet, a significant life advantage.

"But Hayden?" she asked. "He would want this? I mean, not that it isn't a great job…"

"I'm told he's receptive. Why wouldn't he be? It would give him an enormous platform for his projects."

Platform. Think of what she might be able to do with that. At the very least, she might be able to book local gigs again, ones that drew a decent crowd. Sure, her voice wasn't what it used to be, but she could work on that. She suddenly had the desire to work on that.

"What about Mitch?" she asked, referring to the show's manic host. "Is he returning?"

Nolan peered over his shoulder for a second, then stared at her in that steely way he had, almost looking like he hated you, but he didn't. It was part of the persona that had made him famous and took some getting used to. "You didn't hear this from me. But I'm told he's somewhere… *relaxing*."

"Oh…" Piper said, uncertainly.

"From what I heard, he's taking some time off. In a nice place. Where they'll take very good care of him."

Piper's mouth dropped. "Is he in a rehab clinic of some kind?"

"Juuuuuust resting," Nolan said. "Not drugs that I'm aware of. But working wouldn't be a good idea for him right now."

Piper tried to take this in. Mitch in rehab. The contestants had loved him, as he was often the only one who could get between them and Nolan's barbs.

"Nolan's got a bug up his tight royal ass, eh?" he'd once remarked to her backstage after she'd suffered through one of Nolan's patented drubbings ("I felt like I was watching a piano bar performance on the Sunset Strip"). At the time, she'd been on the verge of tears, but Mitch's swipe had instantly elevated her mood. He'd always seemed to have boundless energy, not only hosting *American Star* but also a radio show and producing movies. He must have finally worked himself into a breakdown.

"I hope he's okay," Piper said.

Nolan shook his head and sipped his drink. "We have other hosts in mind."

"When is the audition?" Firio asked him.

"We'd like to get them all done within the next couple of weeks."

"Bella? What do you think?"

What did she think? The truth was, it sounded like a dream, but she was worried about not only having Hayden once again get the better of her, but being pitted against Jojo and putting a strain on their friendship.

"It sounds incredible," she said, her voice coming across more childlike than she'd wanted. No reason to let Nolan think she was desperate, which she *wasn't*. "But… does Jojo know about this yet?"

"No," Nolan said. "I was going to contact her within the next couple of days."

"It's that we're friends." Piper looked down at her soda glass, unable to make contact with Nolan's intense gaze. He was a ruthlessly ambitious person who wouldn't understand prioritizing a friendship over a prime TV gig.

"Then whoever gets it, the other should be happy for her, right?" he asked.

She looked back up in time to see him raising his brows as much as possible given his nearly immobile forehead.

Chapter Five

"*D*id I catch you at a bad time?" Amy Baldash asked.

Actually, it *was* a bad time. Piper was walking to the subway, headed to her recording session, and was running late. But she had about two more minutes before she reached the station, and figured Amy had only called to know if Piper had received the *Loverly* tickets from Hayden.

"I have a couple minutes, Amy. Yes, Hayden tracked me down and gave my husband and me tickets. We loved the show. So thanks for passing my request along. I'd been joking, but I'm glad you did it."

She wiped her forehead with the back of her free hand. She'd gained thirty pounds and hauling it around was a workout.

"Oh, that's great," said Amy in her chipper way. "But that's not why I called. I wanted to reach out because I'd heard that you're being considered for the third judge on the new *American Star*."

Piper stopped dead on the spot, almost causing a man behind her to slam into her; he angled around her, passing her a watch-it-lady glance. "Oh, ah…" she stalled, as a nearby car blared its horn. She jammed one finger in her ear. "Where did you hear that?"

"Afraid I can't reveal my source. But it's true?"

Piper looked around helplessly at the traffic gushing by on Church Avenue. She hated crossing at this intersection. Semi-trucks barreled down it, cars careened around the corner with no thought to who was in the crosswalk. A few months ago, she'd read that a woman about her age had been killed right where she was standing.

So Amy knew about the auditions. What was Piper supposed to say? Nolan had said the auditions were confidential, and she presumed he wouldn't want her talking to the press. She settled on, "That's something I can't really discuss."

"I understand, but I've heard that—"

Panicked, Piper hung up. She stared at her phone, and seeing she had the light, looked both ways several times before crossing. On the opposite sidewalk, she started to feel bad. She'd never hung up on anyone mid-sentence before, at least anyone who wasn't a boyfriend.

Taking a deep breath, she hit Amy's number.

"Hello?" Amy said, cheerily, as if she hadn't been hung up on.

"I'm sorry."

"It's okay, I understand. I'm not here to get you in trouble. I wasn't sure if you could confirm or not."

"No, I can't. I mean, there's nothing to confirm."

Amy snorted out a laugh. "I'm not going to say I spoke with you. It's a small item online, and I'm only going to say it's come from a 'source'—not you."

"But what if someone thinks I'm the source?"

"Don't worry. I'll have called lots of people, and others will hang up on me. It could be anyone."

"I have to go," Piper said, and hung up again.

Walking down the steps to the subway, she wondered if an item like this could put her out of the running.

* * *

"DON'T WORRY, HUN," Jojo said. "She called me too, and I'm sure she called Hayden. And I'm *sure* it was Nolan who tipped her off."

"Nolan?" Piper said into the phone. It was late afternoon, and she'd returned from work fifteen minutes ago, kicked off her shoes, and collapsed on the couch, rubbing one pink, swollen foot. "But he said it was all confidential."

"He doesn't want *us* speaking to the press. But I'm sure he's out there drumming up interest in the new show. That's the way these things work."

"I don't want this out there," Piper said. "I'm not going to get it, it's going to be you or Hayden. I've had enough humiliation in this industry."

"Girl, are you serious?" Jojo chided. "First off, you could easily get it. Secondly, if you're going to get back in this biz, you've got to get used to having no control over the press. Have you forgotten all the crap they publish? Remember that whole 'Hayder' nonsense?

Remember the whole 'Nolan had Jojo voted off' stuff?"

"Ugh," Piper said, wobbling up from the couch to turn on the air conditioner. "Yeah, I remember."

"It's even worse now. And social media will crucify you for pretty much anything. You can't let the haters win. It's all about them, how unhappy they are with their own lives."

An arctic gust of AC chilled Piper's face, and she returned to the couch, plopped down, and drew her palm over the hard roundness of her stomach.

"I'm not sure I'm up for all this right now. It's great money, but is it worth all the hassle?" She paused and allowed herself to say the thing she'd been thinking all day. "I was famous once and I don't think the universe wanted me to be. I should drop out. You and Hayden are more popular. Either one of you deserves the spot more than I do." A loud noise thumped through the phone and she yanked it away from her ear. "Jojo? We have a bad connection."

"Nah, that's me tapping your head," said Jojo. "Hayden doesn't need another success. But you need something good to happen. *You* won. And here you are reading books into a microphone."

"Nothing wrong with that."

"You're a singer, Piper. A singer! An entertainer. It's in your blood and bones. This is me you're talking to. I know how hard you worked. I know how much you loved being big after *Star*. I know you love to *sing*."

"My voice isn't even that good anymore, and

besides, this is a judge job, not a singing job. I'm not sure it's the right time with the baby coming."

"Oh noooo," Jojo drawled. "Whatever will the kid do with a rich, famous mama? Only get into the best schools and never have to worry about money. And if you get on TV, labels will be beating down your door. Why should you give up that dream because you have a kid?"

Piper sunk into the couch cushions and looked around her pretty, airy living room. Life was good for once. Sometimes she thought that the more successful a person got, the more trouble it attracted. Maybe she had no business flying around with the Nolans and Crystals of the world.

"Listen," Jojo continued, sternly. "I'm not going to let you quit. I don't want this thing handed to me, and you certainly shouldn't hand it to Hayden. Where's the old Piper? She kicked everyone's ass." Her voice rose to near oration levels. "You own the *American Star* crown. Only ten winners in the world! That makes you rarer than an albino alligator. There are *twelve* of them!"

Where *was* the old Piper? The ambitious Piper who'd torn through the talent show like an Olympic athlete. She hadn't been the best singer—that had been Jojo. She hadn't been the most charismatic—that had been Hayden. But through sheer force of will and with the help of a four-octave range, a smoky resonance, and the ability to hold a note for forty seconds, she had outmaneuvered them both—not to mention the tens of thousands of other singers who'd auditioned.

She'd played the show like a game of chess, choosing

her moves with strategic precision and giving it her all every night on stage. Had that girl disappeared forever? Piper suddenly missed her young self, ached to have her back in her life.

"Is this about Firio?" prodded Jojo. "Is he against it? Does he want you home breastfeeding and baking bread?"

Piper was mildly insulted. "No, definitely not. He's excited. He thinks this is my second chance, and it will make me happy."

"I think it will too. You deserve it. But I'm still gonna give it my all, because I respect you enough to know you can handle my all. It's you or me, baby. You or me."

"Or Hayden," she said and couldn't help rolling her eyes.

"Nah. He ain't nothing."

They both laughed.

Chapter Six

*A*fter dinner, Firio went upstairs to his office to continue working. Piper was in the sitting room, putting the finishing touches on the baby registry. So many people had asked her what they could get for the baby that she figured it was better to put up a small registry of inexpensive requests than to have people sending her stuff she may not need or want. At twenty-nine weeks pregnant, she should have done all of this earlier but had been conflicted about asking for gifts.

And she had to be realistic about finances. She'd recently read an eye-popping statistic that child-raising costs in New York City were higher than college costs. This little being was going to cost her and Firio a bundle.

The pregnancy hadn't been planned; the pair had dated only two-and-a-half months when it happened. They'd had one of those "meet cute" scenarios that normally only happens in the movies.

On a brisk January day, Piper had been walking in

the West Village towards her old apartment on Perry Street. The apartment was a cheap sublet, offered by a friend who'd moved to Japan to teach English. At the time, Piper had been in Los Angeles, wallowing in the failure of her last indie album, and still heart-sore from her mom's swift and unexpected death.

She decided a new start in New York, a city she'd always loved, might be exactly what she needed. Not to mention that Jojo lived there, and encouraged Piper to make the move. Being offered a job narrating books by a recording engineer who happened to be a fan had sealed the deal. Piper officially became a New Yorker.

The day she'd met Firio, she'd forgotten her gloves. Hands stuffed deep in her puffer coat pockets, she was anxious to get to the warmth of her small studio. She'd passed a little bookstore she often browsed when a man exited and, preoccupied with looking down at his open book, had collided with her shoulder.

As he was apologizing, Piper saw the book in his hands was one of her favorites: *Ancient Surprises* by Lilith Odemay.

She'd complimented his reading tastes, and it dawned on her that the man reminded her of someone. A few moments later, it coalesced that he reminded her of her ex-boyfriend, Marco.

The two men had the same thick-lashed, bottomless dark eyes, slightly unruly black hair, compact physique, and olive-toned skin. But she noticed the man in front of her had a faint cleft in the chin, which Marco did not have, and which lent the man a debonair air, a hint of Cary Grant.

"Sorry about the crash," he'd said, with the barest accent she couldn't place. "Can I make it up to you with a cup of hot chocolate?"

Piper didn't tell him she didn't like hot chocolate, as at the moment, it sounded quite appealing.

"I'm surprised to see a guy with that book," she'd told him as they sat inside a nearby coffee shop. She delicately sipped her cappuccino, having decided to reveal that hot chocolate was not her thing.

"Why's that?" he'd asked. "I've already read it, but I stupidly loaned it to a friend, and she left it on the subway."

Piper imagined his "friend" was an ex-girlfriend or lover—and that was the first sign she was sexually attracted to the man sitting next to her, the ripple of intrigue that went through her at the mention of his female "friend."

"Was she a girlfriend? Or *is* a girlfriend?" she'd asked, trying to sound coy.

"A *friend*." For a moment, he'd dipped his upper body towards her in a possessive swoop, as if he was about to put his arm around her. He didn't. They'd only just met, after all.

"'I saw him and the world sat up straight. I hadn't even realized until that moment that it had been at a slight lean, like the Tower of Pisa,'" she'd quoted, one of her favorite lines from the book.

"'Love is like that—your ancient being calling to someone else's,'" he'd returned.

They'd grinned foolishly at each other, and she had the near-irresistible impulse to lean over and kiss him.

She loved a man with good teeth too, and his were damn good.

There were only one or two men she met a year that caused this kind of internal combustion, and she hadn't found herself sitting across from one in a very, very long time. She hoped none of these thoughts were blinking in neon letters on her face.

When Firio told her he'd moved to the States from Italy when he was fourteen, she wasn't surprised, though he'd lost almost all of his accent. She'd always had a "thing" for Italian culture, cuisine and, yes, men. Marco too was an Italian-American. But there was a lightness and friendliness about Porfirio—he'd told her to call him Firio—that was so distinctly un-Marco-like that she quickly got over comparing the two. Not to mention that Marco didn't read books like *Ancient Surprises*. In fact, she'd never seen him with a book unless it was a biography of some band.

Coffee had led to dinner. Firio was a good conversationalist, laughed at her jokes, and was a gentleman who insisted on opening doors, paying for everything, and walking on the street side of the sidewalk. The kind of guy woefully scarce back in Los Angeles, where the men, with their surfer tans, scraggly goatees, and hairy toes poking year-round out of their slide sandals, were so flaky that Piper had become accustomed to several last-minute cancellations before a date came to fruition.

After dinner, the cold air simply disappeared as Firio took her hand and walked her to her apartment. She'd wanted to invite him inside as much as she'd wanted to be a famous singer, but she'd managed to remain vertical that night, as well as for their next two dates. It was a Herculean effort that she wasn't sure why she was making, but felt she should. Plus, she was enjoying the sexual tension, the fantasies, the gradual build-up to what she was pretty certain was going to be fantastic sex. (She was correct about that.)

Ten weeks later, she was pregnant.

At thirty-four, Piper had been dumbfounded that pregnancy had snuck up on her so easily when she'd neglected her birth control for a couple of days. She'd forgotten to pack her pills on her and Firio's first trip together, a weekend jaunt to the seaside town of Mystic, Connecticut.

She'd especially been concerned that Firio, who was only twenty-eight, wouldn't be ready for parenthood. She'd broken the news on the phone, and he'd seemed shell-shocked, barely acknowledging what she'd said. He claimed he had something to do, and would call her right back. But he never did, and her messages went unanswered.

She began to panic and cry, going over her options in her mind, none of which were remotely appealing. Could she raise a child by herself? She didn't even have a permanent place to live. Her work situation was tenuous. She was paying out-of-pocket for health insurance.

What a fool she'd been, an utter fool! Why had she let her hormones, her biology, override her common sense? The rest of the night had been a nightmare of angst and self-recriminations.

But early the next morning, he'd called her and apologized. "Piper, that was a surprise and I shut down.

I'm so sorry. Please, can we meet and talk in person? Please."

So she'd agreed to meet for brunch. By then, she was frightened but completely prepared to tell him that she would raise the child on her own. Hopefully, he would be part of the baby's life. But the second she saw his smile-bursting face as he stood outside the bistro, she knew whatever doubts he'd had were gone. He too wanted their baby.

A few weeks later, they were engaged.

Her friends, and especially her father, had all expressed barely concealed alarm that she was marrying and having a child with a man she'd known for so little time. But it all felt so right. Even if she hadn't gotten pregnant, Firio had assured her that he'd felt they were on the marriage path, and she felt the same.

They had so much in common and they hadn't even had one big argument. Compare that to Marco. They had barely gone a couple of days without a blow-up, and neither one of them could decide if they wanted to get married.

Piper's parents had told her stories of how they'd fallen in love at first sight and this, she supposed, was what it should be like. Jojo and her boyfriend, Donny, had only dated for a couple of months before moving in together.

This was what it should be—not that on-and-off muck she'd had with Marco. By the time she'd extricated herself from that relationship, she'd hardly recognized herself, felt as if the pair's combined chemical makeup, if allowed to continue to ferment, would have turned them into Bonnie and Clyde or some other crime-spree couple.

But in the short time she'd been with Firio, she'd felt like her strongest, kindest, best self. This was the self she wanted to be going forward. She secretly felt this evolved self is what helped her womb so quickly welcome a baby to its folds.

She and Firio had decided to make it legal but eschew a wedding ceremony, preferring to put every dime into a new house. Neither one of their small studio apartments would do for a growing family.

Besides, both feared a wedding would be too sad, what with Piper's mom gone, as well as Firio's parents, who'd died tragically in a car accident when he was eighteen. Both Piper and Firio were only children, and neither had a large, close social circle.

So here they were—in an old, moldy, drafty, creaky, peeling, but beloved four-bedroom Victorian, built in 1899, with a small backyard and, Piper thought, the best porch on the block—perhaps in the entire neighborhood, a historic area known for its free-standing mansions and manicured lawns, appearing more like a small Southern town than mid-Brooklyn.

It was the Albemarle Road home's broad, wraparound porch—a swoon-worthy luxury in the city—that made this the house Piper immediately wanted. The oval porch wended three-quarters around the house, a decadent amount of space that Piper still hadn't figured out how to best use. She'd put out plants and installed a swing bench, but that was it.

It was surreal to think that when spring arrived she

could sit swinging on the bench with a baby strapped to her chest. The vision thrilled her with equal parts fuzzy anticipation and something akin to stark terror.

* * *

REMEMBERING THAT SHE HADN'T YET retrieved the mail, Piper headed outside at dusk to the black metal mailbox with little butterflies painted on it. She liked the red, green, and yellow butterflies, imagining the artist to be one of the previous owners' children.

Walking back into the house, she sifted through the letters: a few junk pieces, a notice from her health insurance company, and a white business envelope with her name and address printed on it, but no return address.

She placed the mail on the kitchen island, took a paring knife from a wooden knife block, and slit open the business envelope.

DEAREST ONE,

It is my duty to write this letter because I'm a key part of a small but dedicated and powerful society that reaches its tentacles across many spheres. We have been watching you for a long time.

At the direction of one of our high-ranking members, we engineered your downfall. I hold no judgment on these matters. What you did or did not do to deserve this treatment at our member's behest, I can only surmise. It seems quite obvious to me.

Our attention turned from you awhile ago as the

task was completed and your fortunes demolished. But now there has been an unforeseen turn of events, and your fortunes are poised to rise again. This has made our high-ranking member very unhappy.

Dark forces are gathering against you. Our society is the true way and has more power than has already been unleashed against you. You must beware.

Your friend

PIPER SLOWLY TURNED the letter over and saw it was blank. Then she looked again at the envelope, as if a return address would suddenly appear.

"What the *hell?*" she said, aloud.

Her mouth was suddenly very dry and she went to the sink, ran water into a glass, and drank some. Her baby churned and she pressed her palm on her stomach.

Then she picked the letter up from where she'd left it on the counter and went upstairs to Firio's circular office inside the home's spired turret. There was only one turret, with six narrow windows letting in light all around, and Piper thought it the sweetest little room in the house. Her husband was staring into his computer.

"I got the strangest letter," she said, walking over to him.

"Hmm?" he said, still staring distractedly into the computer.

"Honey," she said, sharply, and he looked at her. "I got the most bizarre thing in the mail." She thrust the letter at him.

She watched as he read, his lips moving ever so

slightly, a habit of his when he was reading. Her heart pumped thickly, adrenaline coursing brightly through her. She took a long, deep breath, not wanting to send stress hormones to the baby.

He finally looked at her, his mouth half-open. "What is this?"

"I don't know. It came addressed to me. There was no return address."

He looked back at the letter and appeared to be reading again. "I don't get it. Is this a marketing thing?"

She grabbed the letter from him and stared at it. "What would they be marketing?"

"A horror movie?" he laughed. When she didn't laugh with him, he put his hand out for the letter and she gave it to him. He took another few moments studying it, then said, "I don't understand. What's it supposed to mean?"

"I don't know." She put her hand out for the letter and began reading out loud. "'At the direction of one of our high-ranking members, we engineered your down-fall.'" She scanned more. "'But now there has been an unforeseen turn of events, and your fortunes are poised to rise again.'" She looked at him. "Is it me or does this sound like… a reference to the audition?"

"I—I don't…" he sputtered, holding up his palms.

She looked around the room, thinking. "I feel like this is someone talking about my career. And the audi-tion. What else could it be?"

He reached for the letter again, and stared at it, this time his lips unmoving. "Okay," he said, somberly, the weight of the message getting through to him. "This does sound strange."

"It had to be that item in *Entertainment Daily*. It brought out a nutcase."

She'd seen the item online a few days ago and fielded messages from friends who had also seen it. She'd had to tell them she knew nothing about anything, and most of them understood what this meant and didn't ask further questions.

It's been seven years since a winner was crowned on *American Star*, the influential talent show that produced platinum recording artists Alyssa Alina and Mindy Patel. But sources say a reboot is on the horizon for next fall. Acerbic judge Nolan Ferrari has been lured back from London and Grammy-winning songstress Crystal Pell is set to take her place next to her sometime sparring partner.

But original judge Miles Bennett won't be joining the panel, says an insider. The third judge slot will likely go to either Oscar-winner Hayden Tower, Off-Broadway star Jojo Barr, or *AS* winner Piper Dunner, best known for her rousing girl power anthem, "You Were My Forever, Now You're My Never." All three competed in Season 7.

"That was our most popular season," says the source. "We're hoping to bring back some of its magic. Hayden is the obvious choice, but there's some concern that he and Nolan might clash. Crystal is pushing for him though, as she'd love to remain the only girl on the panel."

Piper wished she hadn't read the comments below the item, of which there were several along the lines of, "I thought Hayden won" and "Piper who?"

"What should we do?" Firio asked. "Call the police?"

"I mean, it's unnerving but not exactly threatening." She stared at the letter some more before half-crumpling it down by her waist. "I knew everything was too good to be true."

"Oh, come on. Don't let this rattle you."

"They know where we live!"

"Honey, anyone can find out anything these days. We have an alarm, and we haven't been setting it. Let's do that. If another comes, we call the police."

* * *

THAT NIGHT, SHE LAY AWAKE LONG AFTER she heard Firio's soft snoring. He'd insisted on putting the letter in his files, in case they needed to show it to the police. The letter's words tossed uneasily around her mind—the ones she could remember anyway.

At the direction of one of our high-ranking members, we engineered your downfall.

Your fortunes demolished.

Her paralyzed vocal cord. The apartment fire that

destroyed years' worth of songwriting and had—no, she couldn't think about that. She shook her head rapidly several times to blot out the encroaching thought of him.

Anyone who followed her career would know about all of it. If they didn't, a half-hearted Internet search would clue them in.

It had to have been written by an irate fan of either Hayden or Jojo. Someone who didn't want her getting the third judge position. *But now there has been an unforeseen turn of events, and your fortunes are poised to rise again.*

She'd had fans like that during her heyday. Like the guy who showed up at every concert stop on her debut album's tour. He always managed a front-row seat and held up a sign that read, "Marry Me, Piper."

Security had figured out his name was Joe Kanabas, he was in his forties, and had money from a settled disability claim. He used the funds to follow her tour bus. But as he didn't make any threats, security never confronted him, only kept an eye on him. He was a paying ticket holder, and despite him creeping Piper out, she was told nothing could be done. It was perfectly within his rights to sit night after night and unnerve her. He'd eventually disappeared. But for years, Piper had worried about running into him on the street.

And there were her diehards, "Pipermints" they called themselves. People who showed up regularly at her meet-and-greets, until she not only knew their faces, but their names, their children's names, and details of their lives until they felt like acquaintances she'd reunite with at various locales around the country.

They'd done so much marketing work on her behalf:

fan videos, social media postings, radio station call-ins. Once, when she'd been trying to get clearance on a song she'd wanted to sing for *Star* but the composer wouldn't allow it, the Pipermints had got wind of this and bombarded the composer with begging postcards. It had worked.

She was impressed at how they'd rapidly organized themselves with military-like precision, without any encouragement from her, as she was living in the *American Star* bubble. They'd loved her in a pure kind of way that left her deeply humbled and appreciative, but a little bewildered by their dead-serious dedication, even referring to her music as her "mission."

Jojo and Hayden—especially Hayden—would have these diehards too. One obsessed enough to send a letter like that?

And what about Crystal? The *Entertainment Daily* item said she wanted to remain the only woman on the panel. Did she want it enough to send a crazy letter to try and push Piper away from auditioning?

She'd looked up the letter's zip code, 10036. It had been mailed from somewhere near Port Authority. So far as Piper knew, Crystal lived in Los Angeles, though most people in the entertainment business came frequently to New York.

Crystal had been one of Piper's kindest supporters, coming to a couple of key shows in her early years and writing her big break-up hit "You Were My Forever, Now You're My Never." She'd even gifted Piper a diamond tennis bracelet after the finale, the first piece of real jewelry that Piper had ever owned.

The idea that Crystal was harboring a pocket of spitefulness under her supportive persona was too much to fathom. Besides, the letter didn't sound like her in the slightest.

Piper regretted giving *Entertainment Daily* her husband's full name. To get her home address, someone had probably tracked down their house purchase through a real estate database, which they'd bought under Firio's name and her married name.

Why hadn't she been more careful and bought under an LLC as most famous people did? But she hadn't considered herself famous enough anymore to draw stalkers, and she certainly couldn't have predicted the "unforeseen turn of events" that would push her into the public eye again.

Even though Firio had made sure to set the alarm before they went to bed, the house Piper loved so much suddenly felt too big, too dark, and too vulnerable.

Chapter Seven

*P*iper couldn't get over how good Crystal Pell looked with her unlined face, glossy black hair with sun-streaked bangs, and tanned arms as slender-cut as a teen's. According to the Internet, Crystal was now fifty-two, but she looked half that, and not in the neurotoxin-injected way that Nolan did, but in a way that crowed of healthy living and winning the genetic lottery.

Crystal had called a couple of days ago, telling Piper she got her number from Nolan and wished to take her to lunch. It sent a *frisson* of anxiety through Piper to know that Crystal was indeed in the city and could have been the one to mail the letter.

They sat at Il Buco, a trendy Italian spot in midtown, with wood-paneled walls, red leather banquets, and so much plant-life sprawling up the walls it felt like they were inside of a greenhouse.

A server poured them sparkling water and took their orders. The pair made small talk about Piper's pregnancy, but as Crystal didn't mention the judge spot, neither did Piper. Crystal smiled at her in that benevolent aunt way Piper remembered from the show—that is, if a benevolent aunt had thousands of dollars worth of luminous white veneers.

"Piper, I wanted to bring you out to talk about that item in *Entertainment Daily*," she said, in her gooey but don't-mess-with-me voice.

Nervously, Piper said, "I'm so sorry, Crystal. The reporter called me and caught me off guard. But I swear I—"

One perfectly manicured hand went up in a stop gesture. "I'm sure it was Nolan who planted it. That isn't what I wanted to talk about. It's what the item said, that I want to be the only girl on the panel."

The waiter came over, depositing a bowl of thick brown bread slices and a dispenser of olive oil in front of them. "No bread, thank you," Crystal said with her megawatt smile, and the man looked marooned in a starstruck haze before whisking the basket away. "Oh my goodness." Crystal shot a glance in the direction of Piper's stomach. "I'm so used to L.A., where no one wants gluten. Let me call him back."

"No, it's fine," Piper assured her. "I've already gained more than I planned."

"What I wanted to say is that it's not true, what the item said," she resumed. "Not in the slightest. I'd love another woman on the panel, and I think either you or Jojo would be great. I plan to bring Jojo out and tell her the same."

"That's nice to hear," Piper said, genuinely relieved.

"I didn't believe it anyway." Not necessarily true, but she felt compelled to say this.

"I called Amy Baldash and told her if she prints another item like that, I won't be talking to her in the future." She smiled sweetly, like a Mafioso might smile sweetly before putting a cap in someone's head. "I'm going to try my best to keep the press from pitting us women against each other, as it loves to do. But the truth is, I don't have any say over who will get selected. It's up to the producers, and I'm sure they'll take Nolan's opinion into account. They've never cared much about mine."

"I totally understand. Thanks for clearing that up, though you didn't have to."

Their salads were delivered, and the two ate in silence for several moments before Piper said, "I have a question for you."

"By all means."

"Do you have any fans who are kind of overzealous? Or even obsessed?"

Crystal's fork dangled halfway to her coral-stained lips, and she smiled in an overly practiced way, with a double row of teeth. "Dear, I've got them all. I once had a woman take over my identity. She tried to move into my house, insisting she was me. I had another lovely lady who told me she'd kill me if I didn't sing at her toddler's birthday party. You name it, I've had it. Any reason you're asking?"

"I received a letter a few days ago that was unsettling. It sounded like whoever it was didn't want me to audition. So I'm trying to think who it might be from…

maybe a fan of Hayden or Jojo, or even a fan of yours? You might not want to be the only girl on the panel, but someone who read that item doesn't know that."

Crystal took a mouthful of lettuce and chewed leisurely, deep in thought. "I suppose it's possible. What did the letter say?"

Piper went into her tote bag and took out the envelope that she'd retrieved from Firio's files, and slipped out the letter. She looked questioningly at Crystal, who nodded and reached out for it.

Piper hoped that Crystal's expression might reveal whether or not she was behind the letter, but her face was smoothly void until her expertly arched brows flew up, then back down. "Do you know what this reminds me of? I don't suppose you've heard of The True Way."

"The what?"

"'A small but dedicated and powerful society that reaches its tentacles across many spheres…'" She placed the letter in the middle of them, sipped more water, and looked at Piper with her kohl-lined, dark-brown eyes. "You see here, how it says, 'our society is the true way…'? There's a group that's active in Hollywood. It's called The True Way. A few years ago, when my career was on a downswing, one of the biggest actors in the world—I can't name him, but you'd know him— suggested I look into it. Supposedly, its members are guaranteed success in anything they ask for in life. Now, this actor, he's been on top of his game for decades. Never suffered a real low in his career. Won an Oscar for a dumb movie he shouldn't have won a toaster oven for. He swears it's all because of this group." She picked up the letter again, drawing one long, butterscotch nail over it. "Here, where it says, 'we engineered your downfall,' that's supposedly what the group can do. Take down your competition."

She put the letter to her side as the waiter appeared with Piper's plate of spring vegetable gnocchi and Crystal's baked lemon salmon, but Piper didn't even look at her food, her eyes fixed on Crystal.

"So I took a few courses," Crystal continued after the waiter left. "Eventually met with a guy—older, weird guy—about officially joining the group, even though I didn't really believe it could do all this actor said. But at the time, I was desperate. I was up for something I wanted very badly, but there was another singer up for it too. She's younger and more popular... Anyway, this man—I remember he had white hair—told me if I joined the group, they could make this young singer go away, not be a threat to me anymore. Make sure the thing I wanted was mine." She blinked her almond-shaped eyes at Piper, and slowly shook her head.

"What did they mean they'd make the young singer 'go away'?" Piper asked, leaning in and keeping her voice quiet. "*Hurt* her... or... put some kind of curse or hex on her?"

Crystal played with her drop necklace, its large diamond so sparkly that its beams periodically stabbed Piper's corneas.

"I didn't want to find out," she said, holding the letter out to Piper by its edge, as if it might bite her. "I didn't like the sound of the whole thing. To belong to the group, I'd have to belong to them. If there were something they wanted me to do, I'd do it. A product they wanted me to endorse, I'd endorse it. A concert they wanted me for, I'd sing at it. A dress they wanted me to wear, I'd wear it. On and on, I wouldn't be in charge of my life anymore. No one but me is in charge of my life."

Piper shivered. She hated people telling her what to do. It was the main reason she'd found fame to be a double-edged sword. Fame, with its cadre of managers, producers, executives, and lawyers, all insisting—sometimes rightly, often wrongly—that they knew what was best for her. Joining a group that promised to give you control over your rivals while simultaneously micromanaging your life sounded like no worthwhile exchange to her.

"That's so bizarre," Piper breathed, staring at the letter with entirely new eyes. "But the way it talks about a 'high-ranking member'—this does sound like some kind of cult."

The idea that Crystal herself was behind the letter began to shake loose its already tenuous hold on her as this other, stranger, and more formidable possibility opened up.

Your fortunes demolished.

One side of Piper's lips tugged upwards in half-amused doubt. But there was a prickly edge to her doubt, the distant abyss of the unexplainable creeping around her consciousness, as one might sense, but not see, a presence in the dark.

Crystal plunged her knife into her lemon salmon steak, cutting off a chunk. "Listen, sweetheart, I wouldn't worry. If the group could do everything this actor said, everyone in Hollywood would belong to it. He's got a classic case of imposter syndrome—can't believe his success. A lot of celebrities are like that, real superstitious." She tilted forward, resting a long nail on Piper's pasta bowl. "I hope you're not going to let that letter stop you from auditioning. There are all kinds of wackos out there, it's part of the business."

"I do remember that," Piper said with faux-casualness, turning to her food. She hadn't eaten in a few hours and was already starving, thanks to her sixteen-inch resident with the monstrous appetite.

Although she hadn't quite made up her mind if she wanted the judge position, she didn't want Crystal to think she couldn't handle it if she got it, so she decided to switch topics. But first, there was one thing she needed to know.

"Crystal, what happened with the thing you wanted? Did you get it?"

"No, I didn't. The younger singer did." She grinned devilishly. "But she got terrible reviews."

Chapter Eight

*A*t home, Piper put the letter back into Firio's files, and went into the living room, taking out the book she was scheduled to narrate, so she could familiarize herself with the characters and think about how she'd want to record them.

The book was titled *Mitzi Tells All*. It was about a glamorous movie star from the 1940s who'd decided, as an old woman, to tell her life story to a biographer. The recording session's producer had thought Piper's experience being a celebrity would bring the narration to life.

Piper was concerned about the parts that called for Mitzi to sound in her eighties. She began reading aloud, striving to make her voice a tad worn-out and raspy, though not enough to annoy listeners. But her mind wandered to her own career and soon it had wandered so far from the material that she put the book aside on the couch.

After she'd been crowned the new *American Star*, there had been a mind-boggling amount of media obligations. She'd appeared on every major talk show there was. Back before the masses disconnected from cable, this meant at least one hundred million people saw Piper on television in the week following her win.

Right after the twenty-city *American Star* tour ended, the machine had rushed out an album that went platinum. She had two hits in heavy rotation on MTV and VH1 (back when that was still a thing, a *big* thing), and she was nominated for the Best New Artist Grammy (it didn't matter that she'd lost, she was just awestruck to be at the Grammy's).

She'd headlined a sold-out concert in Central Park. Her "National Anthem," sung at Game 1 of the NBA finals, if not Whitney Houston's or Marvin Gaye's classic versions, had nevertheless received raves. At her peak, she'd been playing venues that held ten thousand people.

But a little over a year later, it all began to fall apart. One morning, she'd woken up with bronchitis. Weeks later, when it had dissipated, she could barely sing. A throat doctor diagnosed a paralyzed vocal cord. It was two years before she could remotely get back into her range. Two years she spent writing songs, hoping that when she could sing properly again, she'd have a cache of them that the label would be eager for her to record. But then she'd lost all her demos in the apartment fire.

The label, having lost its patience, dropped her.

She got to composing songs again and finally had enough material to record an indie album, but couldn't promote it with a tour because her mother got sick. The indie barely sold anything. Month by month, Piper's assistant would report fewer and fewer traffic numbers on her website. Soon, she could no longer afford that assistant.

She put out another indie album, and though she was convinced she was recording some of the best songs she'd ever written, music tastes had changed, the industry had nosedived, and her window for success had passed.

In those "Who Were the Most Successful *American Star* Winners?" rankings, she was always somewhere near the bottom.

For years, there had been guilt. All of that time, effort, and money the *American Star* machine had put into her with little result. All of those millions of people who'd voted for her, because they'd believed in her. All of that belief she'd be "the next big thing" had been unwarranted, massively misguided.

As the teens were always screaming at her, Hayden should have won. Or as her conscience jeered at her, Jojo. Or anyone but her.

Articles made it clear the music press was disappointed in her. "Piper Dunner Was Your Forever, Now She's Your Never" and "The Cautionary Tale of an *American Star* Winner" were two particularly demeaning headlines. Neither article had mentioned her vocal issues, mother's illness, or fire, but instead concluded the stigma of a goopy, bubblegum show like *American Star* was too much for her to overcome.

There was a chastising tone too—an underlying insinuation that she'd taken a shortcut to the top and now must be rerouted back to the bottom of the heap where she belonged. Voters may have lifted her to god-like heights, but she was a false idol, one that must be torn down so the proper singing gods could take up their rightful places in the celebrity hierarchy.

She'd wanted to call up the reporters and yell at them. *American Star* had the most unforgiving microphone in the business. It would broadcast minuscule sonic inflections clear to the back of the theater and through millions of television screens, with no sweeteners. It could have made the most lauded singers in the world sound like shower-warbling amateurs. Show some respect, damn it.

But neither reporter had bothered to reach out to her or even mention her new indie album.

She might as well have been dead.

Had it all been the result of... a cult member's curse?

Impossible. Plenty of people that had once been big stars faded into obscurity over a number of years. That scenario must be much more common than the ones who managed to hold onto stardom for the long-term. She'd read stories of former celebrities who'd been found bagging groceries, waiting tables, and working in laundry mats. They couldn't *all* have a curse on them, could they?

That was the business. It was random and ruthless. A lucky break here, an unlucky break there, it all added up to a career or no career. In fact, she vaguely remembered reading that Hayden had only been cast in his Oscar-winning role in *Ghosts of Time* because... why?

She pushed herself up from the couch, went upstairs

to her bedroom, and sat in front of her laptop. Typing "Hayden Tower cast in Ghosts of Time" into a search engine, she skimmed several articles before finding what she wanted.

Universal Studios has announced that *American Star* alum Hayden Tower has landed the much sought-after role of Jake Jones in the movie adaptation of the hit Broadway musical *Ghosts of Time*.

Justin Bieber, Justin Timberlake, and John Legend were all said to be vying for the role. But sources say that stage star Anton Bishop, who recently starred in Broadway's *Hair* revival, was cast but had to withdraw after suffering a fall at his house that resulted in over thirty stitches in his face.

"He's very disappointed," said a source in the Bishop camp. "But he can't do a movie with a bashed-up face."

Hayden Tower was the runner-up on the seventh season of the popular singing competition, losing out by a narrow margin to Maryland native Piper Dunner.

"He's excited," said a source close to Tower. "He didn't expect this at all. It's truly unfortunate the role comes at the expense of Anton, whom he greatly admires. But he feels he was born to play Jake Jones."

Piper sat staring at her computer, absently twisting her lower lip.

What a lucky break that had been for Hayden. And what an unlucky break—*literally*—that had been for Anton Bishop. Thanks to Anton's face plant, Hayden snagged the role that won him an Academy Award for Best Supporting Actor. As for Anton Bishop…

His website touted an appearance he'd be making in a Fort Atkinson, Wisconsin dinner theater.

Chapter Nine

*I*t took her a day to open the second letter. It sat on the kitchen island inside of a small pile of mail until she saw it and her heart began to thud. Her name and address, printed. No return address. Postmarked with the same zip code: 10036.

She debated opening it. Whatever stress she experienced could affect the tiny being inside of her. She couldn't believe this person was going to keep sending letters. Had something else to say, something, no doubt, equally as crazy.

But… maybe it wasn't from the same person. Not every piece of mail came with a return address. The midtown zip code contained thousands of businesses. It could be something she needed. Being pregnant, she was on high alert for any piece of information that could potentially affect her health insurance. Was she going to stop opening her mail?

First, she settled herself on a stool at the kitchen island, trying to prepare herself to be calm no matter what she found. She considered waiting until Firio got home, but she wouldn't be able to wait that long, especially as she was never sure exactly when he'd be walking in the door. Some nights, it was six p.m. on the dot; other times, nearly ten p.m.

The thing would sit there, taunting her.

She slit the envelope with a paring knife and tugged out the letter, making the paper crinkle loudly, almost to prove she wasn't frightened of it.

DEAREST ONE,

Your throat problem. Your fire. Your loved one's illness and death. Problems galore!

Did you think this was all poor you bad luck?

Of course it wasn't. It was us. Not me specifically, mind you. But we acted at the direction of our high-ranking member.

Now you want something that our member wants too.

What to do, what to do.

Ooo-ooo.

Will you slink away with your tail between your pretty legs? As you should. It would save a world of trouble, wouldn't it? Dark forces are gathering against you. We went easy on you before. You must beware.

Your friend

PIPER WATCHED with forced detachment as her hands shook. Her heart beat jagged and fast in her throat, making her feel she might choke. The previous letter—even though addressed to her—had been ambiguous enough that part of her could cling to the hope that it was an offbeat marketing campaign that happened to hit on aspects of her life.

But not now. There wasn't a shred of doubt she was the target of a campaign of harassment.

FIRIO STILL HAD HIS BRIEFCASE in his hand and was hardly inside of the door when Piper thrust the latest missive at him. He stood in his light blue work shirt, red and gray striped tie, and black work slacks, staring down at the letter.

When he finished reading, he sighed heavily, then said, quietly, "Bella, let me put down my things."

"Of course. I've been anxious while waiting for you."

She followed him as he walked into the kitchen, placed his briefcase on a stool, shed his suit jacket, sat on a stool, and stared at the letter again.

"Now I know one-hundred percent what it's talking about," she said. "Me and the audition. And it's trying to take credit for all the bad shit that happened to me after I won. Let me tell you, I'm pretty sure I know who's behind it."

"Who wrote it?" he said, looking at her.

"Not sure if he wrote it himself, but I think this is all about Hayden. It says I want something this other person wants too. The judge spot is between me, Jojo, and Hayden, and this sure as hell wouldn't be Jojo. At lunch with Crystal, she told me about a Hollywood cult that claims it can get rid of your competition. Can put a curse on you or something, if a member wants it that way."

"Wait, wait," Firio said, tiredly putting up one hand. "A cult? Like… the Manson family?"

"I don't know! But famous people belong to it, according to Crystal. It's called The True Way and the first letter even said 'our society is the true way.' I didn't want to tell you all this before, because it sounds insane." She jabbed her finger in the direction of the letter. "Hayden belongs to some kind of cult and it either thinks—or it *does*—have the magical ability to screw people over. You know how Hayden got the role in *Ghosts of Time*? The other actor who'd been cast broke his face open."

"Bella," Firio said, pulling at his tie's knot. "How do you know this isn't some wacky person? All that stuff with you… You think a cult can do all that? Bad things happen to people. Trust me, I know that."

Firio's parents had died in a car accident when he was eighteen. The couple had been vacationing back in Italy when it happened, slammed by a truck. "I'm sorry," she said. "I know you had bad things happen too."

"Yes, and it didn't take a cult. It only took a bastard to run a light."

Firio and his parents had immigrated to America when he was fourteen. In four years, his safety net was gone. Luckily, he'd been able to move in with an aunt and uncle in Queens until he could finish college and find a job. She wished that she'd been able to meet his parents, and that her mother had been able to meet the man she would marry.

He came over and gave her an avoid-the-stomach side hug. "I'm sorry someone is doing this. It's someone jealous of my little star."

"I've made up my mind. I'm not going to audition."

"Bella—"

"I don't need to be famous again if this is the kind of thing it draws."

"You can't let—"

"I don't need the stress, and neither does the baby. Let Hayden be the damn judge. He gets everything he wants anyway."

"Should we call the police? Maybe they can talk to him."

"Are you kidding?" she almost shouted. "There's no proof it's him. They won't bother, and it will be even *worse* if they do. He'll run around telling people that Piper Dunner thinks he puts curses on people, like when he ran around telling everyone I was sleeping with Nolan Ferrari. Stuff like that gets out, you're thought of as *difficult*. I may not have much of a career now, but that doesn't mean I don't *ever* want one. Besides," she sighed, "the letter is still vague. I went through this with certain fans. Unless someone makes a direct threat, it's almost impossible to do anything."

Feeling her baby fluttering within her, she closed her eyes to force-calm her racing heart, and sat at the kitchen table, fingers squished up against her mouth.

Seeing her expression, Firio rushed to pour her a glass of water and handed it to her.

After a gulp, she said, "I didn't want the reboot that much anyway."

She stared blankly in front of her, a crushing sensation in her chest. The truth was, she *had* wanted it. Despite her better judgment, she had allowed herself to want it, to imagine what it would be like to have influence and admiration again. Not to mention having steady money, the kind of money that could change her and Firio's life, and the life of their child.

And she'd warmed to the idea of helping to discover the next big star, of mentoring young singers, guiding them in a way she wished someone had guided her, instead of shooting her out of a cannon and being only passingly concerned whether the cannon was facing a mountainside.

Interview the manager they'll want to assign you, she'd tell them. Make sure to take care of your voice and your body, she'd tell them. Get comfortable with saying no occasionally. Try to write as many songs as possible, as songwriting royalties will be the bulk of your income at first. Be mentally prepared for the idea that this might be a short ride, and know you can't control everything.

All the things no one had told her.

Plus, she liked the idea of two women on the panel. While Nolan had said he couldn't be as cruel as he'd been on the show ten years ago, she'd planned to speak up if he took jabs at the female contestants' looks, clothes, or weight. Crystal had always tried to speak up to him as well, but Crystal might appreciate another woman backing her up. Piper auditioning meant double the chance of a two-woman panel.

Firio was staring at her, looking helpless. "You should do what you feel is best. I don't want you to be afraid." For a moment, anger flashed in his eyes. "I want to speak to him myself."

She waved at him. "That's the last thing I need. He'll deny it, anyway."

"I won't. But I want to."

"I'll have to tell Jojo about this. She could be next."

Chapter Ten

*I*n bed, Piper couldn't sleep. Not only because of the letters and their implications but her restless leg syndrome. It had started a few weeks ago, muscles pulsing and scraping inside her glutes. Unbearably annoying.

Not wanting to wake Firio, who had to be up early in the morning, she tried not to make too much motion. She didn't have a recording session tomorrow, and had texted Jojo to ask if she could meet for lunch, but hadn't heard back yet.

Hayden. That little bastard. Had he joined a cult that promised him success in exchange for his undying loyalty? One that turned Piper's career to ashes?

All because she'd beaten him on *American Star*?

She wasn't one to believe in the supernatural or magic powers. But she had to admit that ever since she'd finished the tour in promotion of her debut album, her life had veered out of control so thoroughly that she'd often felt she was cursed. She'd even jokingly said this over the years to various people.

If a curse *was* possible, would Hayden have resented her enough to put one on her? They weren't exactly direct competitors. Sure, they'd both been signed to Diamond Entertainment and Moxie Management. And only one *American Star* contestant seemed to break out every season. But he was Hayden, and she was Piper. There was enough room in the world for both of them.

It was one thing to sabotage someone's career—another thing to kill people. Could the cult *really* have given her mother cancer? And if it could, would Hayden *really* have gone that far? And the apartment fire, which the fire department had blamed on faulty wiring...

How she wished—how she wished she'd been...

Against her will, her mind was yanked back to the thing that she tried to always keep blocked out, the thing that had destroyed her peace of mind more than the rest of it. Her devoted little dog, Marvin, named after Marvin Gaye. A scrappy terrier-mix she'd adopted from a shelter when she was struggling in Los Angeles.

He'd been almost eight years old and no one wanted an older dog, so he'd languished at the shelter for a year. He already had some health problems, and he drooled, and he barked at trees. But he had looked at her through his steel cage with big, beckoning brown eyes, and she'd taken him back to her lonely apartment.

When the fire started sometime in the early evening, she hadn't been home, but Marvin had.

The idea of him dying terrified, in pain, in a fire,

wondering why his mommy wasn't saving him, had wrecked her. She'd cried every day, virtually all day, for a month, thinking of nothing but what her neighbor had told her—that Marvin had been howling piteously, and her neighbor had tried to break the door down, but couldn't manage it. The neighbor said she would always swear that Marvin's yowls had sounded like "Help me."

Piper knew her neighbor was traumatized and only trying to impress how much she'd tried to save him, but she'd succeeded in implanting such unendurable visions and sounds in Piper's mind that she would never speak to the neighbor again.

In bed, Piper tossed as images of Marvin made her stomach ache and threatened to gush tears. Her mother's death—at least Piper had been able to console herself that was from natural causes. But not Marvin's horrid death.

Why hadn't she taken him to her gig that night, as she had many times in the past? This was a post-*Star* lineup at a famous local venue, and sometimes he whined and complained when she was preoccupied, so she'd brought him for a long walk and left him home while she went to her gig.

Then she did what she'd learned to do—push Marvin out of her thoughts. His death was one thought she simply couldn't live with. To this day, she couldn't bear the idea of another pet, of leaving it in a house where tragedy could strike the moment she wasn't around.

While she could accept that Hayden might want her career to fail, she grappled with the notion that he'd kill anyone, animal or human, to make sure that happened.

Her time on *American Star* had been so intense, the contestants' schedules so jam-packed, that much of that chunk of time was a carousel of blurred colors and sounds in her memory. But now individual memories began to surge forth and flash fully-formed in her mind's eye.

The cast hadn't had much time to socialize given their all-consuming schedules of rehearsals, events, media, and filming. But once a week, they'd go to dinner at different restaurants to say goodbye to whoever had been voted off that week.

The "boot dinner" was a sad but funny affair, with people sharing stories of the voted-off contestant. Hayden had been especially adept at coming up with amusing and mildly offensive anecdotes involving whoever was leaving, turning the goodbye dinner into a mini-roast.

After dinner, the cast would pile into however many minivans it took to get them back to the hotel. As the weeks wore on and their numbers dwindled, the dinners became longer and more intimate, and the "*Stars* wrangler," as the woman in charge of getting them all back to the hotel was called, began to loosen her iron grip on their movements.

Piper couldn't quite remember if they were down to five or six the night they'd all decided to head to a nearby bar for a few drinks before going back to the hotel.

No, wait. It was the night Dylan Lopez had been

voted off. He'd finished in fifth place, so there must have been five of them out. No, four of them. Bailie Slinger had been there, but not Cree Omaga who, at sixteen years old, was the only minor remaining.

Dylan, a good-looking guy from Dallas with a bluesy singing style and an Elvis-like swivel in his hips, had been very popular, especially with the young ladies in the audience who'd shrieked when he came on stage like they were being chased with an ax. So his early-ish dispatch had been unexpected, causing Crystal to moan, "You got this wrong, America, you got this wrong."

Dylan was also the jokester of the group, keeping the atmosphere light when their nerves frayed. He was one of Piper's favorites and would be missed. Although the top ten would be reunited for the finale and summer tour, it still felt like a mini-death when someone was voted off, so intense was their daily interactions. Of course, none of them knew that the next year, Dylan would really be dead.

The contestants all managed to keep on a brave face during an elimination, nodding valorously as the judges told them this was only the beginning of their careers, but they all knew the dispiriting truth: leaving the show meant a one-way ticket back to whatever one-horse town or go-nowhere job it had allowed them to escape for awhile.

The night Dylan was voted off, after the "boot dinner," the woman assigned to wrangle them—what was her name again? Cheryl? Cherie?—had agreed that she would pick them up in a couple of hours at The Sunset Idiot, a nearby bar. The wrangler had left with

Cree, the preternaturally talented teen, and Cree's parents, who accompanied her practically everywhere. Cree would end up in third place.

Too valuable to be left unattended, the foursome was chaperoned by a freakishly large bodyguard.

Piper remembered how free she'd felt that night, like she'd been paroled from prison, albeit a prison she desperately wanted to stay in—but not every single minute. At twenty-four, she was one of the older ones in the group, and had been living on her own since she was seventeen. She wasn't accustomed to having her every move watched and micromanaged.

At The Sunset Idiot, they'd toasted to Dylan, downing shots of tequila. Piper had drunk so little alcohol during the run of the show that, despite the meal she'd just had, the booze raced to her brain.

By now, the contestants were so famous that it was impossible to go unnoticed. Strangers began buying them drinks as their burly bodyguard hovered nearby, giving a dead-eyed warning stare to anyone who got too close. The day after an elimination show was their day off, so the gang felt free to keep drinking. They were still in the first flush of fame, delighted and excited that strangers came up to them and *insisted* on buying them drinks, as if they were war heroes.

At the bar, a gaggle of young women wiggled up to Hayden like puppies, doing their *oh-my-gawd-I-loooooove-youuuuu*. When they reached out to paw him as if testing whether or not he was a hologram, the bodyguard stepped in, brushing their greedy hands away.

Then Hayden grabbed Piper's hand and led her to

the small, packed dance floor. They'd twirled and tumbled with drunken abandon into each other's arms. At some point—yes, she remembered it now—they had kissed.

Dylan was next to them, egging them on. "Yes, yes! I knew you two wanted it." Bailie Slinger gyrated around them, pushing their heads together.

Many of the contestants were in relationships, some even married already, including Dylan. But Piper and Hayden were single, and the loneliness and longing for affection could get extreme in that bubble they lived in. The male and female contestants were kept on separate floors of the hotel, and they'd had strict warnings not to "fraternize" after hours, which could lead to an instant dismissal from the show. They all knew that was a euphemism for not getting sexually involved.

But that night, four of them had miraculously found themselves with no eyes on them except those of the wall of flesh that was their bodyguard, with flowing booze, hyper hormones, and a longing for the type of physical connection they'd been denied for months.

And so she and Hayden danced, kissed, and laughed. Hayden was one of the better-looking guys on the show, even in a season that was generally considered to be one of the most attractive ones. He'd started off goofy and nerdy looking—stringy hair and sweater vests —but through the magic of the show's hair and clothing stylists, had transformed into a heartthrob who attracted almost as many shrieks from the heavily female audiences as Dylan did. Adoring signs began popping up: "I

Want to Climb Tower," "Lock Me Into Tower!" and "Tower Power!!"

Although she and Hayden had their moments of tension, Piper had to admit some of that tension was fueled by an unspoken, and somewhat uncomfortable, attraction, mingled with intense competition.

Both of them had flown under the radar for the first half of the show, garnering enough votes to stay on, but not enough to be one of the frontrunners. But those who'd come storming out of the gate eventually turned in a mediocre performance or two with a laughable disco tune or a soppy love ballad. Or worse, tried for a Mariah Carey or Celine Dion song, which only made them seem amateurish in comparison.

As the frontrunners were ruthlessly sent packing, Piper and Hayden started to excel, helped by the fact that they each had powerful but unique voices, and they were each able to take well-worn melodies and freshly rearrange them.

Additionally, both had the quality that was most important in a show like this—more important than great vocal technique, charisma, or originality. They both had resilience. The show was a marathon, not a race.

Week after week, contestants battled brain-draining fatigue, serious illness, demeaning critiques, and cheesy group numbers. Vocal prowess would only get a contestant so far; a steely immune system and mental fortitude were equally as important. (Piper's many nights spent at small performing venues in West Hollywood and Echo Park, waiting until midnight to sing a five-song set for a few dozen people, had unwittingly trained her to with-stand the talent show's grueling late-night rehearsal schedule.)

On the bar's dance floor, their kissing was drunken-sloppy, punctuated by bouts of guffawing and singing, and Piper knew she'd regret it the next day when gossip of the pair's flirting would spread like wildfire to the eliminated finalists, the crew and, for all she knew, the producers and even judges. But in the moment, she didn't care. She was having too much fun.

All too soon, Cheryl (or Cherie) had returned to corral them back to the hotel. In her room, Piper had stumbled to the bathroom and vomited, brushed her teeth, gargled mouthwash, and struggled into under-wear and a sleeveless shirt. Thank goodness she had the room to herself, as Jojo had already been voted off and gone home for a few weeks before she'd have to return for the finale rehearsals.

Piper had wilted into bed when there was a knock at the door. Assuming it was Cheryl (Cherie?), she'd reluc-tantly got up and—trying her best to seem sober—opened it.

Hayden was there, balancing against the wall. He had on his crooked grin, the one with its own thread on the show's forums. Aptly titled HAYDEN'S HOTTTT GRIN, it contained hundreds of screenshots of his mouth. Armed with a laptop, Piper and Jojo had once chased him around the backstage area, trying to force him to look at the photos.

"Have you forgotten me so soon?" he'd half-crooned

while slung next to her door, quoting lyrics from a song he'd done early in the competition.

Even in her inebriated haze, Piper had been startled he'd come to the female contestants' floor. He was putting both of them at risk of being ousted, though she knew the odds of that were virtually nonexistent, given there were only four finalists left. Still, she was a rule follower and didn't want to stir up trouble with the producers.

Whether the producers could *control* the votes was highly debatable, but what wasn't debatable is that they could sway the audience by giving or taking away a contestant's camera time, cutting away or zooming in on a flubbed lyric, or most of all, awarding or denying the performance slot most likely to remain in the viewers' minds—the last one. She didn't want to get on the producers' bad sides when she was so close to nabbing the *American Star* crown.

"What are you doing here?" she'd whispered, probably the dumbest question she'd ever asked in her life.

Hayden had only leaned in and kissed her. She'd let it go on, greatly enjoying his tongue and the light scratch of his three-day stubble, until it occurred to her that any minute someone could come down the hallway and her chance at a big career could be over. No man was worth that, no matter how tempting.

Besides, she hadn't quite forgiven him for spreading that rumor about her and Nolan having an affair; and she was convinced he was its source. If he'd spread a rumor like that, he not only wasn't worth sleeping with, but he certainly wouldn't keep a sexual encounter between them to himself.

"Hayden," she'd slurred, pushing him firmly on the chest, and pretending to be drunker than she was. "You need to go."

"Come on, Pip," he'd said in his soft sexy rasp. "No one will know. I'll leave early."

"We can't risk it."

"What's life without a little risk?"

There was an unexpectedly tender look in his sea-glass green eyes. If they'd said anything else to each other, she didn't remember what. Only remembered that he'd soon slunk off, and she'd shut the door and locked it.

The next day, Piper was suffering from hangover pangs and spent much of the spotless sunny afternoon lounging by the pool in her bikini. Hayden, in sunglasses and a baseball cap jammed down over his forehead, had roamed in and out of the pool area.

Not once did he come over and speak with her, which was fine, as she didn't want to speak to him either. Too awkward.

In bed, Piper let the memories of that faraway time drift away from her. She sat up and adjusted the folded pillow under her knees. Keeping her hamstring muscles elevated was the only thing that helped ease her restless leg syndrome.

Had rejecting Hayden's advances that night fostered

a hatred of her so malignant, so vindictive, that he'd wanted to destroy her post-*Star* success? And he was willing to join a cult and put a curse on her to guarantee her failure?

Something else occurred to her: Dylan Lopez's death from cardiac arrest. As Piper recalled, he'd just signed with a major record label.

Dylan. Hayden's roommate. Also the finalist considered Hayden's closest competition. And he'd snagged a record deal as Hayden's career was on the rise.

This made at least three people—herself, Dylan, and Anton Bishop—who'd gone up against Hayden and lost.

Chapter Eleven

"They're definitely strange," said Jojo, putting the second letter down on the table. "But you're not seriously believing a cult put a curse on you, I hope."

The pair sat in a Vietnamese restaurant close to Piper's neighborhood. Piper's restless leg syndrome as well as her circling thoughts about the letters had kept her awake most of the night. By the time Jojo got in touch to confirm that she could meet for lunch, Piper was exhausted. So her friend offered to come to Brooklyn, saying she wouldn't mind doing some shopping on Fulton Street anyway.

Piper had waited until their bubble tea and summer rolls were delivered, then she showed Jojo both letters and told of her suspicion that Hayden was the "high-ranking member." Jojo had read them, grimacing and blowing out her lips, making brittle exclamations and dumbfounded *Whaa?* noises.

"You don't think it's possible?" Piper asked. "With everything that happened to me after the show?"

Jojo took a sip of milky tea, eyeing her dubiously. "You had a run of bad luck. Since when do you believe in curses?"

"What about Dylan? He died right after getting a record contract. And Anton Bishop? He fell and broke his face open. Thanks to that, Hayden wins an Oscar."

"Shit happens."

Irritated, Piper stuffed the letters back inside of her tote bag. She'd thought that Jojo, with her chanting and insistence on praying before every performance, would believe that invisible forces could impact your life. Not to mention you didn't have to be religious to believe in unseen but potent forces. Isn't that what molecules, electricity, and catching the flu was about?

"I'm not saying I believe in curses," Piper tried to clarify. "But what about everything you did during the show, the chanting and incense burning?" She didn't dare bring up the praying. "You seemed like you believe that sort of thing can alter reality."

"That's different," Jojo said, stubbornly. "They were good vibe rituals, that's all. Besides, it didn't work. I don't mean to be rude," she said, picking up on Piper's mood. "But I think some nutjob wrote them. Someone who wants Hayden to be the new judge, or even me, though I hope my fans are above that. Or someone who wants Crystal to be the only girl judge. Whoever it is knows about everything that happened to you through the media. And saw the item about you being considered for the panel. That's it."

"Even if that's it, you don't think that person could be Hayden?"

Jojo shrugged and spooned some tapioca pearls into her mouth. "Hayden can be a jerk, but he's not psycho. Besides, he seems like he's grown up. He even DM'd me on social and wished me good luck with the audition." Her eyes glazed over as her mouth hovered over her bubble tea. "Funny how I once gave you such a hard time about him."

"Well, it's *somebody*," Piper said, picking apart a summer roll.

"Listen," Jojo said, soothingly. "Do you think I didn't have hate mail while on *Star*? Plenty of turds didn't want a fat woman winning. At one point I had to ask Oliver Corbyn to have someone open my mail for me."

"Oh, no," Piper said. "I'm so sorry. You never mentioned that."

"I needed to keep focused. I'm surprised I didn't get any about the judge position." She glanced up at the waiter as he delivered their meals. "Maybe people are more enlightened these days."

Piper stuffed a piece of grilled tofu into her mouth. The two ate in silence for a minute, then she said, "I've decided I'm pulling out. I'm telling Nolan today."

"Lady!" Jojo rattled her fork on her plate. "If you believe someone cursed you with bad luck, why can't you believe someone blessed you with good luck? You've got a great guy, a baby on the way, a new house, and a second chance at stardom."

"And crazy letters threatening me."

"They're only letters. You've got to ignore the

haters." Jojo shook her fork and went back to her food. "Don't let them win."

Of course, Jojo was right. But Piper couldn't shake a powerfully apprehensive feeling that had settled on her after the first letter, as if she sat cocooned in a darkened theater, watching a disturbing movie she was unable to look away from.

"If it was only me…" she said.

"You can't stop living life because you're pregnant. Show that kid what mama is made of."

"I'll think about it. I only wanted to tell you everything in case whoever it is comes for you next."

"You think I'd let some crap-for-brains keep me from my dreams?" Jojo asked, appearing astonished. "Assholes been wanting me to crawl into a hole my entire life." She leaned forward, locking her big brown eyes onto Piper. "It's not going to happen. The harder they come at me, the more I get into their face."

AT HOME, PIPER PRACTICED some narration and cleaned the kitchen, which was still a mess from last night's dinner. Firio had been working late, and the cooking had fallen upon her, as they'd decided to cook most nights, figuring that would be healthier for the baby than takeout.

Every end-quarter, Firio's hedge fund published its return on investment performance for shareholders. The date for the fourth quarter was approaching and he was more distracted than usual.

As Piper scrubbed a big pan, she thought about what Jojo had said, and whether she should stick to her decision to talk to Nolan and pull out of the running. How brave her friend had been getting up on that stage every week and singing her heart out, despite knowing there were people in the audience who hated her because of her weight.

This brought Piper's trail of thoughts back to how Hayden had snatched up "I Say A Little Prayer" while Jojo was sick when the rest of the cast had stayed away from it, knowing she would want to sing it. And how Jojo had been saddled with that Nancy Sinatra song that spelled her doom.

What was it that Jojo had said about Hayden at lunch?

Funny how I once gave you such a hard time about him.

That's right. When Jojo had returned to Los Angeles for the finale rehearsals, Piper had sensed coolness and distance from her friend. Thinking Jojo was stressed, she'd ignored it for awhile, but when it continued, she'd confronted her one night in their hotel room, which Jojo had moved back into.

"Is something wrong, Jo?" she'd asked.

Piper was taken aback when Jojo had turned on her with her perpetually cheerful expression erased.

"Hooking up with Hayden?" she'd scolded. "*Really?*"

Piper had cringed, the sour realization that her make-out session with Hayden from a few weeks before had gotten around. She'd mistakenly believed she'd escaped the rumor mill on that one.

"We didn't hook up," she'd clarified, weakly. "Just kissed. I was drunk."

"With the dude who stole my song? He's the reason I went home. I thought you were my friend."

"Oh, come on," Piper had pleaded. "You got to go home and get some action from your boyfriend. I've been here for months like a nun buried in a monastery. Hayden's the only guy left who's single."

"You choose dick over friendship," Jojo had insisted.

"There was no dick involved! We just kissed!"

"Someone heard him at the door."

Unbelievable. Nothing got by this group. "I didn't let him in. Be sure to pass that along to Bailie." It had to have been Bailie flapping her lips. She was right across the hall.

Jojo had stood with a pout on until Piper walked over and touched her on her arm. "I didn't know you'd feel so betrayed or I wouldn't have even kissed him. Everyone was drunk, and I've been really lonely. I can't stand the guy."

"Fine," Jojo had relented, softening her posture. But she'd remained cool throughout the run of finale rehearsals, and the incident only seemed to completely fade once they hit the road for the *American Star* tour.

If Piper were honest with herself, with the talent show restrictions gone, she wouldn't have minded reigniting things with Hayden during the tour, exploring an offbeat but electric chemistry she sensed between them, one that the show's viewers had picked up on before she did. But that would have been impossible without antagonizing Jojo. Besides, Hayden had swanned into a heartthrob and disappeared after each meet-and-greet with the fans—presumably with whichever groupie he'd picked out for the evening.

When Marco, the tour band's drummer, began paying her attention, Piper let herself be drawn into his scattered and heavy-drinking life. She'd been a few years without male companionship and her defenses were shaky. Marco could be very seductive when he wanted to be.

Piper placed the rinsed-out pan inside of a dish rack. She preferred to wash the dishes by hand rather than place them all in the dishwasher, as she found the motion of dishwashing to be relaxing.

She stared out the window above the sink into the small but pleasant backyard, filled with sandy-gray old trees and bordered by a green hedge. She especially loved the probably-hundreds-of-years-old Japanese maple that was so gnarled it looked like a contortionist halfway to a backbend. The yard was one of the main reasons she and Firio had wanted the house, so their child would have a patch of nature to run around on.

Over the years, Piper had forgotten how much her friend had held it against Piper that she'd kissed Jojo's "enemy."

An insane idea formulated in her mind. Had her friend's resentment about Piper briefly hooking up with Hayden been enough to make *Jojo* want to ruin Piper's career? It was a little odd how quickly she'd outright dismissed Piper's theory about a cult's curse. And Jojo stood to gain a lot by getting the judge position.

Piper absently watched two squirrels maniacally

chase each other around a big, gnarled oak that separated her yard from her neighbor's.

Come to think of it, Jojo would be a better candidate to join a cult than Hayden would. During the show, she seemed to be doing everything in her power to invoke deities and spiritual forces to help her win the contest.

If some group came along and promised Jojo success in exchange for undying loyalty, would she have taken it? Perhaps, all of these years, Jojo considered herself the rightful owner of the *American Star* crown. But if so, why not sic the cult on Hayden, the guy who'd "stolen" her song?

No. There was no way Jojo would ever want to harm her. Not after everything they'd been through together. The letters were making her mind go haywire.

Piper rinsed her sudsy hands, wiped them, and sat down at the kitchen table. Exhaustion was sneaking up on her. She didn't think she would have the energy to discuss not auditioning with Nolan, especially as he would try to talk her out of it, and he was very persuasive.

With her chin in her palm, she ground the ball of one bare foot into the wood-beamed floors. Barefoot, pregnant, and in the kitchen. She snorted out a laugh, and shook her head. Was she going to throw away one last chance at a big career because of a couple of letters?

She'd survived *American Star*, the most difficult boot-camp in show business. Not only survived it but won it. There was no doubt the tragedies that followed the show had made her more fragile. And now she felt more vulnerable than she'd ever felt, on constant alert for potential dangers to the life inside of her.

Was this who she was going to be from now on—a scared, timid person? One who wouldn't reach for her dreams because of a couple of creepy letters that claimed supernatural powers?

Looking down at her stomach, she said, "I think there's someone I need to talk to."

Chapter Twelve

She stood for forty-five minutes, trying to keep her stomach from being jostled by the six-rows-deep horde of fans lined up outside the backstage door of the Ambassador Theater. But it was an impossible task. After a couple of hard bumps, she moved to the very end of the line to wait for Hayden.

The waiting was an exercise not only in physical torture on her feet, but emotional torture. She used to be on his side of the excitement. There was relief that she no longer was, but she also felt a raw, gnawing ache, an involuntary sense of disbelief that she stood invisible on the fan side.

Hadn't these people all around her watched *American Star*? Hadn't they first been pulled into Hayden's orbit when he lost to her? How was it that no one recognized her? Did she look so different or was it that she'd been completely forgotten about?

She tried to rein in the adolescent foot-stamping going on in her brain, a distinct and unauthorized part of herself, one that might turn to the crowd and vaingloriously shout that ultimate lament of entitlement: "Don't you know who I am?" (If they did, they did not care.)

Hayden, in aviator sunglasses, black leather pants, and a long-sleeved black shirt with silver stenciling, inched excruciatingly slowly down the line signing headshots and sketches, posing for selfies, and taking various gifts and handing them to a man behind him. The man's arms would fill up with bounty before placing it on a nearby folding table.

The scene hadn't changed much from the *American Star* days though the fans now wielded cell phones instead of iPods, flip phones, and digital cameras. She recognized the same sorts of calls she used to hear: "We love you," "You rock," and the perennial, "It's my birthday!!!"

God forbid you missed someone yelling it was their birthday, the next day that person would be in the press with a frown on, and the headline would be something like, "Birthday Girl Left Brokenhearted When American Star Refuses to Sign Her T-Shirt."

Next to her, Piper heard two women plotting a physical assault if Hayden came close enough to them. "I'll bite his arm," said one. "I dare you," said the other. "I'll do it softly," the first woman clarified. "Just a taste."

Coming here had been a dumb idea, but Piper had been consumed with the need to speak to him, and didn't have his phone number, and doubted he'd see a social media request in time for her to make it to the theater when he came out. She'd emailed Amy Baldash for his number, but the reporter had merely routed her to Hayden's publicist. This seemed the quickest, most surefire way to reach him.

As he finally approached the end, Piper's strong voice hollering, "Hayden! It's Piper!!!" was enough to draw his attention over the clamor of the mostly-female crowd. She watched as he spoke into the ear of a large security guard, who moved aside a portion of the metal gate and helped her through.

"Jeez, Piper," Hayden said. "You should have told me you were coming."

"It was spontaneous," she gasped, still in awe at the animalistic gathering, the kind she hadn't had to deal with in years.

She'd forgotten how nerve-wracking unleashed adoration could be, although her crowds had never been this level of frenzied, a level generally reserved for male stars. The teen girls waiting outside for autographs on the *American Star* tour would even ask Piper if she could go inside and fetch Hayden, treating her as nothing more than a messenger. Or they'd chant "To-*wer*-Pow-*er*" in her face.

"Is there any way I can speak to you when you're done here?" she asked him, noting Ava, who was standing like a blonde willow tree several feet away. "Alone?"

"Alone?" He looked quizzical.

"It's—I'm sorry. It's better if it's only you and me, if possible."

"Ahh, hold on." He raised a finger, then walked to Ava, who peeped around his head to eye Piper. Piper gave a toothy smile and waved. Ava smiled back, though she looked uncertain who Piper was.

Hayden drifted once more towards the fans, who were insistently calling out his name. Those calls were like a giant sucking magnet, Piper knew.

"Would you like to sit down?" came the silky female voice in Piper's ear. Ava was smiling at her. "I can go inside and get you a chair."

"Oh, um, that's okay. Do you think he'll be much longer?"

Ava shrugged apologetically. "You know how it is."

Not anymore, Piper nearly blurted but decided that would sound bitter. Piper watched Hayden for about fifteen minutes and, at some point, realized Ava had quietly receded into the theater.

Eventually, Hayden walked over to her and said, "Sorry, I should have wrapped things up earlier," looking at her stomach. He took her by the arm. "Let's get in my car so people don't follow us, and we'll go around the block and come back to Shelby's."

"Sounds good," she said, desperate to get off her feet.

* * *

At Shelby's, the hostess led them to a private table in the back, near the one where she and Firio had sat under the flickering gas lamps with Nolan. The female server greeted Hayden by name and asked, "The usual?" to which he nodded. Piper ordered soda water, though for the first time since her pregnancy, she desperately wanted to slug a glass of wine.

"Pip, Pip," he said, stretching back. "I didn't expect to see you in that mob, and in your condition."

"It's not a 'condition,' it's a pregnancy," she teased. "I thought it would be easier than trying to track you down through social media, but I was wrong. Wow, that was a scene. Just like the *Star* days."

"What's on your mind?"

Earlier, she'd decided that the best way to try to get information from him might be through his ego. Coming straight out and asking him if he belonged to a cult and had put a curse on her wasn't going to get her anywhere.

"First off," she started, wiggling forward. "I want to say how proud I am of you. You really made a success of it. I'm sorry I didn't contact you earlier and congratulate you."

The right side of his mouth, the one that went up farther than the left, resulting in his famous crooked grin, slid obnoxiously towards his cheek. "Oh, thanks. I appreciate that."

The waitress returned, balancing their drinks and a small bowl of salted nuts, which he began popping into his mouth. She poured a bottled beer into a frosted mug for him.

"Anything else I can get you, Hayden?" she asked with no small amount of insinuation, looking down at him like she wanted to devour him alive.

He shook his head and thanked her, and she reluctantly sauntered off.

"I see the ladies still love you," Piper said, laying it on thick.

He shouldn't have been handsome—the green eyes were a bit too squinty, the nose a bit too bulbous at the tip, the jaw a bit too round, the lips definitely too smirky. But it all came together, a handsomeness that wasn't symmetrical but somehow was extraordinarily effective.

"I had to stop coming out to hug people," he said. "A lot of women like to get grabby ass. A few of the men too."

They both laughed and rolled their eyes at each other. Piper remembered how unprepared she'd been for the tornado of demands from strangers after *American Star*. Through its votes, the public had created her—god-ed her into existence. So they fully expected to have a say in her life. They felt perfectly entitled to tell her what songs she should sing and how she should sing them, whom she should and should not date, and even asked her to listen to demos and introduce her to contacts.

And the hugs. Oh my God, the hugs. She'd never realized how hug-starved the American population was until she'd won *American Star*. Once, after leaning over a table at a mall signing to hug each person who'd asked, her back muscles had spasmed, leaving her in bed for twenty-four hours.

"And the babies?" Piper asked him.

Hayden slowly shook his head. "My security fends off the baby tossers now," he said.

In many cultures, it's considered good luck to touch someone of importance. As Piper rose through the show's ranks, more and more people reached out to press their hands against her, even press their young children against her, and occasionally threw—truly *threw*—a baby into her arms. Fortunately, she hadn't dropped any of them.

Hayden traced his nail into the frost of his beer mug, peering studiously at her from behind his glasses. "You happy? Your husband a good guy?"

"Yes, he definitely is."

"That's good." He popped more nuts into his mouth, and stretched his arms, rolling his neck around. "The show is pretty intense. I love it but I can't do it much longer. I'm not twenty-five anymore."

"None of us are." She paused. "I'll get to the point since I'm sure you have places to be. You're up for the judge spot on the new *Star*, right?"

"They've asked about it, yeah. I know you and Jojo are up for it too."

"You want it?"

He shrugged one shoulder, staring past her, examining the oil painting above her head. "Here's the thing. I'd like what you have," he said, dragging his gaze back to hers. "I'm tired of the touring, not having a real relationship. I think I've found someone I want to spend my life with, but I can't do that on the road."

Piper nodded. "I'm glad to hear you've found someone."

"I think I have. No, I'm *sure* I have." He looked around, as if a tabloid reporter might be nearby, and dropped his voice. "I might as well tell you, I'm talking about Ava."

Piper nodded again. This wasn't exactly a surprise to her given the meaningful glances she'd caught them passing each other.

"It's funny," he said, taking another sip of beer. "I was kind of on the fence about it, and then I saw you…" He paused. "How you're all settled down, and I guess…" He paused again, and couldn't seem to make eye contact with her. "It got to me. Everyone settling down. You know how the road is, it can be so… empty and temporary feeling. I want a house, a kid or two, pets, the whole enchilada. A *home*."

"If you think Ava is the one, you should go for it. Plus she understands your career."

"She does," he nodded. "Better than myself even. I was lucky she agreed to take me on when my deal with Moxie ended." He plucked at his black shirt, emblazoned with silver Gothic calligraphy that said LONDON and something else Piper couldn't decipher. "She's smart, beautiful, and gets me in a way no one else has. So I'm going to ask her to marry me. I even bought the ring. I think she'll say yes but I'm nervous as hell."

"Congratulations."

"Thanks much." He tipped his head back, delivering more nuts into his mouth and swallowing it all down with another swig of beer. "So, yeah, I want the gig. It doesn't pay what I'm used to, but it'll be a lot less hustle. There's something else too. I trust you, but please keep this to yourself. I'm starting to have ringing in my ears, tinnitus. My doctor says I need to cut way back on gigs or I could go deaf."

"I'm sorry to hear that," Piper said, and they both said, "No pun intended," in unison and smiled.

"But I'm not going to lie, it's bizarre competing with you and Jojo again. Like we're back on *Star*."

"It *is* bizarre," she said, plotting how to use this opener to maneuver into questioning him about the letters. "I don't like that part of it either. I'm not sure I'm going to audition."

"Oh?" he asked, what looked to be authentic surprise in his eyes. "Why not?"

"For one, you beat me at everything."

"Me?" His hand flew to his chest. "*You* beat me!"

"On *Star* but not any time after that. You've got the Oscar and the Tony."

"I didn't win the Tony."

"You should have." She nodded vigorously and watched as he leaned over the table. Even in the dim of the room, she detected a suspicious glint behind his glasses.

"What's all this about? You're not acting like yourself. All these compliments."

"I'm serious. I think you're so talented and—"

"Pip," he interrupted. "What is this all about?"

She looked down, took a deep breath, and made eye contact. "If you want the show very much, I'd be willing to bow out."

"Why would you do that?" he scoffed. "Whoever gets it, gets it. You got a raw deal after *Star*. I read about some of that stuff that happened to you. I should have gotten in touch, but…"

He fiddled with a round silver pendant hanging

down his shirt. Piper zeroed in on it, trying to decode its design, but he kept his fingers on the pendant almost reverently then dropped it inside the neckline of his shirt.

"I was too caught up in myself," he continued. "I felt if I didn't do everything I possibly could that minute, I'd be sent packing back to Iowa. Back pouring concrete, playing in a bar band. It was terrifying."

"Did you think I'd keep you from getting what you wanted?"

"You?" For the second time, surprise flashed in his eyes. "What do you mean?"

"Do you see me as competition?"

"I did on the show, sure. My biggest competition."

"I mean after the show. Did you think if I was successful, you wouldn't be?"

Bewilderment wavered in his face. She reminded herself that not only was he a great singer, but a great actor. He'd won an Oscar for it. The truth may or may not reveal itself in his expressions. She wished the bar was brighter and he didn't have on glasses so she could better read his eyes.

"Woah. That didn't even occur to me." He leaned back, shifting uncomfortably. "I was selfish for a long time and didn't reach out when I heard about your throat situation and your fire. But I should have. Plus, I —I wasn't sure how you felt about me."

"In what way?"

His mouth turned down and he stared into his mug. "We didn't talk much on the tour. I thought you didn't like me for... that night I came up to your room. I know that got around. I put you in danger of getting kicked off the show. I also had some stuff going on. Stuff I didn't want to tell anyone and it affected my attitude. Anyway…" he trailed off.

She was contemplating how to bring up a cult and strange letters when he snorted and asked, "You want a confession?"

"Sure."

"'Woulda, Shoulda, Coulda,'" he said, naming one of his most famous songs. "That was about you. Kind of regretting how I never made a play for you, other than that one drunken night. I spent some years, um, wishing that I'd, um…"

Peeping up at him from under her lashes, she thought he might be trying to flatter her into complacency. "That's nice," was all she could think to say.

"Yeah, well. Too late, Tower!" He dropped his head and took another sip of beer.

"Hayden," she said, and waited until he looked directly at her. "I have a baby now. I have a life inside of me."

He sat with his mouth half-open, eyes wide. "Yeah? I wasn't—that was—I'm not hitting on you. I only thought you'd find it amusing."

"This is very serious. If you don't want me to try out for the show, I won't. I don't mind not being on it. But I can't—I can't have…"

"What is it?" he asked, sounding concerned. "I'm confused."

She felt her lower lip quivering, and a salty stinging at the backs of her eyes. "It's that—there are people who want you to be on the show, not me. I've been through so much already."

Suddenly, he reached out and grasped her hand, squeezing it tight. "Something is going on. Tell me."

"Just, please. I don't want the show that badly."

"I don't want it that badly either. I'd be happy if you or Jojo got it. Something is going on and you need to tell me what."

She shook her head and gently extracted her hand from his. "There isn't."

He kept staring at her. She could feel the heat of it though she couldn't bring herself look at him. She felt so pathetic that she couldn't come out and ask him about the letters—and about a *curse*. But how paranoid, how *bitter* she would sound—and how *crazy* she would seem to blame her career's nosedive on a *curse*, and specifically, a Hayden-directed curse.

She wouldn't blame him if he laughed in her face. Laughed and said something like, *I know you won, Pip, but it was only by a million votes. You had as much of a chance, more of a chance, to make it big as I did. And you didn't. That's not a curse, that's YOU.*

"I want you to audition, okay?" he finally said. "It's an order."

She made herself look back up at him and saw he had on his crooked grin.

Chapter Thirteen

S he didn't get home until a little after eleven. Firio came out of their bedroom's en suite bathroom in boxer briefs, looking exhausted, with those bluish scoops that appeared under his eyes when he was overly tired. Kissing her with a freshly washed, clean-smelling face, he said, "How was Jojo?"

"She's good. She has a couple of dates at Sony Hall coming up, we could go."

"Sure," he said, giving a big stretch, and plopping into bed.

Piper undressed, brushed her teeth, combed through her shoulder-length, chestnut hair, which was overdue for a haircut. Examining the white ripples that pronged around her drum-tight belly, she realized Shea butter was doing nothing to prevent them. She supposed she'd have to get used to them.

She didn't like having lied to Firio about where she'd been earlier, but had worried he wouldn't want her to confront Hayden alone. If he'd wanted to come with her, she doubted she'd be able to get anything out of Hayden; as it was, she'd choked when it came to directly asking him about the letters.

In bed, she turned off the bedside light. Firio snuggled into her, wrapping one arm below the curvature of her stomach. His arm was heavy, so she could only stand it for several minutes before she'd gently remove it. By then, he'd usually fallen asleep anyway.

His breathing was growing more rhythmic. As he was a fast sleeper, she decided to tell him the truth before he drifted away.

"Honey," she said, quietly. "I wasn't with Jojo. I went to see Hayden."

With a soft grunt, he shifted, seemingly coming out of a half-sleep.

"I wanted to see if I could figure out if he has anything to do with the letters, and I was worried you'd insist on coming."

"Bella," he groaned. "I wish you wouldn't go where I don't know, not now, in case anything happens. But I wouldn't have tried to come or stop you."

She listened to the far-off, wailing warble of an ambulance on one of the busier streets that boxed in the oasis of their neighborhood. There were nights when she heard ambulance after ambulance. She wondered how it was that so many people around her were sick, hurt, or dying, and how it was always there, death. Always the next block over, until one day it was your block, and your house, and your room, and you.

"What did he say about the letters?" Firio asked.

"I couldn't bring them up. It sounds so nuts. So I

hinted at them—that if he didn't want me to audition, I wouldn't."

"What did he say about that?" he asked, sounding sleepier.

She stared up at an orange glow from outside that wavered along the ceiling, then vanished. "He said he wants me to audition. Nothing he said or did makes me certain the letters are about him, or he's writing them. If anything, now I'm feeling like he isn't involved at all."

"Maybe he isn't," Firio sighed, rolling onto his back.

"Then I don't know who is. But he did say that he'd like to be a judge. He's going to ask his business manager to marry him and wants to settle down and stop touring. You remember the woman we met backstage? Ava. The pretty blonde."

"Uh, sort of," he said, and she could feel him stretching an arm over his head. She knew he was tired, he'd been up since dawn doing work, and she didn't want to keep talking and keeping him awake.

"Anyway…" She brought his hand to her mouth and kissed it. "Oh, I need my pillow." With another long grunt, Firio got up, found the pillow on the floor, and stuffed it under her knees for her. He got back into bed.

She heard his breathing deepen, and he said, slurrily, "What about her?"

"What about who?" Piper asked, feeling sleepiness encroach.

"The girlfriend. Maybe…" he sighed and shifted again. "She really wants him to get that job."

Piper opened her eyes and blinked up at the dark ceiling, crisscrossed with cones of muted white light.

"Ava?" she asked, her voice louder, sleepiness chased off. "You think it could be Ava?"

"Just a theory. My personal opinion is that it's some lunatic—what do you call them? Those fans who go overboard for a celebrity?"

"Superfan."

"Superfan," he repeated.

Ava. Her breathing quickened as the pure common-sense of this unconsidered suspect penetrated her thoughts. "I suppose it could be. But why not send letters to Jojo too?"

"That's as far as my detective work goes," he said, pushing up and kissing her on the lips. "Can we talk more tomorrow?"

"Of course. Sorry. Go to sleep."

He rolled over, and within minutes was softly snoring. Good thing she'd gotten used to this sound, even liked it now, or it would have driven her bonkers.

Ava. She could have seen all the things that had happened to Piper after her *American Star* win simply by reading articles. Ava had been in the entertainment industry long enough to have heard of The True Way. The fact that Piper had shown the first letter to Crystal, who knew of the cult, was pure coincidence.

Perhaps Jojo wasn't receiving letters too because Ava had some inside information, knew that Jojo wasn't really a contender. Nolan might have only asked Jojo to audition so he could squash those rumors of him having her voted off, so he could look like a good guy for considering a heavy woman for the judge slot.

But in reality, Nolan had no plans of letting Jojo

actually get it. The position was between Hayden and Piper. And Ava knew this somehow. She knew lots of people; Nolan could have blabbed to someone who'd blabbed to Ava. That's the way the entertainment business worked—lots and lots of blabbing.

Another thing about the letters nagged at Piper—there had been no misspellings. Whoever was writing them was smart, and that's the first quality Hayden had mentioned about Ava that he liked: that she was smart.

Could this be what was happening? Ava was a businesswoman, she had a reputation to uphold. She'd also seemed perfectly nice. But it made a lot more sense that a woman was trying to scare Piper off auditioning so her boyfriend would get the position than that a cult had put a curse on her.

My God, she'd almost fallen straight into this ridiculous little plot. What an easy mark she'd been.

Ava seemed to be a savvy, intelligent, competitive sort. But Ava had no idea who she was dealing with. She was dealing with a woman who, at twenty-four, had won *American Star* by out-maneuvering a hundred thousand people, including Ava's boyfriend.

It was time that young woman, the Piper she used to be, made a return.

Chapter Fourteen

"That was spot on, Piper. Spot on," Nolan clipped out as Piper stood up from the long, glass-topped table, her legs weak with adrenaline. Crystal was smiling at her, and she said in her creamy voice, "You did well. I'm so proud of you."

Piper could feel herself beaming like she used to beam when the judges would give her a complimentary critique after a performance. A tech woman unthreaded the tiny microphone pinned to her blouse front and took off the mic pack from the back of her skirt. Piper knew to wear bright colors, which showed better on camera, so she had on a red, gold, and pink blouse, and gold skirt, an outfit she'd picked out a few days ago. The skirt she'd found at a maternity shop. It had a wide stretchy band that allowed her to get the waist around her ballooning stomach.

Having the pressure of trying to lose the baby weight before filming officially started next year wasn't something she'd thought closely about, nor did she look forward to having all that pressure about her appearance back on her. That is, if she got the job and there was certainly no guarantee of that.

She said a round of goodbyes to Crystal and the tech people who were milling about, none of whom she recognized from the original *American Star*. Nolan walked her to the double doors and stood outside of them with her. The audition had been in the Omni Hotel.

In the wide hall, Nolan turned. "I was watching you on the monitor and you look great, and had some charming natural reactions."

"I wasn't expecting that guy in the insect costume," she laughed.

"We wanted to recreate the types of people you'll see. It was perfect when you said, 'Someone get the Raid.'" He wagged a finger at her. "But careful. No being funnier than me."

Piper felt the blood drain from her face. Seeing her reaction, Nolan grinned. "I'm joking with you. I've been doing this for so long, I've thousands of *bon mots*. Use the same ones over and over, if I'm honest."

Relieved, she said, "I did think that girl Kayla was very good."

"She's a professional brought in for the audition. You had on point comments about her. Telling someone they're good isn't the hard part. It's telling someone they're bad and having to do it hundreds of times. After awhile, they all sound alike."

"It was fun."

"Good job, Piper," he said, solemnly laying one manicured hand on her shoulder. "I mean it. Now it's up to Oliver and the rest, but I'll do what I can." He held her forearm, escorting her to an elevator, apparently thinking she was too delicate to walk on her own. "You have a car home?"

"Yes, the coordinator gave me a number and code."

"Don't want you on the Tube," he said, using the British term for the subway. She didn't bother to inform him that she took the subway all of the time. "We should be in touch within a few weeks." He paused and stared into her eyes; his stare was so unapologetically direct, it was always disconcerting. "You sure you want this? You might get it, you know."

"Yes, I—I do. I wouldn't waste your time otherwise."

"Excellent. I don't enjoy having my time wasted."

With one more flashing white grin, and a jaunty salute, Nolan walked back towards the double doors of the audition room.

Piper took a deep breath and smiled to herself. The audition had been a blast of euphoria, the type she hadn't felt in a very long time.

It was a euphoria linked directly to the deepest part of her, a part as old as her oldest memories of dancing and singing in her bedroom when she was a child, hairbrush in hand, making what she considered "star faces" in the full-length mirror; of sitting on the piano bench while her grandmother, smelling of Chanel No. 5, ran through keys with her.

Around ten years old, she'd started waking up from dreams of fully orchestrated songs, with lyrics and all instrumentation. She'd attempt to sing them for her mother, who would try to figure out what songs they were. Only they didn't exist. They were Piper's songs.

By twelve, she had a busking spot in Dupont Circle, Washington D.C., forty minutes from where she lived with her parents in Silver Spring. Her guitar case would collect a couple hundred dollars each weekend. People couldn't get over this little girl who belted out the songs of Sheryl Crow, Jewel, and Alanis Morissette like a mature woman.

Music and performing was the blueprint for who she was as a human being, the fabric of her soul. Things she'd dreamed about for much longer than she had anything else, including being a mother or wife. It felt right to acknowledge this vital part of her psyche again, even if it meant only watching other people perform.

On the sidewalk, she texted the number of the car service that had picked her up in Ditmas Park. The bustle of Times Square swarmed by as she stood under the Gothic rococo awning of the Omni Hotel. In her thirty-second week, Piper's natural temperature seemed to have increased a few degrees, so despite it being late October, she opened up her long, fuzzy fleece cardigan to allow in some cool air.

Absently people watching, she glanced to her left and saw a man smoking a cigarette. Something about his profile tugged at her memory, but she couldn't place him. Gaunt cheeks, pale skin, an expensive, tailored gray suit. He sucked on his cigarette, looking pensive and nervous at the same time. Then he turned, and it rushed on her why the man seemed familiar. It was Mitch McCabe.

"Mitch!" she called out, automatically.

His expression was a complete blank. Of course, he wouldn't remember her. He'd met so many contestants over the decade he'd hosted *American Star*. Not to mention she was pregnant and ten years older.

She walked towards him. His permatan was gone. He also looked like he'd lost weight, and he had already been skinny. Replacing the flaxen curls was a shorn nest of dull brown hair. Despite the tailored suit, this Mitch looked uncouth, almost sickly, and she didn't know he smoked either.

Then she remembered that Nolan had said Mitch was in a rehab center.

"It's Piper Dunner," she said, only a few feet from him. "From Season 7."

Mitch sucked the last dregs of his cigarette and tossed it to the ground. "Hey, hey, Piper," he said, and she noticed stains of sweat along his high forehead. When he smiled, it wasn't the Hollywood perfect smile she remembered either, but one that was worn, beaten down. "You here for the audition?" he asked.

"Yes. Are you too?"

She figured it couldn't be a coincidence he was at the Omni Hotel on the same day she, Nolan, and Crystal were.

"They called me in for a talk," he said. "I told them I'm not quite up for it, but Nolan practically begged."

His eyes were hollows, the sparkly blues she remembered were deadened and darting, with deep crevices around their corners. His pale hands looked shaky and he rubbed them together. Nothing about him was the manic male pixie from ten years ago. She felt bad for him and wondered what had brought him to this state. Could it be drugs after all? Her stomach was so big that normally people at least glanced at it, especially people she knew, but he didn't seem to notice it.

"Well, good luck," she said, trying to smile at him as if she couldn't see how much he'd changed. "I don't think it will be *American Star* without you."

"Hey, hey," he said, dipping in closer to her. "Hayden is up for being a judge, right? That's what I heard."

"I heard that," she said, noncommittally.

He nodded jerkily, and looked down at the ground, then back towards the revolving glass doors of the hotel.

"You should be careful around him," he said, so lowly that Piper wasn't sure what she'd heard.

"I—sorry?"

"Just be careful." He leaned in more, and his eyes were pools of dark, reflective blue. "I've already said too much. I'll—I'll deny it."

Piper's mouth hung open and she was acutely aware of the surge of people and noise around them. Mitch was moving away from her quickly, but she jogged after him and grabbed the sleeve of his suit.

"Mitch. Is there something about Hayden I should know?"

Mitch looked for a moment as if he'd never seen her before, and shook her hand off his sleeve. "I didn't say that," he said, confrontationally. "When did I say that?" His voice grew louder, and she thought for a second that he might call security on her, like she was a harassing fan.

"Right now. You said I should be careful around Hayden."

"Hey," he said, putting up his palms in a gesture of surrender. "I think you misunderstood me." He stared deep into her eyes with a rabid look, a small animal caught in a trap. "Good luck with the show." He hurried through the glass doors of the hotel.

Piper stood wondering what the hell had just happened. Was there any way she'd completely misheard what he'd said? Perhaps her thoughts about a cult curse had taken over her brain so completely that when Mitch had said something harmless about Hayden, she'd converted it into something sinister. But if so, why did he say he'd said too much, and he'd deny it? She couldn't have imagined all of that.

Her phone pinged and she looked down to see a message that said, "Car #375 is at your location."

In the cool backseat of the town car, she ran the scene again and again in her mind.

You need to be careful around him.

I've already said too much. I'll deny it.

Could Mitch know about this cult? And that Hayden was a part of it?

If so, that meant everything she'd assured herself over the past few days—that there was no cult with supernatural powers that had put a curse on her—could be wrong. Could mean that Hayden was a dangerous person and she was in his crosshairs.

Chapter Fifteen

Entertainment Daily—A source within the *American Star* camp says that auditions were held last week to decide who'll sit alongside acid-tongued Nolan Ferrari and singer-songwriter Crystal Pell for the talent show's revival.

The third judge position is said to be between three competitors from Season 7: runner-up Hayden Tower, who went on to win an Oscar for *Ghosts of Time* and currently stars in the hit musical *Loverly*; Jojo Barr, who came in sixth place and won raves for her turn in the Chicago run of *Rent*; and winner Piper Dunner, whose debut album went platinum, but whose career subsequently stalled.

"Piper was the stand-out," says the source. "She was funny, didn't seem intimidated by Nolan, and could clearly articulate her views on singing. They like the idea of a comeback for her too."

Jojo Barr was a close second, says the source. "Jojo is an exuberant personality, and they appreciated that. But she tended to talk over Nolan and Crystal a little too much."

Hayden Tower, who has had the biggest post-*Star* success by far, didn't gel as well at the judges' table, claims the source. "He was reluctant to give negative critiques. And both he and Nolan have an alpha thing going, and it's a little much for one table. But he has the largest fan base, so that will be taken into consideration."

The source says that Mitch McCabe is also in talks to possibly return to hosting duties. "That's a big question mark," says the source, mysteriously. "They'd love him back, but he's had some personal issues."

*F*riends had sent Piper the item that morning with good luck wishes. She read it several times over. Could this be right? She was leading the pack? They'd liked her more than Hayden? It was incomprehensible.

Though she couldn't imagine Hayden being reluctant to give negative critiques. He certainly hadn't minded giving them to *her* backstage during *Star*.

But mingled with elation at the idea that success and

money could be around the corner was fear over what this could mean for her. She'd finally gotten to a place of thinking the letters were nothing but cranks until Mitch seemed to warn her about Hayden.

However… she wasn't one hundred percent sure what he'd said. Also, if Mitch had a drug problem, could *anything* he said be reliable?

It was all coming at a raw time for her, not only because her pregnancy had advanced to the stage where she was feeling quite uncomfortable and wishing it was over, but she could also tell that something was wrong with Firio. He appeared downcast and distracted, staring into his computer until late at night. When she'd spy over his shoulder, the monitor was filled with rows of numbers, graphs, and charts. She'd tried to get him to open up about what was wrong, but he always shrugged and replied, "Work stuff."

She left her desk and walked into the turret room. He wouldn't be home for another few hours, so if she was going to snoop around, now was the time to do it.

Documents and booklets were scattered over his desk. She pushed the space bar on his keyboard, and his monitor lit up, but was password protected. She shouldn't go sneaking into his computer, but felt unmoored, desperate for information that would explain his mood.

Right next to his computer was a laminated document with a front cover labeled, "Hudson Securities Quarterly Fund Review." There was a yellow Post-It stuck to it. In Firio's handwriting were the words, "Michael—What now??? Advice??? Help!" She recognized the name Michael as a friend with whom Firio occasionally consulted about his fund.

She leafed through the document. The first page was titled "Performance Review," and below that were summaries on various classes of securities, with their return on investment percentages. She leafed through until she got to an orange tab on a page labeled, "Biotechnology Class Review." Firio was the firm's biotechnology stock analyst.

The first sentence of the page was highlighted in yellow and read, "For the quarter, the fund's biotechnology shares were down 26.2%, below the 9.4% advance of the benchmark Nasdaq Biotechnology Index." Next to it, handwritten in black pen, were five panicky-looking exclamation points.

Piper hardly considered herself an investment expert but even she could see that Firio's stock picks had done terribly. No wonder he was so tense and distracted. She wished he'd told her what was happening. True, there was nothing she could do about it, but at least she could support her husband emotionally. He must think she wouldn't want to be burdened, given not only her pregnancy and the letters, but also her audition.

But she was determined to show him she could be there for him during this stressful period, much as he'd been there for her when the letters began arriving. Now how to get it out of him what was going on without admitting she'd sleuthed around in his office.

* * *

"Honey, how are your stock picks doing?"

So much for being subtle. All through dinner, he was morose and uncommunicative; she needed to bring it up, and couldn't think of a cunning way to do it.

Sitting at the kitchen table, he looked at her with tired eyes and rubbed his scalp. "What a question. We don't talk about my work."

"And why not? We've talked enough about mine."

"But yours is interesting."

"Please, baby." She curled his hand into his, grasping his fingers. "It's obvious that something is wrong. I don't like being shut out. Married people support each other."

"They didn't do well this quarter," he said, gently slipping his hand away. "I thought I'd bought at a dip, but it was a plunge. For all six." He sighed and hunched over the table, trying to cave into himself. Piper had never seen him this way. "I thought I saw an entry point. The sector is a little beaten down. But all the fundamentals are sound. Every model I ran said they would rebound. They didn't. Only kept plunging."

"So what does it all mean?" His body language was beginning to seriously worry her.

He turned his dark eyes up, and when she saw the lost look in them, it stopped her breath. "It means the fund is down a couple points for the quarter. Because of me. That doesn't sound like much, but it's tens of millions in fees tied to performance. And investors have already started jumping ship."

Piper gloomily took in this news. She and Firio didn't discuss his job much, but she knew he enjoyed what he did and was good at it. He'd been at the same firm for seven years, since graduating college, and she'd always had the feeling that he was valued there.

"Well…" she finally managed. "This happens, right? No one can get it right all the time."

"Not like this, Bella. Not six companies in the same quarter. Not when the sector did rebound, but not my picks."

"What?" she gasped.

"I don't understand it," he said, weakly. "It makes no sense."

"So… what will happen?"

"This is why I haven't wanted to say anything. I won't get a bonus this year. And my bonus is most of my salary."

Her hand slowly covered her mouth. She couldn't speak.

"Now I have to figure out whether to take the loss or hold and hope things improve. That's why I'm up late at night, running models. If I choose wrong… I don't know if I'll have a job next year."

* * *

THE TWO OF THEM GOT READY FOR BED silently, going through their bedtime routines like the walking dead, the room's atmosphere oppressive. Piper was acutely aware of disaster lurking around the corner: A new house, a new baby, and potentially very little income in the near future. Not to mention losing their health insurance at a pivotal time.

Perhaps they could take on a lodger or two, though

she couldn't imagine what lodger wouldn't mind an infant howling in the night.

Piper couldn't think of a soul she would want to ask for financial help. Her father was living on Social Security and his pension. The thought of asking Jojo for a loan was abhorrent to her. Besides, although she knew Jojo made a decent living, she doubted her friend had enough to spare for Piper's mortgage.

Disaster. They were headed for disaster.

That is, if she didn't get the judge spot. If she got that, all would be well. Firio could find another job if he needed to. They could continue to pay their mortgage, and all the costs associated with the baby. She'd even be back on the Actors' Equity health insurance plan.

Except…

In bed, Firio was distant, not wrapping his arm around her belly as he normally did. She felt helpless to bring him out of his disconsolate state. For once, he didn't drift off right away, and she could hear his light, quick breathing and feel the dreary energy coming off him.

"Firio," she asked. "When did these stocks start to go down? Was it the end of September?"

"Mm, yes," he mumbled.

"Was it… after that item appeared in *Entertainment Daily*? The one about me being up for the judge position?"

He was silent, then said, "I don't know when that appeared exactly. But around then, I imagine."

Piper absently ran her hands over her stomach, feeling a dull moving within it, her baby turning. "You said that's never happened to you before, all those stocks going down at the same time?"

"No. But it's the market. No matter how much you try to plan for it, it's still unpredictable."

"But not *this* unpredictable."

"Not in my experience, no."

He sat up, looming over her in the dark of the bedroom. She could make out the silhouette of his muscular shoulders and arms. "What is it? What are you thinking?"

"The curse," she said, lowering her voice, as if the word had ears, was a physical thing in the room with them.

"Bella…" he groaned, flopping back down. "There's no curse. It's Wall Street. It's volatile."

"You said yourself this has never happened to you before. You said the stocks went down after that item appeared."

He sighed, exasperated, and kicked off his side of their light blanket. "Let's not talk about this right now. I have to clear my head and get some sleep. I meet with the managers tomorrow to try to explain what happened. I don't think blaming a curse on my wife will help matters."

"Sorry," she whispered.

"Please don't worry," he said, and kissed her on the forehead. He rolled away, his back to her.

She lay wide awake, staring at wavering shadows along the far wall.

Dark forces are gathering against you.

It had started already. The curse sending out bad luck—its opening salvo to attack her husband.

But this was insane. She didn't, couldn't believe all of this. How, how? Her entire belief system was upending. There was no way to describe the sensation of having everything she knew about the world shifting beneath her, revealing something new and terrible, something that left her with no control over her fate or the fate of her loved ones.

There was one thing she could control—dropping out of the running for the judge spot. Presumably, once she did that, Hayden and his cult would be satisfied. But she hated the idea of it. Hated not only that her life was being controlled, her chances at doing something she deeply wanted to do being torn from her, but that she was *believing* all of this.

A cult's curse. One that had paralyzed her vocal cord, burned down her apartment, killed her dog, gave her mother cancer, possibly killed Dylan Lopez, and injured Anton Bishop. And now was destroying her husband's career?

How could this *be*?

Chapter Sixteen

"*P*iper Dunner. I'm a big fan of yours."

Anton Bishop shook her hand. He was tall, lean, with salt and pepper hair shorn to his scalp, and appeared somewhere in his forties. The trace of a scar was etched into his dark skin. It started from near the top of his left cheek and reached like an archipelago towards his jawline.

"Oh, you don't have to say that," Piper demurred.

"It's true. I was somewhat of an *American Star* addict. I watched all of your season. When Jojo Barr left, you got my votes." He had a lovely sonorous voice.

The pair sat down in the dimly lit bar/lobby area of the W Hotel in Union Square. Piper had emailed him yesterday, using an address he had on his website, introducing herself and asking if they could chat by phone. To her surprise, he got back within a few hours, and once they ascertained they were both in New York, he offered to meet up for a drink when he got out of rehearsal for a new show.

To get communication going, she'd only said she wanted to ask him about "the business." Luckily, he knew who she was and not only agreed to chat but to meet in person. When the waitress appeared, Anton ordered a cucumber lemonade spritzer, and Piper a non-alcoholic ginger beer mojito.

"So *Star*'s coming back?" he asked. "I think I read that."

Piper sheepishly shrugged. "I'm not supposed to talk about it."

"I get it." He made a zipping motion at his mouth. "So what can I help you with?"

Piper clawed at the pub mix in a bowl on the glass table between them and nibbled on a cheesy cracker-twist. She'd spent all morning trying to think how to phrase everything, and still wasn't sure what to say. She'd have to come right out and ask. If he clammed up, there wasn't anything she could do.

"The truth is, I want to ask about your accident." She made a gesture towards her cheek, in case he'd had more than one accident. "I understand if you don't want to talk about it, but…" She trailed off and, when he remained silent, awkwardly tried to clarify. "I'm curious how it happened."

Anton had a stiff, disbelieving smile on his face. "That's why you wanted to talk?" He didn't sound angry, more mystified.

The waitress returned, placing their drinks in front of them. "Would you like a menu?" she asked. Anton said, "No, thanks," and waved her off in a way that made Piper feel he was about to stand up and walk out.

"I know this sounds nosy," she said with an apologetic tone.

"It does."

A rush of heat tingled Piper's face. She was mortified that she hadn't come up with a better way to approach the subject, but she hadn't.

"It's that..." she tried again. "I'm wondering if anything strange happened right before it."

"Strange?"

"Did you—ahh—did you receive any threats or anything? About the role in *Ghosts of Time*?"

He put his drink up to his lips, glancing out the wall of windows overlooking Union Square. She expected that he would finish his sip, excuse himself, and leave. Maybe he wouldn't even bother excusing himself.

"You can see I'm a black man, right?" he said, unexpectedly.

"Um. Yes."

"And the role of Jake Jones was originated by a white actor. So yeah, I got a few threats. Racists. You're aware there are racists out there, right?"

"I'm aware," she said.

"So yeah, I got a few things. But that had nothing to do with my fall."

"Did you receive a letter? Like a snail mail letter?"

He took another sip of his drink, put it down, and twisted his wedding ring. "One or two of them. And a few emails. Basically saying, this is a white man's role. That kind of thing."

"I'm sorry that happened."

He took a handful of bar mix and chewed it down.

Then stared pointedly at her again. "Why are you interested?"

"The man who took over the role—Hayden Tower. Do you know him?"

"Of course I *know* him. The dude who stole my Oscar."

He said it so fervently that Piper didn't know how to respond, but he grinned. "I'm kidding. I mean, seen him around at events, parties, an awards show. We're not pals." He squinted at her. "I saw him once after he won. He didn't even come over to thank me. You'd think I'd at least get a 'thanks, bro,' or he'd buy me a drink?" The mixture of irritation and amiability in his voice left Piper uncertain how far the depth of his resentment went.

"Did he say anything to you?" she asked.

"Nope. This might be my imagination, but he looked a little guilty, then fled to another room."

"Guilty?"

"Like I said, probably my imagination." His smile was more relaxed. "I don't want you to think I'm being serious. He couldn't help what happened. Someone was going to take over the role and they could have done a lot worse than picking him. At least it wasn't Bieber."

"Look, this is going to sound crazy," she said. "If you get up and walk out on me, I'll completely understand. But you might have read that Hayden and I are both up for being the new judge on *American Star*. Please don't say you heard it from me, but it's out there, so…"

"Yeah, I think I read that."

"I've received a couple of letters that were… kind of

threatening to me. Insinuating I shouldn't take the position if offered."

"I see," he said, blinking his dark, long-lashed eyes. "But I'm a little lost. You wanted to know about my threats or my fall?"

"Would you be willing to tell me about the fall? If not, I understand."

After a few moments of tense silence, he shrugged and said, "I haven't talked about it in the press because it's pretty embarrassing. I have three dogs. Big, goofy dogs. But they're well behaved, I spent a lot of time and money training them." He looked around the bar then brought his attention back to her. "That night, I got home and they were eager to get outside into the yard. I have a place in Los Angeles, small place. Santa Monica." He looked around again, cleared his throat. "That night, I opened the back door to let them out and they… tore off." He shot his arm out. "Like something spooked them. One of them caught me. I stumbled and went down. Hit my face on the patio."

"Something spooked them? Any idea what?"

"No. They were jittery. Like they couldn't wait to get outside. Normally, they sit until I open the door. They're very good about that. But I was a little late getting home that night, and they were eager." He sighed. "It was my fault, I guess. But there was an accident on the freeway and I was late."

Piper nodded, and they sat silent. Then he chuckled and clinked the ice around in his glass. "I can't imagine what Hayden Tower has to do with it. You think he's the one sending you threats? You think he's the one who sent me threats?"

"I'm going to be completely honest with you," she said. "I'm normally not a superstitious person, but I got threats about the judge position, which Hayden is up for. And I saw what happened to you, and Hayden got the role. And I have a history of bad things happening to me after *American Star*, which of course Hayden lost to me. I had a paralyzed vocal cord after my first album came out. Other things happened. And… I guess I'm kind of…"

He said nothing, but deliberately leaned forward, a roguish grin on his face. "You think Hayden put some kind of voodoo on you and me?"

"Well, that's a good word for it." She inexplicably laughed. "I know this sounds insane."

"Yeah," he said, rubbing his head. "It does. But let me tell you something. Before every show, I do a little ritual. I light a candle, it has to be a rose-scented candle because her name was Rose, and I talk to my late grand-mother. I ask her to look out for me." He smiled. "So what is that?"

"That's sweet," she said.

"Right. Sweet." He thrust out a laugh. "But I *have* to do it. Every time. So I guess I believe in that kind of thing. Superstition. Spirits." He looked at her with renewed intensity. "I never thought about how much you and I have in common. He got my role and he pretty much got your career, didn't he?"

"Have you heard of a group called The True Way?"

He pushed his lower lip out, pondering. "True Way?

Nope."

"And the hate mail you got... did any say anything about a 'high-ranking member'?"

"Not that I recall. Whatever I got, I tore up or deleted. High-ranking member. What are you saying? He belongs to some kind of voodoo club?"

"That's what I'm trying to figure out."

"This is blowing my mind," he muttered, gulping down the rest of his drink. "I don't know what to say. Is there any proof he's behind these things?"

"No." She considered bringing up Mitch and what he'd said—or what she *thought* he'd said—about Hayden. But she decided she sounded unbalanced enough.

Ten minutes later, they paid the bill and were standing on the sidewalk.

"This is about the strangest conversation I've ever had," he said, shaking his head and chuckling.

"I know, I'm sorry." Seeing a yellow cab approaching, she hailed it, and the cab swerved over. "Thank you for speaking with me."

"Piper," he said, somberly. "I was out of work for a year after the fall. The scar isn't doing me any favors trying to get movie roles, or at least ones that aren't the villain. My income went way down, and it's only coming back with this new show. There was a time when I was on the brink of being homeless. If you think Hayden— if you think he's got some kind of magic voodoo power —if you *seriously* believe it—you should protect yourself, okay?" He patted her on the back, giving her stomach a wide berth, then peered into her face. "Do whatever it takes. Don't mess with shit like that."

Chapter Seventeen

*A*t home, she absently cut up vegetables on the thick wood sideboard while listening to her latest completed audiobook, *The Secret Between Us*, analyzing her reading technique, homing in on places she could improve.

That slight Valley Girl inflection she'd given the teen girl did the character no favors, making her sound brattier than she'd read on the page. And her male characters could use finessing. The villain sounded too much like a caricature twirling his handlebar mustache during his big "I did it" speech. Yes, areas she could improve.

On *American Star*, she'd done similar evaluations, watching her performances whenever possible, picking them apart, identifying her strengths and weaknesses. When she'd noticed she was disappearing into the cavernous stage at the Hollywood Theater, with shafts of white light cascading down as if from heaven, she began moving nimbly around the stage, taking charge of it—at least as much as she could given the spiked heels that the stylist always forced on her.

When she noticed her face tended to freeze-frame after a performance, looking out into the audience as if she was staring down the barrel of a gun, she became careful about ending with an expression that suited the song—thoughtful for a ballad, energetic for a rock song, perky for pop.

In general, she was a rational person, one who believed in hard work, in breaking something down and scrutinizing its components, in trying and failing and trying again. Someone who didn't believe in the type of thing she'd begun believing—that an invisible force had been launched across the air, found her like a heat-seeking missile, and torpedoed her life.

The day before, she'd spent an hour looking up Firio's six biotechnology stock picks. They'd either been slightly down or were flat until they'd all plummeted shortly after the item about the judge position had appeared in *Entertainment Daily*. Yes, it could be a coincidence, but it sure was a big one.

Last night, Firio had told her that the fund's managers had put him on "probation," and that his next picks would be integral to whether or not he had a job next year. He was so depressed that he'd hardly eaten dinner and shuffled off to bed early.

Her mind again went back to *American Star*. She'd begun a habit of rooting around in her memories, teasing out ones about Hayden, and his attitude to her during the show, and after her win.

She remembered after the finale results, backstage.

The adrenaline rush of winning had suddenly drained out of her and five months of slavish work caught up to her all at once. So exhausted she could scarcely think, she'd desperately wanted to beg off her media obligations and crawl onto the green room couch for a nap. But that was impossible. It felt like the entire country was waiting for her to emerge from the Hollywood Theater.

The other eight of the top ten finalists had returned for finale performances, and backstage they'd rallied around Piper with congratulations, all of them seemingly truly happy for her. Hayden had congratulated her, though she couldn't remember his words.

What she did remember was catching a long glimpse of Hayden's mother's face as she waited for her son to come over to her. Hayden's mother looked uncannily like him, and as Piper fielded more congratulations, the woman stood staring at her with an expression that was difficult to read, but made Piper deeply uncomfortable. Hayden's mother's face was still as glass but displayed an emotion that wasn't quite disappointment or anger that her son hadn't won.

More like... *fear*. Fear, Piper supposed, that Hayden would have to return to Iowa and spend the rest of his life pouring concrete.

A year later, a country crooner by the name of Brooks Keith would be sent packing in ninth place. Yet, his debut album on a small country label would go on to sell millions, while the winner, whose name Piper couldn't even remember, had done middling. But at the time Piper had won, only the winners of previous seasons had truly broken out. Hayden's mom had no way of knowing that her son's career would eventually overshadow Piper's.

But now, Piper wondered if that look could have indicated something darker—a fear that her son would *do* something awful to avenge his loss?

Or was Piper etching a full-blown fiction into these traces of memory?

After the vegetables were chopped, she put them all in a large ceramic bowl and took two packages of tofu out of the refrigerator. She'd been a pescatarian for most of her life. Firio was not, but she'd laid down the law early in their marriage that if wanted meat, he'd have to cook it for himself. As Piper was doing most of the cooking these days, this meant he'd practically been turned into a non-meat eater as well.

She sliced the tofu, and chopped up a garlic clove and an onion, holding her breath while she did the onion. Since her pregnancy, the smell of raw onions was almost nauseating, but she still liked them cooked. She put everything to the side, waiting until Firio got home before she'd steam the vegetables and simmer them with olive oil. She washed her hands, sat at the kitchen island, and pulled over her laptop.

There were so many entities called "The True Way" —companies, movies, books, churches, a diet program, and even a Star Trek fan club—that it took her at least half an hour of various combinations of keyword searches before she found something applicable to the group Crystal had mentioned.

The site was called "Cults Exposed" and there was a

forum post from someone named "FormerTruther" who claimed to have been a member of The True Way for years. But the post wasn't particularly helpful, blaming The True Way for everything from earthquakes to the tsunami that struck Indonesia, to the assassination of JFK, and a claim she couldn't follow that The True Way somehow controlled the Federal Reserve. The poster sounded completely unhinged.

Nevertheless, she sent a reply, giving an anonymous email address she'd set up and asking "FormerTruther" to contact her. She didn't have high hopes as the poster had only posted that one time, and that had been a few years ago.

Then she went upstairs to take a bath before Firio arrived home from work.

THE NEXT NIGHT, Piper was determined to try to entice Firio into wanting to have sex with her. Her third trimester hormones were rampaging and she craved sex all of the time—just when Firio's work situation meant his libido, for the first time since she'd known him, had tanked.

She managed to coax him out of his office with the promise of a massage, which she gave him, her downward facing belly resting on his spine. But things weren't as easy as when her body wasn't playing host to a baby, and she had to do some physical maneuvering to get him into the mood. Fortunately, he wasn't dead yet, and they were able to get things going.

"Sorry I've been so distracted," he said once they'd rolled away from each other, satisfied. It was the first time she felt close to her husband in awhile, and she was relieved about it.

"I understand. And I want to tell you, I've made up my mind to tell Nolan I'm out of the running." Before he could argue, she went on, "Once that happens, you'll see those stocks rebound. I know it."

He made the little "not again" groan he'd started doing whenever she brought up "the curse."

"And if they don't?" he asked. "Then you're not making money, and I'm not making money."

"I make money with narration. After the baby is born, I can take on more hours. I still have some royalties coming in."

"Enough for this house?"

"Um, not for long. But if the stocks don't rebound, and you lose your job, you can find another one."

He sighed. "You don't understand. Most people in my position have a master's in business from an Ivy League school. Hudson took me on after college because my uncle's friend was a partner. They were willing to give me a chance. But that man died a couple of years ago. They have no loyalty to me anymore. This house took all my reserves. I won't be able to afford grad school. And once the stink of picking losers is on you, it will be tough getting another job."

Piper knew about the stink of failure. The entire music industry had run from her, holding its nose.

"We'll sell the house."

"We just bought it. We haven't had it long enough to

get an appreciation. Between taxes and agent fees, we'll lose tens of thousands." He sighed louder, then went to the bathroom. She could hear him running water. "I don't understand why you'd want to give up the chance to make that kind of money doing something you love," he called out.

"Because you can see what's happening!"

She didn't want to argue with him, not tonight, after finally feeling bonded with him again. But it was frustrating that he refused to take anything she said seriously. "That curse has already almost ruined your career. Imagine what's next if I'm named judge."

He came back out, chuckling lowly, then reached over and snapped off the bedside lamp. "Curse," he grunted, getting into bed. "How can you believe all of this?"

"You grew up Catholic. What's the difference between God powers and cult powers?"

"Are you serious…" he muttered.

"Yes, I'm serious. Okay, forget God. What about germs? Those are invisible to the naked eye, but they can cause a huge amount of real problems. You believe in germs, right?"

In the dark of the room, she couldn't fully see his expression, but she didn't need to. She could feel the way he was looking at her—like she'd lost her mind.

When he didn't answer her, she went on, "I'm not sure I believe it, but why take the risk? And what about what Mitch said, that I should be careful around Hayden?"

She hadn't bothered to tell him she'd also met with

Anton Bishop the day before. Telling Firio that Anton's dogs had charged past him, causing him to fall, wasn't exactly hard proof of sorcery.

He turned onto his stomach, tenderizing his pillow with his elbow. "I want you to do what makes you comfortable," he said. "But are you not going to have a career because of a couple of letters? And didn't you say that Mitch guy looked drugged up?"

"We'll figure it out," she said, but could hear the doubt in her voice.

Why was Hayden doing this to her? He had everything now—a Broadway hit, an Oscar in his pocket. Even if he'd gotten those things by getting help from some nefarious cult, Hollywood loved nothing more than a winner. And he was truly talented. He didn't need the judge slot. Something else would come up for him.

She draped one hand under her belly, the other over Firio's backside. "We *will* figure it out," she promised, giving him a squeeze.

Chapter Eighteen

*D*earest One,

Why oh why are you going against your own interests? I've taken it upon myself, at great risk, to warn you. Yet you continue to flaunt us. Could it be that you still don't believe? What does it take? The conjuring has already begun. The next sign will be bigger, as we haven't gotten through to you.

Our high-ranking member is very displeased with the latest turn of events. I'm doing what I can to hold off catastrophe, but you are not making it easy. I wish you would work with me, listen to me, and accept that I'm here to help you. Because I'm the only one who can.

Your friend

PIPER RAN THE LETTER OVER AND OVER in her mind while in her obstetrician's waiting room. A feeling of pure dread had chilled in her chest and wouldn't leave, like the beginning of a bad cold.

She'd left the letter on the kitchen island before coming to her check-up. Firio had originally planned to come with her, as he had for all of her check-ups, but he'd been called into an emergency meeting to discuss the next steps with his poorly performing stocks.

"I'll walk out right now if you want me to," he'd told her. "I won't even give notice."

Of course, she couldn't have that. They relied on his company's health insurance. Their goal was to keep that through the birth, to keep her same doctor. So she'd told him it was fine, the appointments usually took less than fifteen minutes anyway.

She didn't tell him about the latest letter, as it had come after they'd gotten off the phone, and she knew his day was stressful enough. She didn't want him sitting in a meeting with his bosses, trying to save his job while simultaneously worried about her.

Her doctor, Dr. Malhotra, had beautiful buttery smooth skin that Piper marveled at every time she saw her, and short, straight black hair, and perfectly white nails. Piper had chosen her because her friend Taryn, whose son was now two years old, had highly recommended her.

The doctor showed Piper the baby on the monitor (knowing not to reveal the gender) and gave the baby's weight, which was five pounds, six ounces, a little on the large side, which made Piper wonder if the baby was a boy. She had her blood pressure taken.

"One thirty-two over eighty. That's elevated," Dr. Malhotra said, unwrapping the arm cuff. "Are you drinking or smoking?" She kept any hint of accusation out of her voice.

"No, definitely not. Well, I had a few sips of wine over a month ago."

"Are you getting some exercise?"

"I walk a lot. And prenatal yoga once a week."

"Any swelling in your hands, feet, or face?"

"Um, yeah, my feet tend to swell if I've been standing a lot or it's hot out." She felt terrible that she hadn't thought this was an issue and hadn't alerted the doctor to it.

"Any unusual stress?"

"Well..." Piper stared at an anatomy chart on the wall, and it looked disturbingly gruesome to her, the display of red organs and an upside-down fetus, like a naked alien with an oversized head. "Yeah, there's been some stress." She shrugged and laughed. "I mean, there's a baby coming."

"Anything out of the ordinary?"

"Yeah, there are things going on. I'm up for an important job, my husband is having issues at his job, and um..." She scratched at a sudden tingling itch on the side of her head. "I've been receiving strange letters. I got another one today. Could that affect my blood pressure?"

"Any stress can affect blood pressure." The doctor continued to bore into Piper with her large liquid brown eyes. "Are these letters from someone you know?"

"No, it's... You probably don't know this, but I used to be kind of famous."

"Did you?" The doctor cocked her head to the side, as if preparing to humor Piper through a mild delusion.

"Years ago. I was on a show called *American Star.*"

The show's name sent a gloriously stunned smile across Dr. Malhotra's face. Piper was accustomed to that look. She'd met people who'd never seen the show, but not one single person who hadn't heard of it. Deep down, she had to admit she still got a proud charge out of people's reactions.

"I used to watch that with my kids. I—" Dr. Malhotra looked down at her clipboard, then back up, and her mouth dropped a little. "Piper... from *American Star.* Of course. I didn't recognize your name."

"That's my married name. It was Dunner on the show."

Dr. Malhotra planted one hand on her hip. "My husband and I were rooting for you. First time we ever voted. But my daughters, they liked the guy... ah..."

"Hayden Tower."

"Yes! When he lost, the girls screamed so loud I thought they were being murdered. My little one cried so hard she threw up."

"Sorry to disappoint them," Piper said, giving her knee-jerk response whenever anyone felt compelled to tell her they or someone they knew had preferred Hayden.

She was suddenly reminded of the time a pack of teen girls had run to her as she sat in a limousine after a talk show appearance, the window open while she signed autographs. They'd thrown water into her face and yelled, "Hayden should have won!" For a horrifying moment, she'd thought they'd thrown a chemical at her, and she'd be blinded or disfigured.

"Anyway," Piper said. "I guess someone who watched the show has decided to start playing games with me. Sending me creepy letters."

Dr. Malhotra made a series of disapproving clicking noises with her tongue. "That's very shameful," she said, shaking her head. "You don't need stress like that."

"No."

"There's no emergency. But you should do what you can to minimize stress. High blood pressure during a first pregnancy isn't that uncommon, but we need to keep an eye on it. It's very important. I'm going to send you downstairs for urine and blood analysis. Make sure you get enough rest and keep yourself as calm as you can. If reading letters like that is stressing you..." She stared at her with a deadly serious look. "You need to stop."

* * *

AT HOME, PIPER CRIED, guiltily aware that her crying was probably raising her blood pressure even more. But she couldn't help it. This was the first time her check-up had gone anything except swimmingly, and she was completely unprepared for the idea that her baby might be in danger. She wished so badly she could talk to her mom, who would have made them herbal tea and used her calm manner and reassuring voice to talk Piper off the ledge.

She also felt unable to call Firio, who was already

dealing with enough. She'd tell him about the appointment when he got home. Her friend Taryn was at work, so Piper couldn't call her either. She thought about calling Jojo, but worried her friend wouldn't have much sympathy about Piper getting so stressed about a curse that Jojo didn't believe in. But, filled with a need to talk to someone, Piper called her anyway and left a message.

She went upstairs, put on a meditation video, and sat on her bed, willing herself to breathe deeply, imagining her blood flow slowing, her whirring brain becoming still. She tried to make her manic thoughts glide through her brain tissue like water, and out the back of her skull, or be carried up out of the top of her head like balloons.

All the while, she could feel the letter on the kitchen island where she'd left it, its menacing vibrations tunneling up through the ceiling.

After meditating for at least twenty minutes, she went back downstairs and picked up the letter, refusing to look at its words. She took a lighter out of a drawer, held the letter over the sink, and lit it from the bottom.

It flared up swifter than expected into an orange flame, its heat licking her face. She dropped it into the sink before it could singe her thumb. Then she ran water over the dancing flame and charred remains until it disappeared down into the drain. She listened to the dry grind of the garbage disposal while inhaling the smell of burn.

With a cup of chamomile tea in hand, she pushed Nolan's number. When she got his voicemail, an automated female voice that said, simply, "Leave a message," she made her voice as placid as possible.

"Hi Nolan, it's Piper Dunner. I'm so sorry to do this to you, but I'm afraid I can't be considered for the judge position anymore. I can't express enough how grateful I am to you for thinking of me, but I have some things going on with the baby, and it's not a good time. I'm sure the show will be a huge success. Thanks very much. Bye."

Despite the meditation, she sat feeling defeated and resentful, the stirrings of anger throbbing hotly in her chest. But it would be worth letting go of *American Star* once and for all if Hayden left her and her family alone.

Chapter Nineteen

*T*he next day, she was feeling a little better about everything. Her urine and blood work had come back normal. And Nolan had called her the evening before. Although he'd sounded disappointed at her decision to drop out of contention, he was also unexpectedly warm and supportive. "Your baby comes first," he had said. "Hopefully, we can have you on later as a mentor or guest judge."

Piper was relieved he wasn't irritated with her for wasting his time and was touched by the offer of something smaller she could do—though she doubted Hayden would even want her doing that much. She couldn't pinpoint the exact moment when the culprit transformed fully from an unnamed "high-ranking member" to "Hayden" in her mind, but it had happened. It was probably when Mitch had warned her about him.

Firio, while he said he didn't like the idea that she was rearranging her life to suit some crazed idiot, nevertheless didn't want her getting stressed, so he too supported her decision. He'd also given her a firm order: She couldn't open any more letters. From now on, he'd open them.

But she didn't expect to receive any more. Hayden would be satisfied that Piper wasn't to be granted an *American Star* comeback. Then Firio's stock-picking ability would magically be rejuvenated.

But she wondered about Jojo. What if *Jojo*—not Hayden—got the judge position? What then?

Speaking of Jojo, Piper was surprised that her friend hadn't called her back. It was very unlike her. Especially given how upset Piper had sounded when she'd left yesterday's voice message, saying she'd had bad news from her doctor and wanted to chat. That wasn't the kind of message that Jojo—or any of her friends—would have ignored.

Piper also wanted to tell her friend that she'd pulled out of the running for the judge spot before it appeared somewhere as an anonymously-sourced item. While she was almost certain that would happen, if it didn't, she was going to call Amy Baldash herself. Hayden needed to know she was no longer a threat to him.

Jojo's phone didn't ring before going to voicemail, making Piper think that Jojo had her phone turned off or it had gone dead.

"Hey, Jo, I'm not sure if you got my message, but my doctor said my blood pressure was high, and I only wanted to vent. I have some other news too. Not sure how you'll feel about it, but it's a decision I had to make. Give me a call when you get a chance."

She hung up and a feeling of foreboding slithered through her, causing her stomach to clench in a low-grade ache. What had the letter said about *catastrophe*? Something about the letter writer trying to hold it off.

She shouldn't have burned it. But at the time she was so upset with the idea that the letters were causing her blood pressure to spike that she'd reacted, wanting to erase the letter from existence. She would have burned the others too, but couldn't bring herself to go into Firio's files and touch them.

* * *

AT THE DELI, she waited behind a few people at the counter so she could order a small decaf before heading to the subway and into the city for her recording session. She preferred the deli coffee to what she made at home and she'd quit caffeine during the pregnancy.

The server behind the counter saw her and automatically poured her cup the way she liked it, with soy milk and no sugar. As she waited in line to pay, her eyes roamed down to where the newspapers were kept on the bottom shelf of the magazine rack: *The New York Times, The Wall Street Journal,* and the city's two tabloids, one of which skewed liberal, the other conservative. Usually, they had opposing headlines, one saying a particular happenstance was the best thing to ever happen to the city, the other saying it was the worst.

This time, the two papers, lined side by side, had the same photo: a picture of a dark-haired woman on a stretcher being loaded into an ambulance. Piper stared at the double covers, and the woman's smiling face in the smaller photo insets. Her brain lagged in that momentary struggle before recognition coalesces.

One paper blared: "Hate and Run." The other: "American Star Hit by Car."

Piper dropped her coffee.

Chapter Twenty

City News—An *American Star* finalist who won praise for her star turn in *Rent* was injured after a car plowed into her in Manhattan on Tuesday evening, in what police say is a possible hate crime.

Joanna "Jojo" Barr, 32, was walking through a crosswalk near her Chelsea apartment at approximately 9:30 p.m. when an unidentified perpetrator threw what appeared to be grease out of his window before running into Barr, according to the NYPD. Barr was rushed to Lenox Health's emergency room with unknown injuries. Witnesses say the driver, believed to be male, was in a black SUV with no plates.

Witness Eylencia Chaumana said she thought a man in the vehicle yelled, "No fatties on *American*

Star" before throwing the substance out of his window.

"She went down and had this greasy, smelly stuff all over her," said Chaumana, who stayed with Barr until an ambulance arrived. "She was in pain and shock, but talking."

"We will be thoroughly investigating this very serious incident, which is being treated as a possible hate crime," said NYPD spokesperson Det. Sheila Grady. "The area is filled with surveillance cameras, and we will be looking at all of them. We will find the offender or offenders."

Jojo Barr is best known for advancing into the finals of the iconic singing competition ten years ago. A favorite throughout Season 7, Barr was eliminated in sixth place, infuriating fans that thought she was voted off too early.

The talent show launched the careers of Alyssa Alina, Mindy Patel, and Brooks Keith. Season 7 also saw future Oscar winner Hayden Tower come in second place. Since then, Barr has made a name in musical theater, including the Chicago run of *Rent*, and *Hail Lucinda*, which nabbed her an Obie Award nomination last year.

According to *Entertainment Daily*, Barr recently auditioned to be the third judge in a new season of *American Star*, which is returning to the airwaves next fall. The show will include two of its original judges, whip-tongued talent scout Nolan Ferrari and Grammy Award-winning songstress Crystal Pell.

Reached at her home in Los Angeles, Pell said, "I'm horrified. My heart goes out to Jojo. I'm enraged to hear someone might have done this on purpose. I'll be praying for her."

"We're deeply saddened at this news," said *American Star* producer Oliver Corbyn, who would not confirm that Barr is under consideration to be a new judge. "Jojo is part of our *Star* family. I'll be calling her personally to see if she needs anything at all."

Police are urging witnesses or anyone with any information to call Crime Stoppers.

* * *

*J*OJO'S BEDROOM HAD so many flowers in it, it looked like a botanical garden or a funeral home, and the petals intoxicated with their perfume.

Feeling kind of silly to be adding her paltry bouquet to such a spectacular collection, Piper handed her paper-coned flowers to Jojo's boyfriend, Donny. He was a big bear of a man, about six foot three, with a barrel chest and a sleek, bald head. Piper knew he was a lawyer, but had only met him a handful of times over the years, given that Jojo was usually busy traveling, and when she wasn't, Donny was usually busy elsewhere. But those times she had seen him, he'd impressed as a mellow backdrop to Jojo's boisterous personality, grinning at her tales and happily letting her shine. Now, he was somber and solicitous, saying, "I'll put them in some water," and disappearing with Piper's bouquet.

Jojo was sitting up in her Baroque bed, with its elaborately scrolled and carved gilded headboard and footboard. The room was equally as royalty-inspired, with fluted gold columns rising up one wall to the gold-leaf ceiling.

Piper had first seen the bedroom when Jojo had excitedly showed it off to her a few months after moving in. "Built for a queen," she'd preened. With anyone else, Piper might have been turned off by the opulence, but she knew Jojo had made the room look like something a Russian princess would own because she thought it was kind of funny.

Jojo, in a loose white housedress, was sitting up with her slinged arm over her ribs, a white cast on her wrist. Her curly dark hair was swept back with a jeweled headband, and she had bruising on one side of her face. Piper grasped her free hand.

"How are you feeling?" she asked.

"Well…" A shadow crossed her face, the kind Piper had never seen on her friend before, achingly vulnerable. "The wrist doesn't hurt as bad as the bruise." She rolled to the side, hiking up her dress. A garish plum-colored bruise edged with black mapped her outer thigh. "But it's…" She pushed the fabric back down over her leg, and her face fell into that deeply disturbed look again. "It's the smell," she said, staring out of the wall of windows that framed a clear view of the Hudson River. "I can't get the smell out of my nose."

"Of—of the stuff?" Piper asked, delicately.

"Yeah, the… I think it was dishwater or mop water. Like… like I'm dirty or something," she finished.

Piper had never seen her self-confident friend like this, and she despised the person who'd brought her so low, made her feel so worthless and humiliated.

"I want to kill him," Piper said.

Jojo dragged her gaze away from the windows, her eyes haunted. "I'm afraid Donny might if they find the guy. He's so, so angry. I almost hope they don't find him, because I don't want my man going to prison. Of course, I want him found. But Donny… I don't know what he'll do to him." She grinned, though it was a ghost of her old grin. "I hope he leaves a piece of the guy for me."

Piper nodded. She had no idea how people managed to stop themselves from revenge killing the murderers of loved ones. Hoping to lighten the mood a little, she took in the flower-packed room.

"I should have brought some cupcakes. My flowers are going to have self-esteem issues."

Donny came back into the room with Piper's contribution in a gorgeous multi-hued crystal vase, making the contents look less inadequate.

"Put them right here." With her good hand, Jojo moved a book from her bedside table to the bed to make space. "I want them in a prime spot."

"You need anything else, babe?" Donny asked.

"No, I'm good, babe."

"Coffee or water or anything?" he asked Piper.

She demurred, and Donny took an ornate gold chair and moved it right behind her. "Sit," he ordered, looking at her belly.

He left the room, and that's when Piper noticed what she hadn't noticed before—Jojo's finger boasted a dazzling diamond, sparkles pinging everywhere. Piper's hand flew to her mouth. "Oh my God! You're engaged!"

Jojo wagged her fingers. "Six carats. That's my man. Have to wear it on my right finger for now." She glanced at the cast on her left wrist.

Piper got up from her chair and moved to kiss Jojo's cheek. "Congratulations. I'm so happy for you."

"Yeah, it only took ten years," she drawled. "Kidding. That was both of us. We didn't see the need. But an experience like this, it changes you. Suddenly, we both wanted that piece of paper."

"I'm glad a little good came out of it," said Piper, though she felt that came out sounding wrong. However, Jojo said, "Yeah, silver lining. Or diamond lining," and managed a real smile.

"Who is *that* from?"

Piper gaped at a display of white, red, pink, and blue roses that must have been five feet tall. They spelled out GET WELL JOJO.

"Oliver Corbyn. On behalf of all the *American Star* staff."

"Wow."

"I keep imagining how someone must have stayed up all night making it." She pointed around the room at various flower arrangements. "That's from Crystal," she said. The gigantic display had flowers Piper had never seen before—huge, spiky ones that looked like red stars, similar to the red star that flipped within the golden moon in *American Star*'s opening graphic.

"And look," she said, pointing. The pot on the windowsill was deceptively small, but contained five separate crescent-shaped clusters of white flowers attached to bamboo stalks. They arched languidly downwards, like graceful ballerinas. "They're orchids. From Hayden. Donny looked them up, said they must have cost a thousand dollars."

At Hayden's name, Piper felt her blood run cold. It was a cliché, but that's exactly how it felt. Ice water in her veins. "What did Nolan send?" she asked, glancing around, prepared to see the most elaborate floral arrangement of all.

"He didn't send anything." For a second, Jojo looked sad, then she perked up. "But he called and invited Donny and me to cruise the Mediterranean with him on his yacht next summer. Can you believe that?" She shook her head, disbelieving. "Nolan Ferrari. The guy never gave me the time of day after the show."

"Speaking of Nolan…" Piper paused, trying to decide how to phrase everything. "I've pulled out of the running."

"For the..." Jojo started, her eyes wide.

"Yes, the judge position."

"Oh no, girl, don't—"

Piper held up her hand. "I know you've been dealing with a lot, but I left you a message last week. My doctor said I had high blood pressure."

"Yes, I'm so sorry, I didn't—"

"Don't worry about it. My point is, I can't do it."

"Is this about that cult curse thing?" Jojo asked, giving her side-eye.

Piper sat straight up, defiant, ready for the ridicule. "Yes," she said, evenly. "I know you don't believe it, and neither does Firio. But there are other things that happened."

"Do you think…" Jojo said, taking in her sling and wrist-cast. "The cult was behind this too?"

"Yes, I do."

Jojo was quiet, staring at her enormous square-cut diamond. Then she said, "You believe what you want. But I know that there are people out there that hate me because I'm fat. I've dealt with it my entire life. People like you don't understand what people like me go through. And I didn't get a look at the guy driving the car, but I heard him. He didn't sound like Hayden."

"Hayden was on stage when you got hit. He doesn't do the dirty work himself. I don't know how the cult works, how it can cause things to happen. It's unexplainable. I only know that for anyone Hayden sees as a threat, bad things happen to them."

Jojo jutted her chin towards the delicate, arching orchids. "But he sent me that!"

"He's not stupid. He knows what he has to do for appearances. But think about it, Jo. I win *American Star*, and you know all the things that happened to me. Dylan gets a record deal and he dies. Anton Bishop injures his face. Now Firio might lose his job because every single stock he picked last quarter has tanked. I'm getting letters telling me I'm cursed. And now you."

She stopped, deciding she would tell Jojo the key piece that made her convinced of who was behind everything. "I saw Mitch while I was at the audition. He flat-out told me to be careful of Hayden. When I tried to get him to tell me more, he looked frightened and denied what he'd said."

Jojo seemed unsure of what to respond. She brought her engagement ring up to her mouth, vacantly brushing the glittering diamond along her lower lip. "That's all a lot of strange stuff, I'll give you that," she offered, sinking into her white, cloud-like pillows. "But whether this was because of dark magic, or a fatphobic piece of garbage, I can't pull out of the running. That would be letting them win. All those people who want me to crawl into a hole. I won't let them."

Piper dragged her chair closer to Jojo's bed. "I want you to think about it. You don't need to be on *American Star* to have a great career."

"I appreciate that, hun. You're a good friend," she said, smiling indulgently. "But things haven't been as great as you're thinking. The Obie nom hasn't helped me get new roles. Private events are drying up. The show would be life-changing for me. And there should be more big girl rep on TV." She wriggled up from her pillows, staring determinedly at Piper. "I can't let them win. I can't."

Two days later, Piper received several emails from friends, all of them saying some version of, "Sorry!! I'd hoped it would be you!!" with a link to a story broken exclusively by *TMZ*.

Chapter Twenty-One

TMZ—Jojo Barr will be the new judge on *American Star*.

"We're thrilled to have Jojo on the panel, and know her combination of exuberance, heart, and undeniable talent will be a tremendous asset to our show," said executive producer Oliver Corbyn in a statement.

The talent competition will be returning to the airwaves for Season 11 after a ten-year hiatus. Jo-B will sit alongside original judges Nolan Ferrari and Crystal Pell.

The announcement must be sweet revenge for Barr, who was not only prematurely ousted in sixth place during her run, but who recently suffered what the NYPD said might be a hate crime while walking near her home in New York City.

"Jojo was on track to become our third judge," Nolan Ferrari tells *TMZ*. "Her recent unfortunate incident only made us more determined to have her. There is no room in our *Star* family for intolerance."

Jo-B is recovering from a broken wrist and lacerations after reports say a suspect threw a greasy substance on her, called her a slur, and hit her with a black SUV. Police are still searching for the suspect.

The musical theater star is said to have beat out two other *AS* alumni, Oscar winner Hayden Tower and Season 7 champ Piper Dunner, for the coveted panel spot. Insiders say the chemistry between Barr, Ferrari, and Pell sealed the deal.

"I couldn't be more excited," Barr told *TMZ*. "I'm putting that horrible thing that happened out of my mind and am ready to find the new American Star."

* * *

o room in our Star *family for intolerance.*
Piper was galled by the nerve of Nolan Ferrari. Had he completely forgotten that crack he'd

made about Jojo's weight on camera during her initial audition? At the time, it was standard Nolan-talk. He was famous for it. He was paid millions for it. He was considered a "truth teller" in bland, risk-free TV land, where no one dared to say anything remotely offensive.

In many ways, he *had* been a breath of fresh if blunt air in a grotesquerie of insincere coddling. Telling people who couldn't sing that they couldn't sing had been almost revolutionary for the medium. Not to mention that Nolan's off-the-cuff putdowns could be hilarious. But too often his zingers were sharpened with unnecessary cruelty, and that was one of those times.

Perhaps he'd forgotten all about his comment to Jojo. He'd casually thrown out so many barbs over the years that he couldn't be expected to remember all of them. Piper doubted the public remembered it either.

American Star had been popular in a time that when a television show aired, it was dissected the next morning over the "water cooler," and mostly forgotten by noon. There were TiVo and VCRs, but the pattern remained the same. Social media was in its infancy, and not yet in the habit of dragging out a minor disgrace for eternity.

But Piper hadn't forgotten what he'd said. *How big is our stage this year?* No, she couldn't forget it. Not when Jojo had been her roommate, not when she'd seen how her friend had tried to eat hardly anything during the show, despite a brutal, calorie-depleting schedule.

Soon after seeing the news about Jojo's selection, Piper called her. She was determined to congratulate her, despite her fears over the "cult curse" and what it might do now that Jojo had beaten out Hayden.

"I probably wouldn't have gotten it if you hadn't pulled out," Jojo said. "I'm happy, but I feel kind of guilty about it."

"Don't you dare. That was my personal decision. I just can't believe Nolan acting like he's Mr. Tolerance. I remember what he said to you about your weight. I remember he told Ben he looked like a chipmunk. And how he told Marla she looked like a drag queen. And those times he ignored my performance and picked on my outfit."

"But Marla is a drag queen."

"She is? Oh. Well, you get my point."

"The world forgets," Jojo sighed. "Or it's pretty forgiving of good-looking guys with cute British accents. Anyway, it was the aughts and that was his shtick. If he does it now, I'll hand him ass in front of millions."

"That was my plan too, but you'll be better at it," Piper laughed.

After they hung up, Piper tried to tamp down the unease she felt over Jojo's new high profile—and the trouble it could attract. Jojo had been warned and now was out of Piper's hands.

She went to her laptop and spent fifteen minutes plugging Firio's stock picks into a search engine. Most of them appeared no better off than they had been a week ago. But Jojo being named as the judge had only hit the news that morning. Piper supposed even magical cults needed a few days to work their superpowers on the stock market. She only hoped those superpowers wouldn't be redirected towards Jojo, even more than she suspected they already had been.

She took a shower and dressed for work. She always dressed casually, in stretchy maternity leggings and a loose cotton shirt. Sitting in a cramped studio while emoting into a microphone for an hour meant comfort took precedence over appearance.

On the subway, she tried to concentrate on reading the book she was narrating, but her thoughts kept straying to Jojo. A knot of anxiety took up residence in her throat.

She thought about how, if the cult had caused a man to run into Jojo with a car—all in an attempt to get her to back off the judge slot—that the plan had backfired spectacularly.

Sure, once Piper had pulled out, Jojo had been next in line, at least according to what she'd read in *Entertainment Daily*, about Hayden not doing well in his audition. But there was no doubt that Jojo being the victim of such a disgusting crime had brought her attention. Nolan even admitted to *TMZ* that the incident had made the *American Star* powerbrokers want her even more.

Piper's book rested in her lap as she stared absently at the train car walls and their advertisements and remonstrances.

Be Sexy. Be Safe.

If you see something, say something.

A thought, less than a thought, a neurological chemtrail, began to streak its unwelcome way through her mind, brushstroking until it took shape.

That Jojo had come out of the attack on her better than she'd gone into it, at least career-wise. Even in her relationship. She'd gotten a six-carat diamond ring out of it.

Yeah, silver lining. Or diamond lining.

Piper tried to push back the end-thought that was determined to have free rein, snaking and slithering through her brain tissue, then taking hold with a death-squeeze.

The cult hadn't been behind Jojo's hate crime. Jojo had.

Chapter Twenty-Two

It was a shameful suspicion, one she kept forcing to the farthest borders of her mind, like trying to corral an unruly animal.

If Jojo had arranged for an SUV to ram into her in an attempt to draw sympathy from the powers-that-be at *American Star*, surely she wouldn't go so far as to have her own wrist broken, one that might require surgery if it didn't heal after being reset?

Piper had a difficult time keeping her concentration on the book she was narrating, and the recording engineer had to stop several times during her session to tell her she'd skipped words or had misread them. She'd never been stopped that many times before, and she could sense the engineer's frustration with her.

At home, there was the usual drop in the pit of her stomach when she opened the mailbox, anticipating that a letter could be waiting for her. Firio had instructed her to not read them anymore, and she didn't plan to. She would not stress herself and endanger her baby.

That was her resolve up until she saw the envelope.

In a trance, she walked up the stone walkway to the porch and into the house, her thumb pressing determinedly into the letter on the top of the small pile of mail, a foregone conclusion that she would become privy to its contents. What was the difference if Firio opened it and read it to her? Which, of course, he would have to do, because she needed to know if the cult would take credit for the attack on Jojo. If so, Piper needed to alert her.

She decided to read the letter in the kitchen with a tall glass of water right next to her, as its cold, malevolent words always made her throat feel oddly parched. Her hands trembled as she poured filtered water into a glass.

She plucked a small knife out of the wooden block on the island, sat down at the kitchen table, and slit the envelope open. Before drawing out the folded paper, she took several slow, deep breaths to ease her pulse and tried to pretend she was in a movie, that she was someone only pretending this was happening.

DEAREST ONE,

Of course, that was us. Not me specifically, mind you. You know of what I speak. You realize I can say no more.

Obviously, the plan did not reap the intended results. I didn't think it would. But our high-ranking member listens to no one. The member is threatening hellfire and damnation to all involved. I'm doing what I can to calm him, but I fear he won't be dissuaded. Keep vigilant. I'll let you know more.

Your friend

DESPITE HER DETERMINATION TO remain calm and pretend she was in a movie, Piper's heart was hammering, and she was absently chewing on her thumb knuckle. So the cult *was* behind Jojo's attack, or at least wanted Piper to think it was.

What she kept reading over and over was the line, *I'm doing what I can to calm him, but I fear he won't be dissuaded.*

For the first time, the letter writer had used gender pronouns. *Him. He.*

This lent even more weight to the unshakeable feeling that Hayden was the "high-ranking member." The sentence read like a slip-up on the part of the letter writer, who until now had been careful to use gender-neutral nouns.

But Piper couldn't completely discount the idea that Jojo herself was behind the letters. She had as much to gain from getting Piper out of the running for the judge position as Hayden did. Since the hit-and-run, she *had* gained. She'd gained everything.

But if Jojo wasn't behind the hate crime or the letters, she had to be warned about the latest letter. Piper doubted Jojo would do anything about it. Certainly, she wasn't about to quit *American Star*. But Piper had to do her minimum duty as a friend and show it to her.

And if Jojo *was* behind the letters, Piper had to figure out what to do about that as well. Maybe she'd never be able to prove it, but she could, at the very least, never speak to Jojo again, the possibility of which she could barely contemplate.

Piper didn't have many close friends. Her life of perpetual travel had consistently disrupted budding relationships. But despite their mutually packed schedules, Jojo had remained a constant. Hardly a week had gone by in the ten years since they'd roomed together on *American Star* when they weren't in touch.

Jojo had been there with Piper through her mother's illness and death, through her wrenching breakup with Marco, through her long, torturous slide from fame back to non-fame.

And five years ago, Jojo's cherished, energetic little brother had been found dead from a heroin overdose in a hotel room. Piper could still conjure up the sound of her friend's grief-laden wails. Piper had flown to New York and spent several nights sleeping at Jojo's apartment, comforting her in a way that even Donny couldn't. Men tended to want to fix things. Piper knew there was no fixing this, there was only being close.

She and Jojo had supported each other through their darkest times, and celebrated each other's most high-flying victories. Could Piper have not known her friend all this time, not known her at all?

Meanwhile, she wouldn't show the latest missive to Firio. He'd be mad at her for opening it. He'd probably call police, who wouldn't do a thing, as the letter was still so vague, not naming Jojo or even the hate crime.

She had to handle this herself.

* * *

"MORE PROOF IT'S HAYDEN," Piper said, handing Jojo the letter. "You'll see at the bottom, the writer uses 'him.' There's no other male who wouldn't want you or me being on the panel."

They stood in Jojo's living room, which had a sweeping view of the Hudson River. Fortunately, Donny was out somewhere. Jojo was wearing a pale green dress with a black-and-red flower pattern. Piper had called her before she left Brooklyn, ascertaining that Jojo was home, and offering to bring sushi from Jojo's favorite restaurant, one they'd had dinner at numerous times, a few blocks from Jojo's apartment. Given that Dr. Malhotra had suggested Piper stay away from raw fish, she'd had her "sushi" cooked.

Her plan was a very vague one, but she thought it might give her more insight into whether Jojo had plotted her own hate crime; and whether she might be behind the letters. And that plan was to blame Hayden and watch her reaction.

Jojo kept her eyes down, reading the letter. After a minute or so, she looked back up, and simply said, "Maybe it is him."

Not getting the usual dismissive comments, Piper was taken aback.

"I want to show you something." Jojo indicated that Piper should follow her to her bedroom. The room was still bursting with flowers and their perfume hung heavy in the air. But sections of the GET WELL JOJO arrangement were brownish and wilting.

Jojo walked to an antique white oak chest, opened a drawer, and dug around. She pulled out a slightly crumpled sheet of paper. "I couldn't fold it back up with one hand," she said. "Donny opens all my mail. He took it out, but kept it folded."

Piper began to read.

DEAREST ONE,

It is my duty to write this letter because I'm a key part of a small but dedicated and powerful society that reaches its tentacles across many spheres. Our society is the true way.

Your incident was engineered by us at the direction of one of our high-ranking members. You wanted what he wanted. He always gets what he wants, with our help. There will be worse to come if you don't do what you know you need to do. Dark forces are gathering against you. Our society has more power than has already been unleashed against you. You must beware.

Your friend

"AND HERE I thought *I* was the 'dearest' one," Piper scowled. "Is there an envelope?"

Jojo nodded, went to her drawer, and dug around more, pulling out the same type of white business envelope that Piper's letters came in. It was stamped with the now-familiar zip code: 10036. The postmark date was two days ago.

"It came this afternoon," Jojo said. "I was debating whether to tell you. I didn't want to worry you, and I know you'll tell me to quit *Star*." She walked to a nearby loveseat and sat with her sling resting on its arm.

"I don't get it," she said after a few moments of silence. She looked up at Piper, her big brown eyes shining. "I don't understand any of it. How does it work? Hayden... he's... in some cult? Some dark magic cult that curses people?" Her good hand went to her forehead, and she shook head confoundedly. "How am I supposed to believe this, Piper?"

"I wish I could tell you how it worked, then maybe I could stop it. But the only way to stop it seems to be to do whatever they say. Or to not be a threat to Hayden."

"I didn't tell Donny. He's worried enough about me."

"I didn't tell Firio either. Not about my last one. Same reason."

"What are we going to do?" Jojo's expressions were a clashing mix of outrage and disbelief. "Do we let this guy run our lives? Am I supposed to hand the judge position over to him? *Star* might not want him anyway, and then what? He thinks that was my fault too?"

"I don't know," Piper said, quietly. They both stared out of the wall-to-wall windows. Piper watched as a small crop of jet skiers made circles close to the shore, pushing up spirals of water as a white double-decker boat slowly churned behind them.

Jojo having her own letter didn't let her off the hook

as a suspect. Piper knew there was the possibility that Jojo had sent her letter to herself. Could she have typed it out, plus the latest one Piper had received, with one hand?

They went into the kitchen, and Piper set up the sushi on the large marble island separating the area from the living room. Jojo decided she needed a drink, so Piper poured her a glass of white wine and watched her drain almost half of it.

"I'm not going to lie," Jojo said, as Piper squeezed soy sauce into a small dish for them both to use. "I'm a little scared. At the same time, I feel idiotic for being scared."

"Welcome to my world."

Jojo grabbed Piper's wrist. "I'm sorry I was so harsh on you when you showed me your letters." She released her grip and took another gulp of wine. "Should we talk to Hayden?"

Piper grunted. "I tried that. Tried to appeal to his soft side, if he has one. Obviously, that didn't work."

They sat silent again, and Piper tore open the paper sheath around her chopsticks. Despite the drama, she was starving. Remembering that Jojo couldn't open her chopsticks with one hand, she stuck her pair out for Jojo to take.

"Oh, hun, can you get me a fork?" She pointed behind Piper, towards the kitchen. "Second drawer from the fridge."

Piper found the utensil drawer, got out a fork, returned, and handed it to Jojo. She watched as Jojo awkwardly stabbed a crunchy salmon roll with the fork.

The movement was so uncoordinated that it was almost comical.

"Are you left-handed?" Piper asked.

"Yeah, just the luck. The car hit me on my right side, and when I fell, I caught myself with my left hand."

Piper stared down at her food. Jojo was left-handed. Somehow, she'd never noticed this. If Jojo typing out two letters with her writing hand would have been extremely difficult, doing it with her non-writing hand would have been impossible.

Conceivably, Jojo could have written everything *before* she was hit, then dropped the letters inside a mailbox. But that seemed an implausible amount of foresight. There was no real way Jojo could guarantee that a fall would result in a broken wrist.

And Jojo wasn't faking the break. Before the sushi, she'd pulled up the X-ray the hospital had emailed to her and showed it to Piper.

* * *

AT HOME, the remnants of Firio's Chinese takeout were on the kitchen counter and he was upstairs in his study, doing what he was usually doing, staring into his computer.

"How are those stocks?" she asked, slipping up behind him and kissing his temple.

He tried to smile but the attempt quickly wilted. "Bit of a recovery up until a few days ago. We'll see, I guess."

She retired to her bedroom with her laptop on her

thighs, searching out videos of Jojo on YouTube. An hour later, she found a key video that proved Jojo wasn't lying about being left-handed. On *American Star*, during her rendition of "Someone Like You" by Adele, she'd played the ukulele—strumming its strings with her left hand.

An email slid into the corner of Piper's screen and her breath caught when she saw the return address: formertruther@mail.com.

"Hey there," the email began. "Yes, I was a Truther. What can I do for you?"

Piper wiggled her fingers around as she thought about what to say. She typed: "Hi, thank you for responding. Can you tell me if this group is active in Hollywood? And if it promises entertainers that it can bring down their competition?"

She hesitated, then decided to do it. "And do you know if the singer Hayden Tower is a Truther?"

Chapter Twenty-Three

"*B*ella, Bella…"

She was braised with cold sweat, her heart galloping in her chest, and her mouth was twisted open in a half-scream, one she couldn't get out no matter how hard she tried. Realizing it had been a dream, she allowed herself to cry, great gusting sobs, and Firio held her, firmly saying, "Bella, I've got you."

It was the worst dream she'd ever had.

Marvin had been there, his sweet little trusting face blackened and charred with fire, his eyes seized with terror. She had been trying to get to him, to save him, but couldn't move as the fire rose up around her, its smoke acrid in her lungs. She was nailed to the spot, horribly unable to lift her arms, desperately trying to call out to Marvin to jump into them, but her words were dead in her heavy chest. She was going to fail him. And he was looking at her, knowing she would fail him.

Then she had a knife in her hands. She was stabbing it into Hayden, over and over and over. Blood flailed out of him and onto the knife. "You killed my dog," she was screaming. "You killed my dog!" She couldn't see his face, but knew without any doubt the person she was stabbing was Hayden.

The light was on, and Firio was still soothing her, and she was clinging to him. Her heart was beating so crazily, galumphing like thunderous wings under her ribcage. What was she doing to her baby? Her heart was her baby's heart. Her dreams, her nightmares, were her baby's too.

"It was Marvin," she gasped. "He killed him."

"Who?" he asked.

"Hayden, he killed Marvin."

She had never told Firio about Marvin. Was so ashamed she had left him home to die alone. Firio let go of her, turned to the bedside table, and tapped at his phone. "It's three o'clock," he said. "Who's Marvin?"

"I'll kill him," she choked out. "Hayden. I'll kill him. I hate him," she said and regretted saying it, for her baby could hear her words. But she said it again. "I hate him so much."

She had nothing left inside of her, and only wanted the visions of burning Marvin and bloodied Hayden to fade away. But they were still so acute in her mind's eye that she didn't think they would ever leave her.

"He cursed me!" she cried, and at that moment nothing seemed more truthful.

* * *

In the morning, she listened to Firio in the bathroom getting ready for work. By now, the dream's unbearably vivid images had blurred. She was left feeling hollowed out and repulsive, as if all that was good in her soul had been sucked out of her.

Firio came and sat next to her on the bed. He smelled freshly washed, and she could detect the faint scent of his cologne. He looked so gorgeous in his dark blue work shirt and light blue tie, his face soft with tenderness. "Can I get you anything?" he asked, rubbing her arm.

She shook her head. "No. I'm sorry you didn't get much sleep last night."

"Don't apologize for a nightmare."

The tears swelled in her throat, her nostrils burned. She had to tell him. "Marvin was my little dog. He died in the apartment fire. He suffered so much before he got to me, and then that happened."

"Oh, Bella," he said, swabbing her cheek with his thumb. "I'm so sorry."

Her throat was too tight to explain further, and she felt she didn't have to. She could tell by the look on Firio's face that he understood everything.

"Do you want me to stay home today?" he asked.

"No. I'll be fine."

He lay down next to her, his suit pressed up against her naked body. She'd gone to bed in a voluminous maternity nightie, but had ripped it off after the nightmare had sent her temperature soaring, her body aflame with clammy heat. She drew her hand over her belly, rubbing circles on it, trying to let her baby know that it had only been a nightmare and everything was fine now.

"I don't know what to do," she said. "I feel like my emotions are affecting the baby. What if he or she comes out all messed up because of the way I'm acting?"

"That's not going to happen. Please take the day off. Stay home and rest."

"I don't have a session today anyway."

"Good." He pressed his lips against her temple, and stared deep into her eyes. "I wish I could do something. If any other letters come, you won't open them, right? You'll give them to me."

"I will."

"And don't go near him. Hayden. No going up to that theater. Don't do anything stupid like following him around, trying to play detective." He shook his finger in her face. "I have to be all caveman and lay down the law for wifey."

She buried her face in the crook of his neck, inhaling his springy skin, the smell of safety.

Chapter Twenty-Four

The Dallas Chronicle—Singer Dylan Lopez, who was a finalist on *American Star,* has died at age twenty-five, according to multiple sources. The cause of death is said to be sudden cardiac arrest caused by arrhythmia.

"We are deeply saddened to hear of Dylan's passing, and our hearts go out to his family and friends," read a statement on the talent show's website. "He was an undeniable talent, in many ways the heart of Season 7, and had much to look forward to in his life and career. Hopefully, his family and fans will take a small amount of solace knowing how he brightened the lives of millions."

Lopez auditioned with Bill Withers' "Ain't No Sunshine," causing the normally cantankerous judge Nolan Ferrari to remark, "You look like a star and you sound like a star."

He rose through the *American Star* hopefuls until he was eliminated in fifth place, a stunner that prompted judge Crystal Pell to declare, "You got this wrong, America, you got this wrong."

Triad Records confirms that Lopez had signed to its label only two months ago.

"We're devastated at this news," said Triad CEO Darren Silva. "Dylan was working hard writing songs and had some outstanding material. He'd seen the success others like Alyssa Alina and Piper Dunner had after *American Star*, and he wanted some of that for himself, and I believe he was on the verge of getting it. The album would have been a big hit and he would have joined the ranks of the most successful rock musicians. The music world has lost a shining star."

Lopez had recently moved from Los Angeles to his hometown of Glen Rose, outside of Dallas, where he grew up. He leaves behind a wife, Ember, and their baby daughter, Kylie.

A friend says at the time of his death, Lopez was at home with his wife and daughter. "From what I heard, he dropped," said Joshua Briggs, who went to high school with Lopez and played in an early band with him. "He didn't have any health issues that anyone knew about."

Sudden cardiac arrest (SCA) is the leading cause of natural death in the United States, primarily affecting men in their thirties and forties, and occurring when the electrical system to the heart malfunctions. In over half the cases, SCD occurs with no previous warning signs.

"Ember is crushed," says Briggs. "The whole town is crushed. Everyone watched him on *American Star*. He was our big success."

* * *

*T*hanks to Dylan's wife's unusual name, Ember, it didn't take long for Piper to find her on social media, especially as she hadn't remarried and changed her last name. Piper logged into her personal Facebook account, which she only used for close friends and family, and was now under Mae Romano, her middle and married name. She also used a photo of a cherry blossom tree as her profile photo. The public hadn't figured out the account belonged to Piper Dunner of *American Star*.

At the time of Dylan's death nine years ago, the top ten finalists had been scattered all over. Some, like Jojo and Bailie Slinger, were taking advantage of the *American Star* launchpad to try and get a career going. Others had headed back to their hometowns, returning to college degrees deferred or old jobs or new ones.

Of the top ten, only Piper and Hayden had been given contracts with Nolan Ferrari's label, Diamond Entertainment, which had a distribution deal with RCA Records. The rest of the "kids," considered on the cusp of fame during the show, were back to the daily grind of life. (For some reason, *Star* contestants were always "kids," whether or not they were adults with spouses and children of their own.)

Piper didn't attend Dylan's funeral. She'd been in London, set to play a sold-out event for ten thousand people, and it would have been impossible to get to Texas and back in time for her concert. So she'd sent an enormous arrangement of white roses and Calla lilies to the funeral home.

Piper had only met Dylan's wife early in the season, when she and his mother had sat nervous and awestruck in a side room that was filmed during the top 24 episodes. But after Dylan's popularity grew, Ember vanished.

Piper had suspected that Dylan had sent his wife packing back to Texas to keep his marital status out of the minds of his adoring female fans, lest it cost him votes.

Hayden was gaining on him in popularity, not only for his excellent voice and increasingly hunky looks, but because he had something going for him that Dylan didn't—he was single. It didn't hurt to let female voters nurse fantasies that they could one day hook up with the contestant they supported.

Chapter Twenty-Five

"*P*iper Dunner, sure enough I remember you."
Ember Lopez's voice on the phone had a
sweet, mellifluous Southern twang. "I was so surprised
to get your message."

Piper slung one arm under her belly and pressed her
aching back on an overstuffed couch pillow. Quite unexpectedly, within a couple of hours of sending Dylan's
widow a Facebook message, Piper received an answer,
and soon they were on the phone.

"Thank you for agreeing to speak," Piper said, and
paused, not having worked out how to ask about everything. She hoped a guiding force would navigate her
words to the correct ones. "First, I want to say again
how sorry I am about Dylan. He was a wonderful
person and immensely talented."

"Thank you, that means a lot," Ember said as a
high-pitched voice jabbered loudly in the background.
"Hold on a sec. Kylie, darlin', Mommy's on the phone."

The child yelled something and the sound faded as Ember moved to another room. "Sorry about that."

"How old is your daughter now?"

"She'll be ten in February. That was Dylan's birthday month too." Ember sighed and her Southern clang deepened. "It's so nice of you to call," she said, apparently too polite to ask why.

"You're probably wondering why I wanted to talk. I'm going to come out and say this because I'm not sure how else to do it. I need to ask you about Dylan."

"Awl-right," Ember said, confusion edging her drawl.

"Did anything strange happen before… he passed? Did you get any letters, anything like that?"

"Letters?"

"Yes, letters. Sent to your house?"

"Way-el, Dylan was always getting fan mail. We'd only moved back to Glen Rose and he started getting stuff. I don't know how they find these things out, but they sure do. All kinds of stuff. Teddy bears. Drawings. A few women sent…" She giggled. "They sent lingerie. What's he supposed to do with that? I did get some nice things though." She giggled again.

"But was there anything… threatening?"

"Threatening? Mmm. Not that I'm aware of. I'm sure he would have mentioned something like that. His fans could be a little out there, but they weren't dangerous. At least not that he ever told me."

"Was there anything else unusual that happened around the time of his—what happened to him?" For some reason, she couldn't bring herself to say "his death."

"Not that I recall. Things were going so well. He'd been signed to that record company and was spending every day writing songs. We'd moved back here to be close to family, but it was also so much cheaper than L.A. He made our barn into a recording studio. He enjoyed that so much. It was a great place for folks to come and collaborate with him."

This wasn't getting her anywhere. Piper felt ghoulish, getting a young widow on the phone and prodding her with questions about her dead husband. "It's just…" she started, awkwardly. "With the tenth year anniversary, I began thinking about him. I'm sorry if I've brought up painful memories."

"Oh, I always enjoy talking about Dylan. But if you don't mind my asking," Ember said, in that painfully polite Southern way, "what do threatening letters have to do with anything?"

"It's—it's complicated. Can—can you tell me, was Dylan still in touch with Hayden Tower when he passed?"

There was what Piper felt was a rather long pause. It went on until Piper said, "Ember?"

"Yes, yes. Way-el, you see, it's that… Hayden was the last person to see him alive besides me."

The baby's foot thumped against the wall of Piper's stomach so hard that she winced, not because it hurt, but because the kick was so strong and odd-underwater feeling. She sat with her mouth hanging open uselessly until she was finally able to summon her voice. "He was? Can you tell me more about that?"

"Oh, he was here working out songs with Dylan. Stayed with us for about a week. But he left the day before Dylan died. He left kind of suddenly. Dylan seemed a little upset afterward, like they got into some kind of argument. Do you still speak with Hayden?"

"Ah. A little." Nausea was marching from her stomach into her throat, as if her baby had kicked a ball of it upwards. She tried to swallow it down. "You say they got into an argument?"

"I'd thought Hayden was staying longer. But he drove away one day, didn't say goodbye to me or Kylie. Like I said, Dylan seemed a little upset. I could tell because his face would get red when something upset him. But he wouldn't talk about it. He could be like that. Alpha male, you know. Didn't share his feelings too much."

Piper covered the phone's mouthpiece with one hand, and groaned softly, the nausea quaking in her chest. She couldn't throw up at such a pivotal moment. "Ember, can you tell me anything else about Hayden and Dylan's relationship? Were they competitive?"

"Oh sure," Ember said. "They'd sit here on their guitars, one strumming one thing, the other trying to outdo it. Hayden would sing, and Dylan would jump in and sing louder. But they laughed about it. Called themselves Lennon and McCartney. They pushed each other to be better, you know."

"And have you seen Hayden since Dylan passed?"

"Yes, sometimes," she said. "He's a big star now, so

it's hard for him to get away. But he was here last year for a few days. He likes to see how Kylie is doing. He's a very good man."

"I'm sure he is," Piper said, unable to keep the needle of sarcasm out of her tone.

"Is something wrong with Hayden?" Ember's Southern politeness sounded like it was being worn thin. "I'm a mite confused with all these questions."

"I'm sorry. I've had some threatening letters. The police have asked me not to get into details," she lied. "I'm calling other *Star* finalists to see if they've had anything similar."

"Oh," Ember said, not sounding like she bought the explanation. "And you think Dylan had got these letters too before he passed on?"

"I'm looking into all angles."

"Are my daughter and I in any kind of danger?"

"No, no, nothing like that." Great. The poor woman had been through enough, and now Piper was making her think she was unsafe. "Can you do me a huge favor and not mention this call to anyone? Not even Hayden if you speak to him. It could disrupt the investigation."

"Awl-right," Ember said, her honeyed voice unable to disguise her puzzlement. "Should I talk to the police? I could tell them—"

"No, no. I've got it covered. Thank you so much."

After the pair hung up, Piper sat staring at the floor, taking deep breaths to lower the nausea. She waited until the baby stopped gyrating, then pulled up Hayden's Wikipedia profile on her phone and ran the timeline.

Hayden's debut album was close to making its appearance at the same time as Piper had been struck by vocal cord paralysis and Dylan had been signed to Triad Records.

She pictured the entire scene. Hayden had gone to Glen Rose to visit Dylan. There, Dylan had played songs for him that would be on his debut album. The songs must have been good, so good that Hayden felt threatened and left prematurely. Dylan was bewildered by his friend's attitude, and Ember picked up on her husband's mood.

Hayden, realizing that his old *Star* rival was going to have a smash album on his hands, couldn't have that. So he'd called in his cult. The next day, Dylan died. Both of Hayden's immediate *Star* competition, Piper and Dylan, had been neutralized.

"Son of a bitch," she rasped.

Chapter Twenty-Six

"How are those stocks doing?" she asked, slipping a large knife out of the slit in the wooden block, stopping to admire its silver reflection before plunging its side into a lettuce heart.

Firio stood at the kitchen island, loosening his tie. "The lettuce is dead, honey," he joked. She could feel him watching her as she hunched, working the lettuce heart into inch-long slices. She looked up at him and gave a loud *ha*, then stopped and waited for his answer.

"I'd rather not talk about the stocks." He unthreaded his tie from around his neck and deposited it on the island, landing it in the S-shape of a snake. He started on his buttons and was shirtless before her. It was his usual after-work routine; he couldn't wait to peel off his work-self. "I'm beginning to regret I ever told you about them."

"Why's that?" The knife jutted towards the ceiling, gripped upright in her hand.

"Because I can see it's disturbing you."

"You need to share anything with me that affects our finances," she said.

"Yes, and it would be nice if you shared with me anything that's affecting your mental state, but I don't think you're doing that."

She put down the knife, scooped up the lettuce shreds and dumped them in a big salad bowl. Then she picked the knife back up, and again its gleam held her attention before she pumped its un-blunted side into a large carrot.

"I'll tell you what's affecting my mental state." She kept her voice even, each word carefully enunciated, like her narration voice. "I talked to the wife of a guy from *American Star* who died of cardiac arrest. Hayden was the last person to see him besides her." She lifted the diced carrots and deposited them in the bowl, and raised the knife. "Also, I got another letter. And no, I didn't show it to you."

"Unbelievable," he moaned. "Why didn't you tell me? What did it say?"

"It basically admitted that the cult had caused someone to attack Jojo. And Jojo got a letter too, essentially telling her to drop out of *American Star*."

"Then we need to—"

"Let me tell *you* something," she said, emphasizing the words with a jab of the knife. "The police won't do a thing. The letters are too vague. And besides, what are they supposed to do? Stop every person who drops an envelope in a box near Port Authority?"

"Maybe they could dust them for fingerprints or something."

"Really? You think this person would leave their fingerprints? You think they're that stupid? Don't you watch crime shows? Even if you manage to get fingerprints, the writer would have to be in a criminal database to make a match. That's highly unlikely. Even if cops decide to take this seriously, which they won't, it will take months to get anything going with analyzing the envelopes. You think they're going to give this the time of day when they've got murders and rapes to investigate? Meanwhile, Hayden is going to have Jojo killed."

"Killed?" Firio looked alarmed, his brows flew up, though she couldn't be sure if his alarm was for Jojo's safety or her own behavior.

"Or neutralized somehow. Paralyze her. Take out her legs or her voice. He *killed* Dylan. Stopped his heart!"

"All right, Piper," Firio said, a little snappishly. "But if we can't bring the letters to police and you won't stop reading them, then what? You have high blood pressure and this isn't helping. You're getting obsessed with this Hayden character. Him becoming more famous than you isn't the worst thing in the world."

It felt like a javelin had been thrust into her ribs. Firio probably didn't realize that was an unimaginably insensitive thing to point out at the moment. "That's not what I'm upset about. Don't you get it? I need for you to take this seriously."

"Fine. It's serious. Now what? How do we fight *magic powers*?"

He'd almost had her. But she caught the nearly

imperceptible condescension in his tone. No one else would have heard it, but she did.

Putting down the knife, she came around the island, rubbed the sticky-sweaty muscles of his shoulders. "I'm tired of talking about this."

"You are?" He sounded dubious.

"Yes." She placed her head on his chest. His musky man-scent journeyed through her nostrils and intoxicated her brain stem, basic and primal. The roundness of the child they had made together bumped against his abdomen. She tilted her face up and kissed him. "Go change. Dinner's almost ready."

He moved dazedly out of the kitchen, defused by her pliancy. Piper listened to the scuff of his shoes on the wood boards. "Fool," she hissed out under her breath.

She'd given him his chance, his chance to be on her side as she mobilized forces deep within her. He'd chosen not to be on her side, so she'd neutralized him. And it hadn't taken a curse, only agreeableness.

Chapter Twenty-Seven

She watched him. Coming down the metal-gated pathway in a denim jacket, past the throng of fans holding out Playbills and eight-by-tens of his face. She watched as he leaned sideways when someone thrust out a phone and snapped their photo together. Watched how he spoke briefly to each person, with direct attention, like the person was important to him.

The crowd was at least five rows deep, but there were grooves and tunnels of space through which she could see him, sometimes only his shoulder or hair or the side of his face, could see him darting in and out of her line of vision like an animal being hunted.

She was going to confront him with everything: Dylan's death, Jojo's attack, Anton's fall, her vocal cord paralysis, and the fire. She wasn't going to tell him about the letters, because she worried that the letter writer, her "friend" who'd claimed to be sending them at great personal risk, would pay the price.

No, she was going to tell Hayden she'd heard of The True Way, and knew what it claimed it could do, and demand to know if he was a member. He would deny it, of course, but she would be calm and reasonable, and then she would tell him she was going public.

The media, naturally, wouldn't run with such a story. But she knew plenty of online places that would. The name Hayden Tower would be everywhere, permanently linked to a murderous cult, as other celebrities' names were said in the same breath as the Illuminati. She was also going to lie and say she was working with a cult investigator, and that former members were willing to talk, and they were all going to split the cult wide open.

That is, unless Hayden backed off of her, Firio, and Jojo. Unless he stopped punishing people he considered his competition. And she was going to say that this cult investigator and these former members knew she was meeting with him, and if anything happened to her, the plan would go into immediate effect.

"Little flat at the top, Tow-*er* Pow-*er*," she sing-songed quietly, digging her nails into her palms.

He was close enough to her now that she could have easily called out to him and be heard. But as he got even closer, so close that they could have made eye contact if only she had been a little more in front and he looked in her direction, her resolve began to waver.

The resolve that had sent her fleeing from her house after texting a message to Firio, who was working late, that she was going to visit Jojo. The resolve that had made her formulate a plan in her mind, how she could get Hayden to leave her loved ones alone. And what made her waver was the life inside of her swollen belly.

If Hayden's cult had the power to give her mother cancer, injure Anton, and stop Dylan's heart, surely it could do something to her baby. Her threat might be enough to ward him off, but it might not.

Dejectedly, she stepped backward on the sidewalk and bumped a person behind her. "Sorry," she murmured, but the young woman was focused on Hayden, neck craned hopefully for a view.

At the crowded corner, the red traffic light seemed to pulse strangely. Rubbing at her eyes, she wondered if she needed an eye exam. For the briefest of moments, she couldn't remember if a red light signaled stop or go.

A black town car turned at the corner, and something about it drew her gaze. Black town cars all looked alike, but this one had some kind of aura about it, the way it slunk almost malevolently by her. It stopped and a man got out. A man in a denim jacket with a dark baseball cap pushed down over his forehead. Several people parted in front of her and she caught sight of the man's face, or the lower half of his face.

Hayden. She'd recognize that jaw anywhere.

He closed the door of the town car and walked down the sidewalk. She found herself speeding up and following him, the brisk night air coursing along her cheeks. Normally, she had one arm boxed around her belly when she walked in crowds, but this time, her belly stuck straight out, her arms hung down at her sides.

Nothing could harm her. Not right now.

Hayden turned a corner, and she walked straight

past him to the cross street. She peered back over her shoulder, preparing to call to him as if she'd happened to see him. Standing inside the doorway of the glass building, he looked furtively around before digging into his jacket and taking something out that he patted against one palm. It was only when she saw a tiny orange flare that she realized he was lighting a cigarette.

He took several puffs, staring off towards the rush of cars along Forty-Fifth Street. There was so much humanity spilling out from the nearby brightly lit theaters that, though she was only about fifty feet from him, she was camouflaged as if she crouched in a thicket of deep woods.

Something about observing him in his private ritual seemed more important than alerting him to her presence. She was fact-finding, gathering essential information. She clutched a nearby streetlamp, its monolithic steel hiding half her body.

Hayden examined his phone for a minute or two while dragging on his cigarette and tossed the end butt to the sidewalk, grinding it with his foot. Then he was on the move again.

He dipped down the subway stairs, and Piper followed, holding carefully onto the railing, trying to keep up with his rapid pace but convinced she was going to lose him.

He passed the MetroCard machines and she dug into a front pocket on her tote bag where she kept her card. He moved through the turnstile and she followed. He took a left towards the uptown platform and she was behind him, with several people between them on the escalator. If it had been stairs, she was certain he would have gotten away from her.

He stopped at the end of the platform, pulling his cap lower. She passed him, and stood behind a subway map display, peeking around it.

She would get on the train car with him. She'd ask him if he'd like to go somewhere and have a drink. That she had something important to talk to him about. If he refused, she'd say everything on the train. He'd be a captive audience. But preferably, he'd go somewhere with her. She didn't want anyone to over-hear her.

The platform underneath her feet quaked with tiny vibrations, sending them skittering up her legs. Suddenly, her skin flash-intensified with prickly heat in an odd way she'd never felt before.

Her legs had an empty-weakness to them and dizzi-ness tilted her stomach. She looked for a bench to sit on but there wasn't one nearby.

She remembered on the *American Star* finale when something in her brain took over another part of her brain.

She and Hayden had been assigned three songs each for the finale. For the second song, they each had to sing a new one written by an unknown, one selected by view-ers. Piper's was called "Over the Mountain" and Nolan had hated it. Called it "treacly" and her performance "average."

Backstage, she'd tried to shove aside his harsh and humiliating critique. She had to sing another song in ten minutes, her last one of the competition, and she had to be at her best. But his words glued in her mind. *Average. Average. Average.*

During the bridge of her next song, she'd felt herself slipping away from herself. A small but steadily rising panic in her brain: *I can't do this, I can't do this.*

She was an average singer who had fooled everyone, fooled them into believing she deserved to be here more than any of the contestants who'd been eliminated, or even the ones who hadn't made it past the first attempt in a line of thousands.

Fooled everyone, that is, except Nolan. He knew she had no right to be standing on this stage in front of millions. The sense of inadequacy was so bright it was fluorescent. She stumbled on the lyrics, said *cleave* instead of *weave*, couldn't remember where the rainbow led, and her throat began to screw shut. She only wanted to give up, walk off, and let Hayden have the win.

One more instant and the mental intruder would have taken her down, but a lull in the band happened, and she heard a girl scream, "We love you, Piper!"

That's what she focused on: that girl's voice. Whoever that girl was, her call of support had buoyed Piper enough to fight off the swelling panic. She'd relaxed, swooping back into the song, blasting up to an F6 whistle tone, then plunging three octaves to an almost-growl, bringing ten thousand people in the Hollywood Theater to their feet.

A train boomed into the station; she felt its rush of air on her face. Hayden turned, turned right towards her. She caught a glimpse of his face, his eyes registering recognition as she squatted down to the platform, activating her thigh muscles, grunting with the effort, trying to get her alien body to the solid ground with her baby safely upwards.

* * *

At first, she could only see the ceiling of the station, something she couldn't recall ever having looked at before. A grid of off-white coffered squares spidered with brown cracks of water damage and silver pipes running alongside.

"Oh my God," was the first thing she heard anyone say, and it was a woman's voice. She lay there, studying the ceiling, wondering what would happen next, embarrassingly aware of her stomach bulge, the clumsy-wide, obscene splay of her legs. Thank god she'd worn leggings.

"Piper. Are you okay?"

Hayden was sitting her up. A thin crowd was peering down, a few people got on their phones, whether to call for help or to make personal calls, she had no idea.

"I'm fine," she said, patting her tote bag, which she hadn't let go of. A New Yorker holds her bag no matter what. And as she sat with her arms propped behind her, she did begin to feel fine. The flash-flood of prickly heat and revolving dizziness had eddied away. She was mortified sitting on the dirty platform with her fat ball of a stomach and open legs, strangers milling in slow motion around her with their luridly human curiosity.

A woman thrust a bottle of water into her face, and

she took several gulps. When she tried to hand it back, the woman indicated she should keep it.

"What happened?" Hayden asked her.

"I was about to come over to you," she said. "I saw you. Happened to see you. I'm headed home from shopping."

"Is help coming?" he asked someone, looking up.

"I'm fine. I only got dizzy." She rocked on her haunches, trying to gather enough momentum to stand. Limber as a turtle on its back.

"No, Pip. Relax," Hayden said, propping a bended knee behind her back.

She wilted onto his thigh, relieved to feel like a little girl being taken care of. It was so hard to believe he was pure evil.

"I saw you smoking," she murmured for lack of anything else to say, staring at the black hair-strands on his wrist peeking out of his jacket sleeve.

"Oh God. Don't tell Ava. She'd kill me."

She glanced quickly at his face, wondering if he'd said that as a test, to see if she knew about him, but he was looking up at the onlookers. "Help is definitely coming?" he asked no one in particular.

"I called 911," someone said and someone else said, "I'm going upstairs. I'll get someone."

"I feel really stupid right now," Piper said.

"Don't. I'm going to tell you something. I've had some health issues. I was told not to smoke anymore. So." He pushed his mouth up against her ear. "I'm down to one a day, Glory Note. After the show. But please, you can't ever mention it to Ava."

She shook her head, inexplicably feeling a small partnership with him, sharing this secret. "I won't tell."

He chuckled into her ear. "I get my driver to drop me off, smoke, and… Oh, forget it. What am I talking about this for?"

He looked up, as if about to ask another person to find help, but Piper pulled on his jacket sleeve. "Go on. Don't leave me hanging."

"Anyway, I take the subway home, change, and shower so she doesn't smell it, then go to her place. On nights she comes to the show, I can't. Almost go out of my mind for awhile."

"Heh. You're very sneaky." She paused, fishing for further information: "Why don't you get back into the car?"

"They send the same drivers for the cast. Everyone gossips. Thanks to a driver, I know one cast-mate is having an affair with another. I can't risk anyone in the cast finding out and passing it along to the wrong person. They've got insurance on me. If they knew I was smoking, even just one, they wouldn't be happy. So the driver thinks I prefer to hang with the rabble."

They said nothing, her arm draped over his thigh and arm. She hoped she wasn't holding up the train. Just as she thought it, she heard the train announcer's barely-intelligible warble, the ding of the doors, and the train squealed out of the station.

A cluster of burly-shouldered men in black helmets and black firefighter garb with fluorescent yellow stripes ambled authoritatively towards them. One of the firemen placed what looked like a large bright-orange boogie board next to her, and another man with a round, baby-face, almost like a teenager, knelt in front of her.

"What happened here, ma'am?" he asked, as staccato voices squelched through his radio.

"I'm fine. I only got too hot." Hayden tried to unlatch himself, but she clutched at his sleeve. "You should go before someone recognizes you. I don't want this all over the press."

"I could come with you."

"I don't want to go anywhere, I'm fine." She looked at the baby-faced fireman. "Can you help me up? I want to go home." If she went to the hospital, Firio was going to know she wasn't with Jojo and she didn't want to deal with the repercussions.

"Ma'am, you should get the baby checked out," the baby-faced fireman said.

"You really should," Hayden added. "I can come with you."

"No! Please, *please* leave. I don't want this out there. I'm going to call my husband. It's nothing serious." And yet, she wouldn't be able to forgive herself if she didn't get checked out and something was wrong that could affect the baby.

"Ma'am," the teenaged-looking fireman insisted. "We need to put you on the stretcher."

In a flash, one of the firemen had his hands under her armpits, and another one had his hands under her knees. She was swiftly layered onto the bright-orange boogie board and carried off up the stairs.

She could no longer see or hear Hayden.

Chapter Twenty-Eight

*I*t was about four p.m. when Piper decided to go outside and face Firio, who'd been in the garden working for the past couple of hours.

He'd called in sick to work and they'd slept in until about noon, having returned from the hospital around four a.m. A technician had strapped a heart monitor to her stomach for three hours, and she'd sat listening to the reassuring sound, like horse hooves galloping over a distant tin street. She'd had urine and blood tests run on her before finally being cleared to leave.

So far as anyone could tell, her near-fainting episode had been a combination of being dehydrated and having slightly elevated blood pressure. She was told the usual things—drink lots of water, get enough sleep, don't stress yourself, etc. The most important thing was that her baby's heartbeat was strong.

The ambulance had taken her to the nearest emergency room, Mount Sinai West, which was far north of Chelsea, where Firio knew that Jojo lived. "I decided to take a walk," she'd told him when he'd questioned where she'd been, but it was clear he didn't believe her, and he'd dropped the subject. But all early afternoon, he was tense and quiet.

In the garden, she walked to where Firio was kneeling, digging into the dirt with a spade, pulling up clumps of weeds in their overgrown garden. He had on black training pants and a white jersey, and was grunting as he slammed the spade into the dirt.

In another hour, it would be pitch-dark, but now the air had a bluish-gray cast, the horizon was burning tangerine, and a faded half-moon hung high in the sky. She'd brought out two glasses of homemade hot lemonade with cinnamon and nutmeg and tried to give him one, but he shook his head and kept pumping the spade.

"Are you going to speak to me?" she asked.

He silently worked for several seconds, then said, "What's the point? You're only going to lie to me."

"I don't understand what you're angry about," she said, though she knew.

He stopped and stared at her, his face glistening with sweat despite the chill air. "You weren't at Jojo's. You wouldn't walk all that way almost nine months pregnant. And if you did, you shouldn't."

She sat at the little wrought iron table and sipped some husky-warm lemonade, her stomach clenched with nerves, trying to come up with something to placate him. She settled on a rather unconvincing, "My doctor said to take long walks."

"What I think," he said, standing with the dirty

spade on his hip. "Is that you went to that theater, the one where Hayden Tower does the show. It's right near there."

Staring off past a thicket of mottled, twisty sycamore trees into their neighbor's backyard, she said, "What does it matter? You don't believe anything I tell you anyway."

"I said I'd speak with him. You said not to. But now you keep doing it yourself."

"What are you going to say to him? He'll just deny it."

"I tell you what I'd say to him," he growled, pointing the spade. "I'd tell him to leave you alone or I'll kill him."

"Oh great! You know what will be in the news the next day? '*American Star* Piper Dunner's Husband Threatens to Kill Hayden Tower.' Your name won't even make it to the headline. But *mine* will be all over."

"So what did you say to him?"

"Nothing! I didn't even see him. I decided against it and walked to the subway."

She hoped like hell that someone hadn't recognized Hayden and a video of his "heroics" wasn't currently crawling around the Internet. She'd checked a couple of times already, but seen nothing.

She and Firio stood at an impasse, his jaw clenched, her hand steely around her glass. He tossed the spade to the ground, walked over, and grabbed the other glass of lemonade, guzzling down half of it, his Adam's apple bobbing in his throat. He wiped his forehead with the back of his hand, raked it through his black hair, sweat-wet strands curling around his face.

"You can't be running around like this," he said. "You're putting yourself in danger, and the baby too, and I have some say about that."

"What do you want me to do?" she asked, her voice rising to a girlish pitch. "Not go anywhere?"

"I want you to do what I asked you to do before. Don't open any of those damn letters. If one comes, give it to me. And don't go near that guy."

"All right," she said, sullenly. "I won't."

"Do you promise?"

"Yes."

He drank some more, and sank into the opposite wrought iron chair. "You have no idea how worried I was last night." He paused, the silence between them charged in a way that warned he was about to say something she didn't want to hear. "I know we didn't know each other very well before this happened. The baby. I suppose I'm…" He stopped, wiped his forehead again, and went on, "I'm getting to know you now. I didn't realize you had these beliefs about cult curses and things."

"I didn't!" she said, louder than intended. "I didn't until the letters came and I put it all together. You have no idea what it's like to have everything and it's all torn away from you. Yes, there were times that I didn't like being a star. But for the most part, I felt so lucky. To get to do what I love, and do it for millions of people who liked it as much as I did. I prepared my whole life for it, finally got it, and it was ripped away from me and there's no getting it back."

Unexpectedly, Firio came over and knelt in front of her, causing a swell of tears to rush threateningly behind her eyes. "I do know what it's like. My parents were taken from me, and now my career. Not as much as you, but I have an idea what it's like to lose the things you love."

"Then please understand. I've had so many bad things happen to me, and to those around me. I can feel it. This thing, like a dark cloud. It's always hovering over me. Like no matter what I do, I can't get free of it. I could never understand it. Why me? But *now I know why*."

"I know you're trying to make sense of why things happen to you, but it's not a curse, okay?" He put his hand on her knee. "What happened to the theory that it's his girlfriend sending these letters? What's her name?"

"Ava," she said, despondently, her bottom lip quivering.

"She could be jealous of you and Jojo because she wants her boyfriend to be on the show."

Piper wiped at a few tears that had trickled out and were gliding down her cheeks. "I considered that, but not after Mitch warned me about Hayden."

"Ask him what he meant by it."

"I tried, but he clammed up. Denied he'd even said anything." She gave a shuddery exhale, and rubbed her wrist along her dripping nose. "Besides, Ava couldn't have anything to do with Dylan's death. Hayden was managed by Moxie at that time, not her. She wouldn't have had any reason to kill Dylan."

"Piper. The man died of a heart—"

"See? See?" She pointed her finger in his face.

"I'm sorry. But you can't seriously believe people are being killed with a curse."

"I don't know what to believe," she said, slowly shaking her head. "I don't know what to believe."

THAT NIGHT AS SHE LAY IN BED, with Firio's soft, familiar snoring beside her, a little bit of peace settled on her. She remembered how the stoplight on Forty-Fifth Street had strangely pulsed, how her memory of a simple thing as to whether a red light meant to stop or go had, for a disorienting moment, abandoned her. She hadn't mentioned either occurrence at the hospital, worried the doctor might not let her go home.

Could that brief episode have been due to pregnancy hormones? According to her reading, pregnancy hormones could cause about anything.

Add in the letters, and she was being driven out of her mind. This thought gave her a degree of peace because it was preferable to believe that someone, a plain old human being, was trying to drive her insane than to think she was in the crosshairs of a cult with the power to kill her in an instant if it wanted to.

Hayden. If he were trying to drive her mad so she would drop out of the running for judge, why had he sent her another letter *after* she'd done exactly that?

The way he'd tenderly helped her as she lay sprawled and defenseless on the subway platform—it seemed impossible he could act so compassionately towards her, and yet be evil enough to do everything she was imagining he'd done, even killing one of his good friends.

The stark realization of how much danger she'd put her baby in with her irrational behavior stabbed through her like an icy knife as she stared at a muted beam of outside light straying across the far wall.

She was done with it. There was no cult curse on her. Hayden—or even one of his superfans like she'd originally surmised—was trying to mentally torture her. And she was letting him do it, had let him play her perfectly.

Firio was right. She was still unable to accept the unfair hand she'd been dealt just when she'd gained everything she'd always wanted. This is what was making her susceptible to Hayden's manipulations. It seemed unfathomable that life was so random, so cruel. But it was. Life sent typhoons. It sent earthquakes and wildfires. It sent war and terrorists.

So life had sent her a fire that killed her dog and destroyed her songs. Sent her a paralyzed vocal cord. Sent her mother cancer. Sent Dylan cardiac arrest.

Life, life.

Tomorrow, she would start focusing on reality. Reality as she *knew* it, not imagined it.

In four weeks, there would be a baby in the house. She hadn't even packed the hospital bag. Nor had she done any holiday decorating. Though that hadn't been all her fault. Twice, she'd asked Firio to string up the white Christmas lights on the porch and he still hadn't done it. She hoped it wouldn't be like this with the baby. Would he even change a diaper without being asked a hundred times? She had to incubate the baby, push it out of her, breastfeed it—what the hell would *he* do?

Screw it. She'd string up the lights on the porch by herself. She couldn't get them high up, but she could drape them around the wall. And she would go buy a pine wreath, a real one not one of those plastic ones, and figure out a way to get that attached to the front door.

She tried to let her mind drift into sleep, but something continually niggled at her, a piece of the puzzle that didn't fit. Mitch. He'd warned her to stay away from Hayden, she was certain she hadn't misunderstood him.

This meant he knew *something*.

Chapter Twenty-Nine

*M*itch looked different, much better than the last time she'd seen him.

His hair was longer, the blond curls resprouting. His skin tone wasn't the ghastly pale she'd seen last time either, closer to his permatan but with a pinkish cast, coloring from the actual sun, not a bottle or booth. He must be spending time somewhere sunny. He was dressed casually, in a light blue T-shirt emblazoned "ROGUE" and black workout pants, and was carrying a red gym bag that he plopped on the floor near to where Piper sat waiting for him at a lunch spot on Madison Avenue.

A few days ago, she'd remembered that post-*American Star*, she'd spoken to Mitch several times on his radio show, and one of those times, he'd given her his private number in case she ever wanted to call in. After finding six old cell phones tucked away in a box in her office closet, she'd charged them all. The pre-smartphone phones were silver and cutely fit in the palm of her hand. One of them had his phone number in it.

She had no idea if he'd be reachable at the old number, but he was. She also had no idea if he would agree to meet with her, but luckily, he seemed to have forgotten all about their exchange outside of the Omni Hotel or was at least acting as if he had. He took her up on her lunch invite, saying she'd gotten him just in time, as he was headed back to Los Angeles the next day.

After their greetings, he'd smiled with that spirited, magazine-ad smile she remembered from *American Star*, and said, "Welcome to satellite radio."

She'd lied and told him she'd been offered a radio show on Sirius. As a server poured them tap water, she said, "Thanks, I'm hoping you can give me some advice." During her years in the entertainment business, Piper learned that show business types loved to give advice, thrived on the sound of their voices preaching the ins and outs of the industry.

"I'll try," he said. "What's your show going to focus on?"

"Music."

"Ah, that makes sense."

A different server appeared, and the pair ordered sparkling water, and Piper a shrimp Cobb salad and Mitch a chicken salad sandwich.

"So how did it go with Nolan?" she asked casually, as if she was only asking to be polite. "Are you coming back to *Star*?"

"Not sure yet. I have a lot of stuff happening in L.A. I took a long vacation and ignored my production company for too long." He stared beyond her, submerged in thought. "I had to straighten some things out." Then he snapped out of it. "I'm feeling better."

"That's good," she said, deciding not to press further, not wanting to alienate him before she was able to ask her questions. She smiled and said, "I'm hoping to get some of the *Star* alum to come on my show."

"Absolutely," he nodded. "You've always been generous with your time with me, so if there's any way I can repay the favor, let me know. Interviews, contacts, whatever."

"That would be amazing. Especially with *Star* being on-air again, there will be a new crop of kids who might like some publicity." She felt a little guilty about how far she was taking this, as if these new "kids" might actually be expecting to be booked on her non-existent radio program.

"You should talk to Nolan or Oliver Corbyn about that," Mitch said.

"Oh, I plan to," she smiled. "And I still have some contacts. There's Jojo. She's a good friend of mine and now the third judge."

The server reappeared, carrying their meals. Piper watched as Mitch inelegantly scarfed down several bites of his sandwich. "Jojo's a good contact for you," he said, nodding in that eager way she remembered from the show, like a little boy asked if he'd like to get up to some mischief.

She waited until he seemed like he'd swallowed and said, "And Hayden too."

His blue eyes darted down to his plate. "Mm-hmm," he mumbled.

"We still speak occasionally, so I'm hoping he'll come on."

"Sure," he said, gulping sparkling water, as his little boy energy transformed before her eyes into tense, wiry energy.

"Do you think that's a good idea?"

"Why not?" he asked, avoiding eye contact by using his fork to pick at some chicken chunks that had escaped onto his plate. "He's a big star."

"Yes, he is." She forked some salad into her mouth, watching as he nudged his fallen chicken around. "Funny how he's the big star. I mean, he was the runner-up and I was the winner. Yet there he is, and here I am."

"Life is strange," Mitch offered.

"Isn't it? Sometimes I wonder how things happen. How one person has a ton of success, and another person, equally as talented, perhaps even more talented, doesn't. Might be a good topic for the show."

He nodded absently and she could swear there were beads of sweat forming along his hairline.

"You'd be a good person to speak to that," she plowed on. "You've seen it all. How Brooks Keith got famous even coming in ninth place. How some of the winners don't go anywhere." She laughed. "Like me."

"Oh. But you…" He hesitated. "You had some issues, I'd heard."

"I did. Right after the debut album. Things seemed to fall apart."

"It's pretty random, all right," he said. "Even me. I never thought I'd be so successful. I have no real talent other than talking to people and acting excited." He flashed a plastic smile but his eyes were flat.

"So what do you think makes one person a success and another not? Is it all luck?"

He shifted, and looked down at the floor, towards his gym bag. "Hard work. Talent. And luck," he said, finally looking back at her. "Luck for sure plays a part. Could be as simple as you're up for something you want, some kind of job, and another person who's up for it too gets sick and can't make the audition."

"Random, right?" she said, putting her finger into the air. "That's how I read Hayden got the role in *Ghosts of Time*. He took over from an actor who'd had an accident and needed stitches in his face."

Mitch looked supremely uncomfortable, murmured, "I'd heard that," and shoveled his sandwich into his mouth.

"I wonder if…" She laughed a little, trying to appear thoughtful. "I wonder if there's a way to *guarantee* good luck. What I wouldn't do for that."

"What *would* you do?" he asked, unexpectedly direct.

"If someone could guarantee my radio show would be a success? Anything."

"Huh." He looked around her, through her, and then at her. "Would you… what if you were successful, but only if it meant someone else wouldn't be?"

"Like an exchange?"

"Yeah, something like that."

"Hmm." She took a bite of salad, though it was a

bad idea. The lettuce stuck in her throat. "I'd consider that, I guess." She laughed like it was a joke and glanced sideways at him. "I don't suppose you'd know how to make that happen?"

There was a long pause as the question hung in the air, and she wondered whether she'd gotten her point across, and whether he knew she'd gotten her point across.

"Piper, I think…" he said deliberately, his blue eyes bluer than she'd ever seen them, radiating intensely. "That you'll do fine on your own. I don't think you need any help from anyone."

"So… so…" she said, her heart sinking. "You won't help me?"

"Of course I will. I said I would. But…" He shook his head, and out came his showbiz, nothing-is-wrong smile. "I think you'll do fine."

Damn it. She'd lost him. She decided on one last big push. "If there *was* a way to guarantee the type of success you and Hayden have had, you'd tell me, right? I have a baby coming and a mortgage. I sure could use your secret."

"Piper," he said, a tinge of impatience in his tone. "You'll do fine. Don't go messing with—I'm sure you'll do fine."

Bastard. He knew about the cult. "Okay," she said, sighing dramatically. "But if you ever want to spill your success secret, think of me. I won't share it."

* * *

OUTSIDE ON THE SIDEWALK, Mitch hiked up his gym bag and gave her a half-hug. For the rest of lunch, he'd acted his usual self, smiling, telling stories, handing out tips on how to interview. But there had been an unmistakable current zapping between them, the tension of the unspoken.

"I'm sorry it didn't work out with *Star*," he said.

"It's fine, I dropped out."

"You did? Huh. Why's that?"

"Decided it would be too much to commit to with a baby on the way."

"I see. I'd thought they'd decided on Jojo. After that attack on her, seemed like the right thing to do. Kind of fortunate for her in a weird way, wasn't it?"

"Not really. She's got a broken wrist and that was very hurtful for her."

"Of course, I didn't mean—bad joke. But there you go. You drop out, so Jojo gets the spot. *Luck*." He put his hand on her shoulder and locked her with his deep blues. "It was nice seeing you. I'm sorry things didn't go as planned after *Star*. You're very talented. One of my favorite winners. You should be as famous as Alyssa Alina."

"Or Hayden," she said, pointedly.

At that, Mitch turned from her and hailed a yellow cab. "Gotta run, lots of packing to do before I catch the redeye." He leaned in to air-kiss her cheek before opening the cab door. "Call me if you want me on your show."

The door was open and he was about to get in. She was going to lose him and was seized by a last-ditch

236

impulse to be more straightforward with him. It might be her only chance.

"Mitch, about Hayden. Let me ask—"

"Bye, Piper!" he called, either not hearing her or pretending not to.

He hopped inside of the cab and it rolled off. She stood watching as it hit a line of traffic and stopped. She wanted to run up to the cab, knock on the window, and demand to know—point-blank—if he and Hayden were members of a cult that could curse people.

But what was the use? He would only deny it and likely get insulted. It was unwise to make an adversary out of a man with as many professional contacts as Mitch had.

Sighing with defeat, she opened her car lift app and put in her home address. On a whim, she checked her email, and saw she had a response from "Former-Truther." Her heart flipped as she clicked into it.

And do you know if the singer Hayden Tower is a Truther?

He sure as hell used to be. Probably still is. He and his *American Star* pal Mitch McCabe. For your own protection, don't let them know you know. They can be dangerous! For my protection, this email will destruct right after you open it. We're not supposed to take photos, but I managed this one secretly.

Attached was a photo. It was dark and grainy. With

shaky hands, Piper opened it and enlarged the photo with her fingers.

She recognized Hayden and Mitch, or at least their profiles. They were both staring at a man standing in the middle of them, who appeared to be talking.

The man looked to be in his fifties... and had bright white hair.

Chapter Thirty

*M*itch.

It was Mitch writing the letters.

"Mitch," she whispered, staring out the car service window at the glassy-gray East River streaming by as the car drove over the Prospect Park Expressway back to Brooklyn.

How hadn't she put it together before? After all, he'd flat-out warned her about Hayden in front of the Omni Hotel. He was part of the cult and he knew Hayden was too. Not wanting to put himself in harm's way, he'd written letters, and made them sound as unlike himself as possible. He knew what Hayden was capable of with the help of The True Way. He'd seen what had happened to Anton and Dylan.

This is why Mitch hadn't wanted to be part of the new *American Star*. He'd wanted to stay far away from Hayden, in case Hayden got the judge position. And he must be worried that something would "happen" to Jojo, causing the slot to go to Hayden after all. That's why he was still wary about returning as host.

She realized Mitch was doing what he'd done on *American Star*—looking out for the contestants. Though he was certainly choosing a strange way to go about it.

The T-shirt he'd worn at lunch. It had said "ROGUE." And he was The True Way member who'd gone rogue on the cult. He could have worn that shirt as a signal to her.

Perhaps Mitch or Hayden was the one who'd tried to bring Crystal into the cult, not some world-famous actor, as she'd claimed. Goddamn, everyone involved with *American Star* could be a member. Nolan. Oliver Corbyn. Alyssa Alina and Mindy Patel. Brooks Keith.

Some twisted part of her wondered why she hadn't been invited too—but that was presumably because Hayden got in, and his first order of business was to "demolish" Piper, the one who'd bested him on the show.

As FormerTruther had warned his or her email would disappear after being closed, Piper took a screen-shot of it and emailed it to herself.

* * *

AT HOME, SHE DECIDED SHE WOULDN'T mention the photo to Firio. What was the point? He would still come up with some way of mocking her fears. And if the photo *did* make him believe everything, she worried he'd find a way to confront Hayden, and possibly get himself arrested after making a threat. She didn't need a husband in trouble with the law, especially not with a baby due.

She needed to pack her birth bag, but her mind was so twisted around Hayden and the cult that she could barely rein it in, pull her focus back to the biggest event in her life she was about to experience, bigger than her mother's death, bigger than her *American Star* win: giving birth. An itch was in her brain, and it had inflamed to the point of being untamable.

She sat nervously checking out the window, waiting for the mailman to show up, which was usually around five p.m.

When she finally saw him, she walked out, greeted him, and took the mail from his hands. She had a feeling that Mitch would have sent another letter before he left for Los Angeles so that the postal stamp would have the same midtown zip code. Before the mailman had even turned around to continue down the street, she'd quickly sifted past the junk pieces and saw the familiar white business envelope with her name printed on it.

Inside, her breath quickened in a way that signaled oncoming hyperventilation, so she stood with eyes shut, breathing deeply for at least a minute to slow down her heart rate. She sat at the kitchen island, and took the paring knife out of its wooden block.

DEAREST ONE,

I've held off our high-ranking member from his plans for revenge for as long as I can, but he is determined. You and your friend are in danger. He's said he'll take out your baby too. I don't know what he's planning exactly, he won't tell me. But I know it won't be good. He's out of control. You *know* who it is.

There is only one way to stop him.

Make sure you destroy all of these communications. Protect me as I'm protecting you.

Then make it look like an accident.

Your friend

Chapter Thirty-One

$\mathcal{S}$he stood clutching her stomach, shimmering in her rage. A rage she knew her baby was feeling too. It was down, down, down deep, down deep in the skeleton, down deep in the middle of her, lodged in the marrow of her spine. She could see nothing, but heard a loud, rushing, thumping in her ears.

How dare he. How DARE he! Threaten her *baby*.

Hayden. The sick son-of-a-bitch.

It was one thing to hate Piper for winning. It was one thing to hate Jojo for getting picked to be the new judge.

But her innocent baby?!

How DARE he! He'd taken everything. Everything. And now he wanted the most precious thing she had?! How DARE he!

And had he really given her mother cancer? Was he capable of that?

Her proud, supportive, lively mother who for years had dutifully driven her to auditions, state fairs, and singing contests. Who'd dutifully waited with her in the cold, drizzling, predawn rain for her preliminary *American Star* audition. Piper could clearly see her mother. Her face was still plump and youthful, her short auburn hair still thick. She was wearing a black shirt with little flowers sewn onto the front.

After six hours of waiting outside the convention center in L.A., Piper's bones had been chilled, her fingers numb. A cold front had unexpectedly wafted into the area and she hadn't dressed appropriately for it; had, like most of the other women in the line, wanted to look like star material in her flirty, thigh-length dress. *Pick me, pick me, I'm cute, you see?*

A man with a bullhorn had stalked down the mile-long line, announcing that they would soon be closing the auditions. *Thank God*, Piper had thought. Now she had an excuse to go home and get warm. How was she supposed to sing well under these kinds of conditions anyway? Her throat was brittle, her teeth chattered in small bursts. If she even made it into the arena holding area, there would be another hours-long wait, and she'd get perhaps twenty seconds in front of a screener who'd already heard thousands of people bust out their lungs that day. It all seemed so pointless.

"Mom, we should guh-go," she'd said.

"We're here now."

"But they'll be closing the audition. We're not going to make it in."

"Let's see."

"But I'm fuh-fuh-reezing."

"Piper." Her mother had looked at her sternly, something she rarely did. "We're not quitting now. I have a feeling. It's overpowering, do you understand? This is where we belong."

She started their little chant, the one her mother had been chanting at Piper for as long as she could remember, saved for those times when Piper didn't want to do one of the myriad things a child, teen, or adult doesn't want to do that her mother knows she should do.

We're just gonna do it
That's all there is to it

Piper was in no mood for their little chant, but her mother was so determined and energetic that Piper joined in for a couple of refrains.

We're just gonna do it
That's all there is to it

Several people around them joined in too. Intermittent singing, dancing, and all manner of goofing around had been going on for the six hours they'd been in line so it was another way to pass the time.

We're just gonna do it
That's all there is to it!

Suddenly, a harried-looking young woman appeared out of nowhere and handed Piper a label with a number on it: 7123.

The woman stopped handing them out at 7125.

A few years later, Piper's mother would be gone. As would her sweet, hyper little Marvin, who loved her no matter how her career was going, and it hadn't been going well. Five years in Los Angeles. Dropped out of college and nothing to show for it but a lot of broken promises and half-empty performance venues.

Until she won *American Star*.

She'd rightfully and finally won a place in the music world, one she'd worked so hard for that she still felt the dim ache of that hard work in her bones. She deserved to have her place. Hayden shouldn't have been able to knock her out of it by making an evil and unfair pact with a cult. She'd beaten him on equal footing, equal terms.

Now what?

He would take his revenge—on her, on Jojo, on Firio, even on her helpless, innocent baby. At her next check-up, Dr. Malhotra would discover something wrong. Hayden would cause her to have a stillbirth, so she'd have to hold her dead newborn in her arms, just as he'd forced Ember Lopez to hold Dylan's lifeless body after his heart stopped.

Then he'd take down Jojo. He'd send another maniac in a car, only this time the maniac would run her over, finish her off.

Then he'd make sure Firio was destroyed, taking his career down in tatters, so they'd have to sell their beloved house and move somewhere cramped and roach-infested.

Finally, he'd turn his attention to Piper. He'd send her some malady, some illness. Or strike at her vocal cords again, so she couldn't do narration anymore. And when Piper and Firio were homeless and childless, he'd send a calamity to kill them both, put them out of their misery. He wouldn't be satisfied until he'd taken it all.

She stopped shaking and moved up the stairs, then

stood staring blankly at the cream-colored wall in her bedroom, feeling hollow, wracked, empty.

There is only one way to stop him.

Slowly walking to the bathroom, like a ghost, a shell, she looked at her red-splotched face in the mirror and grasped her protruding stomach, felt the life thrumming inside of her, the life she would kill to protect.

Make sure you destroy all of these communications.

A sense of relief and calm settled on her, an unexpected strength and determination suffusing her soul.

Make it look like an accident.

She opened her mouth.

And she sang. She couldn't remember the last time she'd spontaneously burst into song, something she used to do all of the time until singing was as much a part of her daily routine as talking was for other people.

It was the first song that came to mind. Her voice sounded clear and resonant in the tiled walls of the bathroom. She sang the chorus of "I Will Survive."

Because she would survive.

But Hayden would not.

Chapter Thirty-Two

The subway. That's how she would do it. That's why she'd happened to be standing at the corner when Hayden had slipped out of his town car and furtively smoked a cigarette in a building's doorway. That's why instinct had told her to follow him, why she'd collapsed, and why Hayden had confessed that he smoked after each show as long as Ava wasn't around.

Piper didn't have a cult, but she had a force on her side. Call it God, call it The Universe, call it Fate. Whatever it was, it wanted to rebalance The True Way's power, rebalance it in her favor for once.

It couldn't be more perfect. She knew where and when Hayden would be standing in front of a gulley that, if he happened to topple into it at the correct time, would kill him.

How else could she know this unless a force, a supernatural overseer, was helping her out? How else could it be that Mitch wrote, "Make it look like an accident," as if Mitch too was part of this divine plan, a plan he

248

didn't even know he was already part of? This guiding force, this God-like plotter, had given her permission. Permission to do the most unforgivable thing a person can do to another person.

What more proof did she need that Hayden had killed Dylan, had killed Piper's mother, had burned Marvin to death? Had almost killed Jojo, had scarred Anton Bishop's face? This universal force was on her side, and telling her it must be done, and she was the one who must do it.

There is only one way to stop him.

She would have to do it as soon as possible. Before he put his revenge plan into action. Before Piper went into labor. Couldn't exactly bring a newborn to an assassination.

Now to think what glitches could pop up.

If Ava came to a show, he would leave with her, and not go for his secret cigarette break. But obviously Ava didn't come to all the shows.

The letters. Piper had burned all of them she had left and, for good measure, buried the ashes in the garden.

Crystal knew about the letters, but didn't know that Piper had suspected Hayden was the "high-ranking member."

Jojo knew about the letters, even had one herself, and also knew Piper thought Hayden was the curse inflictor. But Jojo would want to get rid of Hayden too.

Anton Bishop. He knew. But it was abundantly clear he had no love for Hayden, the man who'd stolen his Oscar, who may even be responsible for the scar on his face. Anton would have no reason to step forward and tell anyone about their discussion. He'd even told her to do what she needed to keep herself safe.

Firio. He knew about most of it. But she was pregnant with his child. And he loved her. He wasn't going to risk the mother of his child going to prison by telling police that his wife was convinced Hayden Tower had cursed her.

Even if for some unfathomable reason he *did* tell police this, she could deny it. There was no proof. None. She'd never confronted Hayden about the letters.

Mitch. Of course, Mitch was the one who knew everything. But Mitch wouldn't tell. He was her "friend," after all. He was the hand through which this force was telling her what needed to be done.

She'd have to delete the photo that FormerTruther had sent her. No one knew she'd received it, and FormerTruther wouldn't reveal it, as that would put him or her in danger from The True Way. Besides, the person had no idea who she was, as she hadn't used her real name on her email.

Sure, the law may suspect she'd planned it, but suspicion wouldn't be enough for a jury to convict her. *Beyond a reasonable doubt.* That was the bar. And she didn't meet it. There was plenty of reasonable doubt.

She had high blood pressure.

She'd almost fainted once before, and she had hospital records.

She had no motive to kill Hayden. Nothing to gain from his death, not even the *American Star* judge position, as both she and Hayden were out of the running.

The only thing she had to gain from his death would be the fantastical notion that murdering him released her from a cult's curse—and who would suspect that except her best friend and her husband? Two people who had no reason to turn against her.

And if they did? She would deny, deny, deny. She didn't believe in curses, didn't believe in supernatural powers, in dark magic.

The most, the very most that would happen would be a short stint in prison for manslaughter, or even involuntary manslaughter. She had no previous arrests; she'd been a model citizen.

She'd be out in five years, even less with good behavior. She could handle that. Firio would take care of the baby in the meantime. They'd visit her often.

But no. No. A jury wouldn't convict a pregnant woman who'd fainted. Simply fainted, and had the horrific luck to fall into Hayden Tower as she did so.

She had no choice, did she? It was her or Hayden. Her and her baby or Hayden.

He had no one to blame but himself.

The "He had it coming" refrain from *Chicago*'s "Cell Block Tango" came to her, and she whisper-sang a few bars.

A tiny part of her flickered to life and, with astonishing rationality, told her she'd gone insane, but quickly retreated.

Chapter Thirty-Three

*H*ayden threw his cigarette down and smashed it with his foot, his leg twisting back and forth. Folding his arms across his chest, he stared into the traffic gushing by on Forty-Fifth.

Piper worried that he was about to hail a cab. But no, after canvassing the snarling lines of vehicles, he must have decided that a taxi would take too long and the subway would be the best bet. He turned and started down the stairs. Piper abandoned her spying spot behind the streetlamp and darted down the stairs after him, her hand coursing along the steel of the railing, tight enough not to topple over, but loose enough not to slow her down.

There were so many people, and she had to dodge around this body and that body to keep up with him. He was wearing the same black baseball cap as last time, so she could track his head bobbing down the stairs. It must be the cap he wore when he wanted a degree of anonymity.

Piper knew how it worked, how a star could turn it on and off—one minute, ooze pixie dust and draw attention, then slump the shoulders, dial down the magnetism, pull a cap over the eyes, and fade into a crowd.

Hayden hit the turnstile with his card. About six people back from him, Piper swiped her card through and pushed on the turnstile, but it refused to open. She glanced at the card reader and it said, "Swipe again at this turnstile." Damn it!

She glanced back up and noted his baseball cap disappearing down the escalator. She swiped again, trying to hit the sweet spot between too fast and too slow, either of which would make the turnstile reject the card. Her chest tightened in panic as the card glided through the reader, and it turned green, allowing her to pass through.

She came down the escalator, sweeping her eyes from one end of the platform to the other, not knowing which way Hayden would have walked to wait for the train. She hoped there weren't too many people on the platform, which would make it difficult to get close enough to him.

There was also a chance he'd stand away from the yellow caution line, back far enough that crashing into him wouldn't send him over. But she knew what it was to be famous. He'd want to stand close to the edge, so that people were behind him, not to the side of him, giving them less opportunity to recognize him.

She knew that surveillance cameras were now recording her every move, so she couldn't appear to be searching for or following him. She'd spent an hour inside the nearby Buy Buy Baby, paid for a bassinet, and left instructions for next-day delivery. She and Firio already had one, but her story would be that she wanted a rocking one too.

Now she was headed home.

Everything had to look spontaneous, so she made her stride appear casual while her eyes darted back and forth on high-alert for Hayden's black baseball cap.

Then she spotted it—and him. Standing not quite to the middle of the platform. She turned her face away so that she wouldn't appear to have seen him and walked farther down the platform.

It was a busy station, with a woman cutting up and selling mangoes; another woman with a Churros cart; and a man playing guitar and singing, with a speaker spilling backing track music. Piper pretended to watch the busker, while her gaze rolled up to the digital timetable that showed that a train was three minutes away.

In three minutes, she would be a murderer. In three minutes, Hayden would be dead. In three minutes, the people who loved him—Ava, his parents, his friends, his fans—would have their lives upended.

She imagined she could be arrested, but for how long would they keep her? She could be sent to jail for awhile, and would get no health care for herself or her baby. It would be cold, damp, scary. The other female prisoners might hate her, as she'd once been famous. God help her if there were any Hayden fans in there.

And the news. Oh, my God. The news. It would be everywhere.

Academy Award Winner Hayden Tower Dies in Subway After Pregnant American Star Rival Falls Into Him

They wouldn't even bother to mention her name in the headlines.

The timetable turned to two minutes.

The worst part was wondering where and how she'd give birth. Would they let her go to a hospital? Or did women give birth inside some kind of clinic within the jail? Would she even get an epidural?

Her mind went even darker. How much would he suffer before he died? In that split-second as he fell, would he experience terror?

What if he fell but didn't get hit? What if he got hit but didn't die, lay under the train in unbearable torment? He'd declared war on her and her family. But she couldn't stand the idea of him under the train's ribcage with broken, bloodied legs. Then she remembered Marvin howling in petrified agony, and thought of her mother, her vitality drained away, drained down to a skeleton in a diaper.

She began to shake uncontrollably, her stomach gnarled into icy, queasy knots, with cold, coppery adrenaline flooding her mouth. She tried to take her water bottle out of her tote bag, but her hands trembled so badly she knew she wouldn't be able to hold onto it. She pulled her hand out of her bag, surprised to see the bottle was tightly clutched in her bowed fingers.

One minute.

She felt the soft tremors of the approaching train vibrating under her feet, but they were very, very soft. So soft she wondered if she was only feeling her own quaking body, which was trembling so violently she didn't think she'd be able to walk closer to Hayden. She closed her eyes and opened them wide, commanding herself to focus.

She looked at Hayden as if she'd just seen him and was in the process of recognizing him. Yes, yes, it *is* him.

Closer, get closer. Closer. Remember to turn to the side so that when you fall you can come down with your arms outstretched and not land on your stomach. She'd practiced it in her living room. The fall looked contrived and might break her hand or arm, but there was nothing to be done about it. She couldn't let her stomach hit the platform.

One minute, one minute.

She pressed her palm to her forehead, swaying slightly.

Now she definitely felt the rumble under her feet, the savage energy of tons of steel hurtling through the tunnel. She heard the ferocious roar of the train's engine. Hayden turned his head to the right, towards the tunnel. She moved around a couple of people and positioned herself about ten feet away.

There was a telltale breeze on her face. She saw the train's headlights in her side vision, saw the glimmer of white light that would transition one part of her life into another, usher life into death. There was no going back.

No going back.
No going back.
NOW!

Chapter Thirty-Four

*"P*iper!"

The sound made her gasp, stumble, and drop the water bottle.

"Piper!"

With the *wahhhn-wahhhn* squall of the horn and *boom-boom-clang-clang* of the metal wheels along the electrical rails, the train bulleted into the station, sending wind sweeping along her face.

There was a woman next to her, a heavy-set woman in a bright red coat. Red hair, red lips. So much red.

"Piper! Oh my God! It *is* you. I *knew* it."

Piper turned back towards the train, which slowed and stopped. She heard the ding of the train doors open and knew she'd lost her opportunity.

Forever.

For standing there staring at her, eager-eyed, with that *you remember me?* expression on her face was—no mistaking it—a fan.

Piper hadn't been recognized in public in something like a year, and here stood a fan at the worst time imaginable; a fan that could easily become a witness for the prosecution. There would be no second chance, not with a fan that could tell police she'd seen Piper Dunner in this station before.

It was over. Over. She'd lost her chance. Lost it.

She watched Hayden step inside the train car with a crowd of people. The woman bent and picked up the water bottle and tried to hand it over. It took Piper a few moments to realize she needed to take it from her.

"Sorry to scare you," the woman said, placing her hand over her heart. "It's Megan. Megan Donnelly from San Francisco."

"Hi, yes, Molly, it's so good to see you," she said, instinctively launching into her fan-patter.

Years spent pretending she was happy to see fans when they may have approached her at an inopportune time—when she was starving, exhausted, sick, or looked terrible—had trained her to slip into fan chit-chat under any circumstances.

One could never, *ever* seem ungrateful to a fan. Even if that fan ruined your meticulously plotted murder and you wanted to punch her in the face for it.

"Megan," the woman corrected. "Are you all right?"

"Yes, yes. Megan. You startled me." Her vision focused; she began to see the woman as a human being and not merely an atrocious force that had ripped away her chance to save herself, her baby, her husband, her friend.

In fact, the woman was looking more familiar,

thanks to her distinctive stuck-in-the-fifties hairdo, teased high into a mound and flaming auburn. She was a "Pipermint," a diehard who'd been to many of Piper's West Coast meet-and-greets, a woman about fifteen years older than herself.

Could Megan have deduced anything from watching as Piper stealthily took position behind Hayden? Could she have seen, even through the thicket of humanity, Piper's shuddering body and the expression in her eyes, which must have been both terrified and lethal?

If so, Megan was giving no indication of it. She was smiling with the "fan face"—mouth half-open in amazement, eyes bugged.

"I can't believe it," Megan said. "I haven't seen you in so long. Was—was that…?" Slowly, she turned, her hand raised towards the train as it whisked out of the station. "Am I imagining things or was that Hayden Tower?"

Good God, only an *American Star* diehard could have picked him out of that crowd, with his baseball cap rammed over his forehead. Piper stood staring into Megan's eyes. Her unnaturally thick lashes were clearly fake, her gray and silver eyeshadow slathered all the way up to her overly tweezed brows. What could she say that would align with whatever Megan had seen?

"Was it?" she asked. "I didn't notice."

"That's right, *Loverly* is at the Ambassador. Had you just seen it?"

"No, no. Going home."

"Oh." Megan smiled, befuddled. "Congratulations

on the baby." She paused, beaming, as if the baby was hers as well. "Can I hug you? I'll be careful."

Piper nodded, allowing her still-trembling body to be swallowed in Megan's smothering, spice-scented embrace.

Chapter Thirty-Five

She awoke instinctively feeling it was morning, though the heavy drapes blotted out most of the leaden morning light.

Normally, Firio's phone alarm would have roused her, but the house was ghostly still and vacant-feeling, no water gurgling through the rusty old plumbing, no comforting smell of freshly ground coffee wafting up to her from the kitchen where Firio would be making a pot before he left for work. She must have slept right through his getting-ready routine.

She was a light sleeper and normally even the sound of his drawer sliding open was enough to bring her to semi-consciousness, but she'd plunged into a coma-like slumber, barely recalling a faded chain of nightmares—the subway platform, the wind-blast of the train, her trembling body, the back of Hayden's black baseball cap, the clump of fake lashes and manic, adoring gaze of a superfan.

Last night seemed so far away, and she had the

feeling of having escaped doom. The hot rage she'd felt in the aftermath of her plan being thwarted was completely gone, all she felt was immense, soul-melting relief. How different things would be this moment if Megan Donnelly hadn't appeared out of nowhere.

Piper would be in a police station, in a stale-smelling fluorescent room, being asked the same accusatory questions over and over until she confessed all. Or she'd be on a cold, hard cot, in a cold, hard prison cell, with a cold, hard cellmate who was silently plotting to shank her to death.

Or would she have gotten away with it? Would she now be snug in her bed, finally free and safe from the curse—free and safe from Hayden? At this thought, a portion of her anger hazily reassembled at the borders of her mind.

With much difficulty, she managed to roll up out of bed, realizing she was at the point where even one more day would mean she couldn't do this on her own. In the bathroom, she brushed her teeth and spent a long time scrubbing her face. In the shower, she lathered her hair and worked all of the crevices of her body, her armpits, the folds under her milk-engorged breasts, the crease between her legs, the one she couldn't see to shave anymore.

All her muscles ached, as if she'd run a marathon the day before, the imprint of the adrenaline that had gushed through her on the platform.

After blow-drying her hair to near-dryness and pulling it into a ponytail, she put on a maternity dress and flats and headed downstairs to make breakfast.

Thank God Firio had been working in his office when she'd gotten home last night about 11:30 p.m., so he didn't see her face as she'd traipsed zombie-like into their bedroom, undressed, dropped her clothes on the floor, and crawled into bed without saying goodnight to him. She knew her face would tell him everything—that she hadn't been to buy a bassinet at Buy Buy Baby, as she'd texted him before she'd left.

There are two lines human beings live with and manage to mostly wall off from their consciousness before suddenly finding themselves near the line: their own impending deaths, and the desire to kill another human being. It didn't matter that, physically, she hadn't crossed that line after all. Mentally, she had. Something had tripped off in her brain and she was not the same person. Now she knew, with undeniable certainty, that she was capable of taking a life.

He would see it, the man she loved, father of her child. He would see it in her pupils, in the lines of her mouth, in the contours of her flesh, as much as she was certain she would see the same in him. Perhaps he'd even smell it on her, the pungent stench of killer, and at that thought, she put it together why she'd spent so long cleaning herself. She was Lady MacBeth.

In the kitchen, Firio was sitting at the island, in his work clothes, his head down, examining a scuff on the wood planks.

"Honey?" she asked, surprised to see him sitting in eerie silence. "What's the matter? Are you sick?"

He lifted his head, and his face… he knew. But how, how? He knew before he'd even seen her.

Her phone was in his hand. He cradled it, palm out, the display pink and white, the colors of the car lift service she normally used. Last night, she'd walked three blocks to Church Avenue before summoning it.

"Ambassador Theater. It's right here in your phone, so don't bother denying it."

She closed her eyes, took a breath. Opening her eyes, she said, "Okay." It was the only thing she could think to say.

"So what is this, Piper?" he asked, his voice dull with resignation. "Are you… what is this? An affair? With Hayden Tower? Is that what this is really all about?"

"Affair!" The accusation was so unexpected, so ludicrous, that she hung between wanting to laugh and wanting to scream at him; her words came out a roiling combination of the two. "I'm having a baby in two weeks. Are you mad? You think men want this hot body?!"

"Well, what is it? Why do you keep going to see him when I've asked you not to?"

Her jaw unclenched. So he hadn't seen homicidal intent on her face or smelled it oozing off her skin while in bed. He was still clueless. And, being a man, his brain went to the ultimate man-reason for irrational behavior —sex. What a simple creature he was.

She walked to the island and hiked her bulk up on a stool. There was no point in denying that she had defied his orders to stay away from Hayden. She had to be extremely circumspect how she looked and sounded, of how much she might inadvertently reveal.

"I wanted to talk to him. About the thing you don't want to talk about."

"The killer curse."

"Yes."

"And did you?"

"No."

"So you keep going there to talk to him, but not talking to him."

"Yes."

She snatched her phone back from where he'd placed it on the island. What a fool she was. Police could have seen Ambassador Theater in her car lift app. How did anyone get away with murder these days? No wonder Megan had been sent to stop her from her plan; she'd messed up and it hadn't been the right time.

"I don't appreciate you going through my phone," she said, wondering how he'd even gotten into it. It was password protected. Then she remembered. After Dr. Malhotra had given them the baby's expected due date, she'd changed the password to the due date in the car on the way home and told Firio what she'd done. Idiot.

"I was worried about you. You didn't even come to kiss me last night. I knew something was up."

"I have a photo an ex-cult member sent me of Hayden and Mitch McCabe," she said, her flat tone indicative of her hopelessness that Firio wouldn't believe anything she said. "They're with a guy with white hair. Crystal said the leader of the cult has white hair. The person confirmed that Hayden and Mitch belong to it."

She wanted to tell him the contents of the last letter from Mitch—with the warning that Hayden was going to target their baby. This information could be enough to ignite Firio's protective instincts and bring him over to her side. Then she would finally have a partner in this madness.

But she was still cunning enough to know she couldn't reveal anything that sounded like a motive for murder. Because she'd already begun murkily weighing the idea of trying to kill Hayden again.

Firio paused for what seemed a very long time before saying, "Let me see these things."

"I can't. I got rid of everything."

Another pause. Then, as if he was speaking to a child, "And why would you do that?"

"Because I don't want evidence of what I know on my phone, in case anyone from the cult comes after me."

They sat quietly, a barrier between them—one that might never come down. How could it come down? She was on this side, the side of those who know what it feels like to kill, or at least come a second away from it. She was on the side of knowing there were things in this world that were simply unexplainable. He was still on the side she used to be on, the side of logic, laws, and civilized behavior.

"All right," he sighed, pushing up from the island. "I'm running late. I couldn't decide whether to wake you or not." He stood looking at her, his expression almost pitying. "What if we went to see a counselor together?"

"Counselor!" she practically spat. "Why don't you stop being so condescending and open your eyes. You have a wife with a brain, who isn't being delusional, and who is trying to fight off a real threat. Without your help, I might add."

She'd said too much, enough to hang herself with. But she could always deny it.

"If you feel that's what you're doing, fine," he said, exasperation having dwindled into resignation. "You do what you need to do. I have nothing left to say."

Taking up his briefcase, he walked out of the kitchen.

Rubbing circles on her stomach, Piper sat feeling morose and resentful at the same time. Fine for him to tell her to do what she needed to do. He hadn't turned into someone else, hadn't been *forced* to turn into someone else.

If he were any kind of man at all, he'd be figuring this out with her instead of fighting her at every turn or acting like she was a nutjob. This is what she got for not being more selective with her choice of procreation partner. If he wasn't going to help her, he could at least stay out of her way.

Maybe he was. That could be the meaning implicit in his, "You do what you need to do."

"Goddamn right I will," she said, nodding at nothing.

Chapter Thirty-Six

$\mathcal{T}$he doorbell chimed. Had to be a package delivery person. Gifts from the baby registry had been regularly arriving. Onesies, swaddle blankets, teething toys. She'd already received five nail kits and was looking into where to donate four of them.

As Piper's fans hadn't figured out where she lived, most of the gifts were coming from various people she'd worked with over the years, friends back in L.A., Firio's work colleagues, and her father's social circle.

She grimaced when she thought about the gift her father had sent her, which had not been on the registry: A thing called BabyTrakker. A smooth, flat, brightly colored oval-shaped device that, once you looped it to your child's clothing, or used the belt that could adjust to fit an ankle, wrist, or stomach, would monitor your child's whereabouts via your computer or phone. The belt and device couldn't be removed except with a key.

Piper had seen a flaw in the system—a babynapper could simply remove the child's clothes or, God forbid, the limb on which the device was fastened. But the device looked like a colorful piece of plastic jewelry, so hopefully a kidnapper would mistake it for such. Her father had paid for a year of the monitoring service, so she supposed she'd use it, despite its gruesome implication. She hadn't mentioned anything about the letters to her dad, knowing he would go ballistic. But it was as if he sensed danger around her and the baby. At least one male in her life seemed to care.

Opening the inside wood door, Piper's mouth dropped. Hayden Tower was standing there.

In a red and black flannel jacket and dark jeans, his hair was tousled and his eyes startlingly green in the clear morning light. Piper felt as if a ghost was staring at her, as if he'd gone over that subway platform after all.

"Hi, Piper," he said before she could get anything out of her mouth. "My assistant found your address. I didn't mean to scare you."

Piper's mouth was still open and she knew how absurd she must look. *Get control of yourself.*

"Um." She floundered, desperately trying to think why he'd be here, and if she should let him in, and what kind of excuse she could use to not let him in.

"I wanted to talk to you," he said, enunciating loudly, pushing his voice through the outside glass door. "It will only take a minute."

Unable to think of any reason to deny him access, she opened the door. He came into the foyer, bouncing on his heels. "Nice neighborhood," he smiled. "Hope it's okay I parked in your drive."

"I was going to make some coffee if you'd like some."

She surprised herself with how collected she sounded as her mind reeled off reasons why he would be here, the most obvious being that he'd come to harm her. But to do it directly wasn't his way. He used his cult. It was probably something about *American Star.*

"Sounds good," he said.

In the kitchen, she got down the ground coffee and began scooping it into a filter. She hadn't told him where to sit, but let him figure that out for himself.

"Gorgeous house," he said, looking approvingly around the kitchen. "Just the kind of place I'd like someday."

She poured water into the machine and turned, circling her hands protectively over her stomach. "So what's up? You didn't want to call? Nolan has my number."

"I thought it would be better to do this in person."

Shit. Someone had told him what she knew about the cult. Who? Jojo and Firio were the only ones who knew her suspicions about Hayden. Could Jojo have possibly told him everything?

Wait, there was Anton. Oh my God, Anton. He must have run into Hayden at some event. They'd probably had a good laugh about it—Piper Dunner's gone off the rails. Much as Anton was the only one who took her fears seriously, he'd only been humoring her. Or his desire to get in good with a big star by sharing this juicy tidbit of gossip had overcome him. Or—he *did* believe Hayden was responsible for his scar. And he'd seen

Hayden and confronted him, revealing his source as Piper. Now what?

"I saw you in the subway last night," Hayden said. "As the doors closed."

"Oh!" Piper exclaimed, then froze. She didn't know where he was going, or what her reactions should be.

"Your face was… it was so… I guess my question is…" He asked, "May I?" and sat on an island stool when she nodded at him. "I guess what I want to know is, are you following me?" He tilted his head curiously at her. "This is the third time I've seen you outside of the theater. The first, you had something on your mind, but wouldn't tell me what. Then twice in the subway. But you live way out here. I looked up the recording studio where you work. It's downtown."

He leaned forward, tapping his chest. When he made his taps, her eyes were drawn to the silver pendant hanging around his neck, the one she'd noticed when they sat together at Shelby's. Now she could see the design was a triangle inside a circle.

"Pip, it's me, fellow Glory Note. We went through *American Star* together. That makes us like Vietnam buddies."

The gurgles of the coffee maker slowed, hissing air. She turned and took two mugs out of a cabinet. "Do you want soy milk?" she asked.

"Black is fine."

She poured two mugs, handed him one. "It's decaf. I don't drink caffeine right now."

"No problem." He sipped, looking up at her over the rim of his mug. Then he put the mug down and wrapped both sturdy hands around it. "So that's why I'm here. I can tell there's something strange going on with you and it has something to do with me." He crossed his arms and grinned confidently at her. "I used to study you. How was Piper feeling today? Was she going to blow me off the stage tonight? I watched if you touched your throat, if you talked less, if you didn't laugh as much, anything to let me know how the performances might shake out. All that studying gave me a little insight, I think. Even now."

Piper's movements around the coffee machine had given her whirring mind just enough time, but she was still at the mercy of her imagination, which would now be put to the test in a way it never had before. She was a singer, not a storyteller. But her songs. The best ones were like little stories. Somehow, she trusted that whatever was about to come out of her mouth would be enough for him.

"I'm not following you. I mean, not *quite*," she said, pushing out a breathy little laugh. "This is going to sound pathetic."

He shrugged and took another sip of coffee. "Hit me."

"Well…" She leaned against the kitchen counter. "Sometimes I miss all that *American Star* excitement. It never left you, but it left me. Fame—it's a huge adjustment, but you adjust quickly. You have to. When it starts to slip away, it's like… sand falling through your fingers." She dug at the air. "You can't grab hold of it. I feel like I've fallen back to me, but a 'me' that doesn't fully exist anymore. Fame is an unnatural existence, but losing it seems even more unnatural. It's hard to explain."

He looked at her, his head cocked to the side. "I think I'm getting it," he said, though it was clear he wasn't, and was bewildered as to where her speech was headed. She wasn't quite sure herself where it was headed, but it felt real, because she was giving voice to all of those thoughts she'd already had, had for a very long time. Now she only needed to link them to why she was following Hayden.

"Remember when we were sitting in that ugly hotel room, that holding area, waiting to see if we'd be picked to be on the top 24? That was the last time you were completely not-famous. And remember we were all chatting, and you and I were talking about whatever it was. Probably how long we'd been trying to make singing work and getting nowhere."

"I remember. I also remember that I asked you, for some reason, if you liked Beef Jerky. They caught that on camera. Friends razzed me about it for awhile, thinking it was a double entendre. But it wasn't. I was nervous."

"Ha," she said, taking a sip of coffee. "The carpet was maroon with these triangles of gold and green. I remember it because I spent hours staring at it, waiting to see if my life would change. You never came back to that room. You got into the elevator, went upstairs, became a star, and are still a star. But I'm back in that room. When everyone went away, it felt like I'd been the victim of a big hoax or prank."

She paused, sipping more coffee. Everything she was

saying was so natural, so true, that it easily could have been the reality of why she was following Hayden, and she almost felt she lived in that alternative reality, where her motivation was professional jealousy, not murder.

"Lately," she continued, "doing nothing except narration and getting ready for the baby, I've been missing how it used to be for me. So I go to the theater sometimes, and watch you come out, and see the reaction of the fans. Then I reminisce. I was supposed to be the 'last Star standing,' but it was really you."

"Wow, Pip," he said, his bright green eyes growing dewy, whether with pity or self-congratulation, she wasn't sure. "I didn't know you were thinking all of that."

She sighed and hung her head, staring into her coffee. "You can see why I couldn't bring it up at Shelby's. How badly I wanted the judge spot, so I could get some of that fame again." She squinted back up at him, wondering if that last line had sounded too melodramatic.

"Hmm." He rubbed at his stubbly chin. "You seemed like you didn't want it. Something about people not wanting you to have it."

"I'd heard from Nolan that the network wanted you, not me."

"Listen, you don't need to sneak around the theater spying on me. Come up whenever you want. Hang backstage."

He was smiling—happy. Oh yes, he would be happy, wouldn't he? Thinking the winner of *American Star* was scheming to soak up some of the runner-up's fame, hoping its stray beams might land on her, and temporarily enliven her failed life. How he must relish the idea that the real winner is getting jostled in the gray-faced crowd, no one even recognizing her as the runner-up makes his autograph and selfie rounds.

"That's so nice of you," she said, and smiled back at him. "Would you excuse me for a second? Pregnancy means the coffee goes right through me."

He nodded, waved.

She walked to the front door and peeked through the glass side panel, alertly taking in all of the neighborhood that she could see. In one fluid motion, she flicked the top and bottom locks.

She continued to the downstairs half-bath by a small laundry room, and went to the toilet, because she hadn't been lying about the coffee going straight through her. As she came out, she took a left down the hallway rather than a right, which brought her to the back porch door. She checked that it was locked, then wended her way to the kitchen.

Hayden had his coffee mug to his mouth, his head tipped all the way back. Looking at her again, he almost appeared glowing. Glowing with the ego pumping she'd given him, no doubt.

"More coffee?" she chirped.

"Nah, thanks. I got to head back into the city, get some rest before the show."

"Your glasses," she said, indicating them. "They're cool. Where'd you get them?"

"Um." He took them off to glance at their insides. "These are the Armani's."

"I had no idea you wore glasses. You didn't on the show."

"I was a young lad. My eyes weren't nearly as bad as they are now. Stuck to contacts on *Star*. But my eyes get all dried out if I wear them too long."

"Huh. I thought you wore them for fashion."

"Nope. Blind as a bat without 'em."

"Can I see them for a sec? I might need glasses too."

"Uh, sure." He handed them over, and she watched as his eyes narrowed into fluttery slits.

She pretended to inspect the glasses, then hooked them on her dress neckline, reached over to the wooden knife block, and slid out the top knife, the biggest one. She wrapped her knuckles over the handle and, with her other hand, drew the knife block towards her so he couldn't reach over and grab a knife of his own.

"If you move, I'll stab the shit out of you," she said.

"What?" he laughed, but his face drooped, his expression wavering in the space between belief and disbelief. He looked almost as he had when he'd first auditioned for *American Star*—pudgy and insecure.

"All the doors are locked. If you move, I'll kill you. I'll say you attacked me."

"What the fucking hell are you talking about?" he said, his voice rising sharply as the reality of what was happening hit him.

"You're going to tell me what's going on with you and that cult. And you're going to tell me the truth, because I know more than you think I know."

"Cult?" Unexpectedly, he stood up, the stool toppling to the floor with a thud.

276

"Don't move!" she screamed, lumbering around the island like a bulldog, the knife raised at him. "I'm not joking. I'll flay you open!"

"Jesus Christ, Piper!" He held his hands up, thrusting his palms out in a defensive motion. "What the fuck cult are you talking about? You've gone crazy."

"You'd like that, wouldn't you? I know about The True Way. I know about Anton and Dylan. I know how you got famous. Call your people, call off your plans. I need to hear it."

"The True Way? What—why—why are you bringing that up?"

"So you admit you belong to it."

"I—not really. Not anymore."

"Who else belongs? Mitch?"

"He was the one who told me about it."

"Crystal?"

"I heard she'd gone to a few meetings, but that was about it." He kept his palms crossed in front of him, eyes blinking disorientedly. "What has The True Way got to do with anything? Give me my glasses back. Put down that knife."

"You paralyzed my vocal cord. Set my apartment on fire." She raised the knife higher. "Killed my dog and my mother!" She jabbed the knife forward. "Took my career. I won. *I* won!"

"I swear on my life—on my parents' lives—I didn't do any of that. Killed your dog and your mother? Listen to yourself! I thought your mom died of cancer!"

"I know about it all and it all matches up. Even Mitch warned me about you."

"Have you lost your fucking mind?" he yelled aggressively, then seeming to feel he needed to try a different tack, modulated his voice. "Can we talk, please?"

"Then talk!"

He waved one hand in a circle, blinking and squinting, sputtering out his words. "The True Way. It's—it's a personal growth group. They—they have this thing, where they help you manifest things you want in your life. Mitch said the group's 'technology,'—that's what he called it, but it's like mental exercises—was responsible for his success. So I tried it. Went to meetings, took courses. It was expensive. But—but it's this underground kind of thing. You have to be sponsored by a member to get in. Mitch sponsored me. What do you mean he warned you about me?"

"I'll ask the questions! Was one of the things you wanted the role in *Ghosts of Time*?"

"Sure, that, and other things, too. I was having a hard time writing songs for a new album. I was trying to get out of a bad situation with my old manager. And I wanted to quit smoking. I'd had a stroke, a small one. I was told if I didn't quit, I could have another. Maybe that one would kill me. But I couldn't quit. I wanted *Ghosts of Time*, but there were lots of things I wanted. Some I got. Some I didn't."

"Anton falls and needs stitches in his face, and loses the part. Surprise, surprise, you get it."

"I—okay, yeah. But I didn't ask for that to happen to him. When it did, President—that's the guy that founded the group, I don't know his real name—President said it had manifested that way. No one can help the way things manifest; it was destined to happen. That Anton's fall was actually good for him, because it would open up the pathway he was meant to be on. But it scared me. And they were putting pressure on me to recruit more celebrities. They never shut up about it."

"Sounds like a damn cult to me!"

"Whatever it was, I haven't seen any of them in at least two years."

"And you expect me to believe you didn't 'manifest' my downfall too?"

"Piper, I swear to God, I didn't even know about The True Way until long after you won *Star*. I was worried about myself, not you."

"What about Dylan? I spoke to his wife. You're the last one to see him before he died of cardiac arrest. Just when he'd signed a record deal."

He shook his head and his expression crumpled. "Listen." He appeared to come to a decision about something. "I'm going to tell you the truth, but you have to keep it under wraps. Dylan didn't die from cardiac arrest. He drank himself to death. Alcohol poisoning is the official cause, but Ember didn't want anyone knowing about that, so she came up with this cardiac story, and the media didn't bother to look deeper into it."

Suddenly, Piper remembered the night Dylan had been voted off, when the remaining finalists had been out drinking at a bar. How Dylan had downed shot after shot. And how while on tour, he'd always had a beer or a drink of some kind in his hands. At the time, Piper had chalked his heavy drinking up to his new rock star status.

"I—" She felt the knife trembling weakly in her hand. "How—how do I know you're not lying?"

"If you want, I can talk to Ember, you can listen in. I'll think of a way to bring it up, but it's not a thing she likes to discuss. You could try to get the coroner's report somehow." He splayed his fingers out on his raised hands. "I went down to Glen Rose to see if I could talk him into rehab or joining The True Way, which I thought might help him. But he was in denial and got angry with me. So I left. That was the night he died. How I wish I'd stayed. It's the biggest regret of my life. Look, can I—" He made a motion towards his chest, and she realized he was waving at the silver pendant hanging around his neck. "Can I show you this?"

"No! Keep your hands up."

"It's a gift from Dylan. He gave it to me about six months before he died. If—if you look on the back, you'll see '100' in honor of his one-hundred days of sobriety, and our initials. The 'A' and triangle is for Alcoholics Anonymous. You can look it up!"

The knife felt lead-heavy in her hand, her shoulder muscle was burning.

"Why would Ember tell you the real reason he died?"

"Because she was hysterical. I was the first person she called after she found his body. He'd been drinking in the barn studio all night. After that, it was all kind of hushed up. She didn't want Kylie knowing how her father had died—worried she'd feel her daddy had chosen booze over her. That's not what happened, but she's a child."

"And what about Jojo?"

"What about her?"

"She was hit by a car. You're going to tell me that wasn't you either?"

"That I hit Jojo with a car? I was doing *Loverly* that night. How the hell would I manage to do both things?"

"You sent someone. Manifested it. You—you…"

Their eyes locked and it flashed through her mind that if he were lying, he would look away from her. His eyes would dart and shift around. But, even without his glasses, his sea-green gaze had landed on her face. His look was direct and unwavering, the expression of a man who wanted answers.

He was telling the truth.

It crashed on her how she sounded—and looked— like a complete lunatic. She'd created and embraced an alternative reality, one where she'd been cruelly punted back to obscurity by supernatural forces. But her decline had simply been the sad, slow slip of life; the odds of achieving and holding onto fame stacked too far against her, too far against anyone, except for the lucky few, like Hayden.

"Piper," he said, seriously. "You're a blurry blob right now but if you come near me with that knife, I'm going to fight like hell. You won't win this one. Do you want to put your baby in that position?"

She said nothing.

"Why are you thinking I've done these things? Is someone telling you all this? Is it Mitch?"

Her throat tightened, her shoulder muscle ache intensified, and she put her other hand around the knife, to give her hold more support. But the knife was drawing away from him, its handle resting against her chest.

"It's someone who wants you dead," she said, so quietly she could barely hear herself. "And who wanted me to be the one to kill you."

Chapter Thirty-Seven

"It was the perfect plan," she said, as Hayden backed—cautiously—into an easy chair in the living room, after she'd waved blithely at him. "Oh, can I get you anything? More coffee? Tea? I've got some croissants."

"Uh, no thanks. I've kind of lost my appetite." He touched his glasses, double-checking they were back on his face.

In the kitchen, she'd returned his glasses and put away the knife. She'd given him a brief rundown on the letters, and how she'd become convinced he'd put a curse on her through The True Way. She fully expected him to flee and call the police.

Instead, he'd asked her to tell him everything.

"It has to be someone who figured I'd be the perfect pawn to talk into killing you," she said, gripping the armrest and awkwardly lowering to the couch.

He shook his head, lifting a brow. "You were going to do it?"

"I don't—" The impulse to lie to him was too strong. She couldn't admit what she'd been a second away from doing on that subway platform. "I was considering it."

"Great. Makes me feel better." He paused. "You believed I would kill your mom, Piper? Kill your dog? Kill *Dylan*? That's what you think of me?"

The look on his face was more hurt than angry. It seemed impossible that she'd gone to the place she'd gone to, had stuck her toes into a boiling river of emotion that at first had tickled her feet then sucked her along to the craggy edge of madness.

"Try to understand," she said, leaning forward as much as she could. "I can't show you the letters, because the last one said to get rid of them all. But they were convincing. Then some things happened that must have been coincidental. Firio made a bunch of bad stock picks. Crystal knew of The True Way. There's Anton's fall and Dylan's death. These were things that happened naturally, but this person knew I'd connect everything. When Jojo got hit, the person used that as well." She pointed at him. "Someone wants you dead, and they either wanted me in prison or thought I'd get away with it."

"That's why you were standing behind me on the platform?" he asked, his hazel eyes darkening. "The plan was to push me over?"

"I—no, no, Hayden." She vigorously shook her head. "I was getting a sense of your routine. I hadn't decided to do it. I—I don't think I would have gone that far."

"You seemed ready to go that far back in the kitchen."

She stared at the hard roundness of her stomach and silently asked her baby to forgive her for what he or she was about to hear.

"I truly believed you were a danger to me, and the last letter threatened the baby too."

She looked back up at him, the threat of tears stinging the backs of her eyes, her bottom lip beginning to quiver, but was determined not to cry. She didn't deserve his pity.

"I'm asking you to understand something I myself don't understand. How I… lost myself. I'm not going to deny that I've been jealous of you. But I haven't been angry at you. What I've been angry at is life. Fate. When someone convinced me you were responsible for that fate, *then* I got angry with you. But I see now I was being manipulated." She paused, and said with as much dignity as she could, "If you want to report me to the police for threatening you, I won't deny anything."

He remained silent for so long that her soul folded, expecting to hear his voice on the phone to 911.

"Can't imagine NYPD will give a crap about a pregnant woman waving a knife around. Pregnant women get pretty bonkers, don't they?"

Something—probably relief—made her start laughing. She was even more relieved when she heard his laughter mingling with hers.

"Man," he said, rubbing at the side of his head. "What I wouldn't do for a cigarette right now. When did you start believing in curses, anyway?"

"When did you start believing in 'manifestations'?"

He crossed his arms and smiled ruefully, as if to say, *touché*. Then he said, "I believe that someone is manipulating you, Pip. But we have to figure out who."

"Yes, yes, we do!" Gratitude, palpable and exhilarating, coursed through her like liquid. Someone believed her, took her seriously, and might even help her. The irony of the someone being the person she came close to killing wasn't lost on her. "I'd thought it was Mitch writing the letters to help me. But it could be him trying to get me to kill you. He warned me about you when I saw him at the audition, said to be careful around you, then refused to admit he'd said it. Could he have it out for you, Hayden? How did he feel about you leaving The True Way?"

Hayden shrugged. "We didn't talk about it. I've been living here and him in L.A. I wanted out and didn't want to give him or anyone a chance to talk me back in. I don't even know if he knew I'd left." He gave an exaggerated shiver. "Nah, I can't believe he'd want me dead."

"I was sent a photo of you and Mitch talking to that guy with the white hair. It looked like none of you were aware the photo was being taken. So it could be someone in the group or who knows someone in the group. Would The True Way want you gone?"

"Hell if I know," he said, staring out of the front windows. "I kept telling them I was busy with projects, couldn't be a member anymore. Eventually, they left me alone. I'd signed an NDA, that I wouldn't reveal anything about their program, and I haven't."

He sighed, shed his flannel jacket, putting it to his side. "There's a thing they do to help you break through destructive emotional patterns. They record you talking about your darkest times. I recorded the truth about how Dylan died. I'm always worried they'll release that recording. Kylie, his fans… they don't need to know how he died."

"Sounds like they got blackmail material from you, to keep you under control."

"I suppose that's one way to look at it." His face sunk into dejectedness as he leaned on his knees, kneading his hands. "I don't know why they'd want to kill me. I'm no threat to them. I'm surprised whoever wrote those letters would even mention the group or me."

"Well, they didn't."

He looked up at her, blinking in dismay.

"What do you mean? You said someone was sending you letters saying they were from The True Way and I'd put a curse on you."

"That's—that's what… I mean…" She locked her hands on her forehead, embarrassed and frustrated. "That's what it was *implying*. That's how I put it all together."

"So the person may not have even been talking about *me*?"

"Don't you get it? That's how brilliant this person was. They didn't even have to say your name. They hinted around at it, and after enough hints, it all led to you. They said enough to make me want to kill you, but not enough that I could ever bring anything to police."

He clung to the chair's armrest, probably stopping himself from leaping up and running out the door. "Okay, let's pretend I can understand that. I still have no idea who'd want you to kill me."

"What about Anton?" She settled back, remembering her conversation with him. "I met with him and he didn't act too happy you won an Oscar. He was the only one who seemed to believe in the curse, too. He told me to protect myself."

"Uh-huh. Or..." He shifted around uncomfortably. "Jojo."

Piper opened her mouth to argue but stopped. Deep down, she knew it was something she had to consider.

"She's the one who'd gain the most from both of us being out of the picture," he said. "She wanted to get the judge spot."

"I thought about that," she said, recoiling with the sickening idea that her best friend would go this far to revive her career. "But there were two letters after her attack, one of them to her. She has a broken left wrist and she's left-handed. I don't know how she could have typed them herself."

"Maybe she used voice software."

"I've used voice software. Gave up on it because it's so bad. The letters had no misspellings, the language flowed easily."

"Translation service."

"Would she risk someone knowing what she was writing though? And I got another letter about you even *after* she got the judge position. Why would she bother with that?"

"Or…" he said, rubbing at his knees. "It could be *anyone* from *Star*. Someone who thought they should have won. News of the reboot pushed the person over the edge." He folded his arms, staring pointedly at her. "What about The Chosen One?"

Piper's mind went utterly blank, and then, it came to her.

A sweet-cheeked seventeen-year-old with a halo of raven ringlets and a pure-as-a-natural-spring tone, Corey Stanhope, a former *Star Search* winner, had been considered a shoo-in to take the *American Star* crown. The judges—even Nolan—consistently raved over him, leading the media to dub him, "The Chosen One."

But around the three-quarter mark, The Chosen One started to choke: forgetting lyrics, hitting clunker notes, and selecting songs that were bafflingly (and laughingly) unsuitable.

After a cringeworthy performance of Sir Mix-A-Lot's "Baby Got Back," he was voted off in seventh place and, for the most part, never heard from again. Could he have spent the past decade stoking a desire to avenge himself on the winner and runner-up?

"I suppose anything is a possibility," Piper said. But in reality, she couldn't reconcile the rosy-faced, Jesus-loving teen she once knew with the Machiavellian letter writer. "I have to ask you something you're not going to like."

He said nothing, waiting.

"Ava."

"Not a chance," he snapped.

"I know it's—but, is there any reason she'd—"

"No, Piper." His tone indicated he wasn't going to consider this possibility for a second. "She loves me. We're getting married. Besides that, I'm her biggest client. There's no reason, absolutely none, she'd want to get rid of me."

"You haven't cheated on her or anything?"

"No! I know you don't know me very well away from *Star*, but when I'm with a girl, I'm *with* her."

"I'm sorry. I had to ask. We have to think of all possibilities because whoever it is probably won't rest until you're dead. And once they realize I won't be the dupe who kills you, they might do it on their own. And they could take me out too."

THEY HAD A QUICK LUNCH and kept an eye on the time. Hayden wanted to get back to the city by four p.m. to rest before the show. And they wanted to wait until about nine a.m. West Coast time to call Mitch, even though they suspected he was up at the crack of dawn.

"Let me ask you something," Piper said, handing him a cloth napkin.

"Shoot."

"Sometimes you were so rude to me on *Star*. I think that's what convinced me you hated me enough to put a curse on me."

He put down his egg salad sandwich, absently peeling the crust off of one half. "I know I acted like a jerk. There were a couple of reasons. My parents were having issues before the show, on the verge of divorce, though my mom didn't really want it." He stared down into his lap. "When I got onto the show, it kind of reignited their relationship. Every single time I was up on that stage, I was worried I'd get voted off, and their reason for being together again would disappear."

Piper now understood the look of fear Hayden's mother had given her backstage after she'd won. With the show over and her son emerging the loser, Hayden's mom must have been worried about how her marriage would fare.

"That's a lot of pressure," Piper said. "There's enough pressure being on the show, let alone feeling responsible for your parents' marriage."

Noting a bit of egg salad stuck to his upper lip, Piper made a tapping motion on the corresponding spot on her own lip. Hayden wiped his mouth with the cloth napkin and they fell into grinning at each other, like this was nothing but a casual lunch between old friends.

Then he said, "As the show went on, I saw you were my biggest competition. I mixed you up with getting in the way of saving my parents' relationship. I'm not using that as an excuse. I was twenty-three and not a mature twenty-three. I apologize."

"Okay, so that's one reason you were rude to me. I forgive you," she said with mock solemnity. "But you said there were a couple of reasons. What's the other?" A tingly excitement fluttered through her, a fore-shadowing.

"Yeah, um…" He looked down again, wiping at his lap. "Despite that, I'd started to have feelings for you. *Those* kind."

She lifted a brow. "Pretty sure I remember that, or at least some of it."

"Not only sexual. I liked you. As a person. Um, a romantic interest."

"Hmmm," she said, feeling her cheeks warm and unable to control her smile. "Usually a guy is nice to a girl he likes."

"Well, I wanted to win too. Mentally, I had to keep you in the enemy camp. To paraphrase Joan Jett, I hated myself for liking you."

There was a thick silence, each unable to make eye contact. Piper finally broke it with, "I liked you too. But it was a bad time. Besides, you were spreading rumors that I was sleeping with Nolan."

He bowed his head before raising his eyes impishly at her. "I apologize. Again. In my defense, you did sing 'Nobody Does It Better' straight to him."

"I did not! You know the lights blinded you to panel!"

He laughed and began thumping his foot on the floor. She heard a melody that had a jarring familiarity to it and, without any thought, she joined in, knee bouncing rhythmically, her voice and Hayden's rising together in perfectly melded, well-oiled harmony:

Don't stop singing
Don't stop singing
Don't stop dancing
Don't stop dancing
Ya gotta dance, dance, dance, dance, DANCE!

Piper clutched her stomach with laughter. It was the closing song of their *American Star* tour, a song they'd sung several times a day for weeks in rehearsals, then for six nights a week for four months in front of thousands of screaming fans.

To think that the silly tune had worn grooves so deep in their temporal lobes that they could instantly access it after a decade. If she wasn't blimpish with pregnancy, she had no doubt they could have seamlessly stepped into the song's choreographed dance moves around the kitchen.

After they stopped laughing, there was an indefinable, alive current between them before Hayden said, "Oh man, those were the days, eh? The good news is my parents worked out their crap and are still together. Not because of my career, but because they figured out a way back to each other that wasn't centered on me."

"I'm happy to hear that. Hayden, what…" She paused, feeling pathetic for wanting to know all these years later. "What did you say to me on stage after Mitch said my name? I couldn't hear you. Do you remember?"

He stared past her and she assumed his words were lost to history. But then, he dictated them from a faraway time: "I said, 'You earned it and you deserve it.'" He looked at her. "I still feel that way."

She tried to smile at him, but a feeling of grotesqueness crawled through her as she remembered standing behind him on the subway platform.

A mental gate started to shutter down, not fully, but enough that she could block most of that memory behind it.

She wouldn't have done it. Not *really*.

But the part of her mind that hadn't been gated off refused to submit to her magical thinking, whispering to her in a continual loop: *murderer, murderer, murderer.*

* * *

AFTER THREE TEXT messages that went unanswered, Hayden called Mitch. When he picked up with a terse, "What is it, Tower?" Hayden placed his cell, which was on speakerphone, on the table.

"Hey, man, long time no see. Wanted to check in about something."

"They've got my NDA and my collateral. I'm out. Don't harass me."

"Hey, hey," Hayden said, shooting his eyes up to Piper, who sat trying not to breathe too loudly. "I'm not in either. Haven't been for awhile."

"*Right.* That's why you have me on speaker. Who's with you?"

"It's only Piper." He nodded at her, and she said, "Hi, Mitch. It's me."

There was a long pause before Mitch growled, "Make it quick."

"We think someone in the Way is sending Piper letters, telling her whacked out stuff about me. Do you know anything about it?"

"Letters? Listen, don't get me involved with whatever this is."

"Why did you leave the group, Mitch?" Piper asked.

"You've got my NDA and my collateral. Hold up your end of the deal. I'm out."

There was silence.

"Mitch?" Piper asked.

Hayden picked up his phone and tapped at it. "Guess he doesn't want to talk," he said, wryly.

"Wow. He sounded terrified."

Hayden stretched back contemplatively, his fingers making a dull thudding on the table. "Nolan told me Mitch had been in rehab," he said.

"That's what he told me too."

Hayden stopped his finger drumming. "Mitch was much higher ranking than I was. Something bad could have happened."

A sharp spear jabbed inside Piper's chest. "Higher ranking," she said. "That's the language the letters always used, saying the person who'd cursed me was a 'high-ranking member.' So whoever wrote the letters sounds like they were in the cult."

"That's what I was about to say. What if something bad happened and Mitch left… and went to get deprogrammed?"

"Deprogrammed?" Piper said, a grin inching across her face. "So you *do* believe it was a cult."

He emitted a lone sigh, shrugging in a gesture of defeat.

"So if Mitch defected," Piper continued, "he has no motive to want you dead. But that explains why he warned me about you, he thought you still belonged. And he apparently believes The True Way *can* make bad things happen to people."

"Maybe it can."

"Or maybe it can't. But if the cult gets a member to

ask for enough 'manifestations,' then any time there's a 'success story'—even if another person's misfortune is responsible for that success—the cult takes credit for it. That does two things: makes you believe the group has supernatural powers, and makes you think those powers could be turned against you if needed."

They said nothing, staring at their greasy plates. Finally, Hayden said, "You must think I'm a dope falling for all of this. I honestly felt it was a self-empowerment group, though a pushy one. And it did help me in some ways."

"I don't think you're a dope, Hayden. I fell for it too."

Fell for it so hard, she'd almost killed him. That part she kept to herself.

* * *

At the door, Hayden asked, "So what do we do now?"

"I think we wait to see if I get another letter. If I do, and the postmark is the same, it's not Mitch sending them, as he claims he's in Los Angeles. Can you ask your PA to look in a photo database to see if paparazzi got recent shots of him there?"

"Sure."

"If I do get another letter, I think we need to take it to the police. Tell them everything. They may not be able to do anything, but at least there will be something on file."

"Listen," he said, shuffling his feet. "I'd rather not do that. The whole thing could get leaked to the press.

For Ember and Kylie's sake, I don't want the stuff about Dylan's death getting out there. And I'd rather everyone not know I was in this group."

"But you have to—"

"I've got private security. No cops are going to do a better job protecting me than they will. But you need something too. I can have one of the guys come out here and watch your house."

"No. Don't do that. It's better if whoever is behind this doesn't know I'm on to them. As long as no one knows we had this talk, the letter writer could still think I'm going to…"

"Kill me?"

"Um. Yes."

He nodded and she unlocked the door and opened it for him. "Hayden, other than your security, you shouldn't mention this to anyone. Not even Ava."

"I wouldn't tell her this, she'd go nuts. Probably want me to quit *Loverly*."

He started out the door into the pale early winter light, when Piper pulled his elbow. "Can you do something for me?"

"You got it."

"Do you have a lawyer who can hide a home purchase? Once the baby is born, Firio and I should move. I don't like this person knowing where we live."

"There's my estate guy. I met with him last month, actually. He can probably recommend someone."

"Okay. You have my number now. Let's talk soon." Eyes lingering on his silver pendant, she said, "I'm sorry about Dylan. I know you two were very close."

He nodded, turning the pendant outward. "One-hundred, see? He fought hard."

They were quiet for a few moments, the cool air shivering along her neckline.

"Hopefully I'll survive long enough to meet the little Pip," he said, looking at her stomach. Bending towards one ear, he added, "By the way, after I knew I'd have to sing about Jell-O and marshmallows, I didn't mind losing. You should have won the Grammy for singing that tripe without laughing."

He winked at her as she lightly slapped his arm. She had the most comforting feeling of being at home, as if none of the past several weeks had happened; even that none of the intervening years since she won *American Star* had happened.

Standing so close to Hayden, she was again young and hopeful, bursting with newfound success, her entire sure-to-be-charmed life ahead of her.

Chapter Thirty-Eight

_T_he next day, she finally put together the duffel bag that would act as her birth bag: newborn diapers, unscented wipes, several cotton onesies, two swaddle blankets, a cap, socks, and mittens. She stared at the stash, wondering if this was all a baby needed.

She couldn't get over the mittens. It was surreal to think in a couple of weeks she'd be a mother, putting those miniature mittens over two miniature, miraculous hands. The thought of it made her insides tingle with a special kind of feeling, one she recognized as nascent mother-love. Closing her eyes, she whispered, "It's almost time to meet your grandchild, Mom."

Her father, who'd retired to a hand-built cabin in rural New Hampshire, was a volunteer fireman who wasn't able to get a week off until shortly after the baby was born. It pained her to think that her child would only have one grandparent, given that not only her mother but Firio's parents had passed.

She started on her own hospital bag: Loose clothes,

a hair cap, ponytail holders, cotton nightgowns with buttons she could undo for breastfeeding, several pairs of "granny" underwear, and flip-flops for the shower.

"Don't forget sanitary pads," her friend Taryn had advised her. "I'd assumed the hospital would have some, but they were out and it took ages for them to get more!" She'd also recommended a mini handheld fan. "You're gonna burn up!" she'd warned. "Those baby hormones and all that pushing will incinerate you and you can't open the windows!"

Piper was glad to get the straight talk from Taryn, but the whole thing had her rather terrified. Could she do this? It's not like she had a choice at this point. "I'm just gonna do it and that's all there is to it," she muttered to herself while packing. Women had been pushing out babies for centuries, and most of them without sanitary pads and mini-fans.

Later that night, she sat in her office and logged into a site called Fame Chat. It was a new site she'd discovered a few weeks ago when, worried about Firio losing his job, she began combing for alternative sources of income. Not confident she had enough fame left to monetize, she was happy when the site accepted her as "talent."

In the morning, she'd received a text message from the site that a dozen people had paid fifty dollars each to get a fifteen-second personalized video from her. She was pleasantly surprised at the number of people still wanting to hear from her, and hope bloomed within her that she could have a reliable source of secondary income.

The clients sent messages requesting what they'd like her to say and, no shocker, the first five were from people requesting birthday messages, either for themselves or someone else.

But the sixth request piqued her interest. It was from someone calling themselves "PM #278."

She knew what that meant. Her hardcore *American Star* fans, the Pipermints, had numbered themselves on the show's forums to keep track of their population. "PM #278" must be an old diehard.

Clicking into the message, she saw: "Piper, I have to speak with you. In person. It's VERY important!!! PLEASE meet me at the skating rink in Prospect Park. Let me know when you can do it. SOON!!! An angel has nothing!"

Piper read the message over again; its insistent words and liberal use of exclamation points made her heart flutter.

Did this Pipermint know something about the cult and the letters?

Or… could the Pipermint be behind everything?

Or… could this *not* be a Pipermint?

But the last sentence pointed too strongly to the messenger being an authentic Pipermint. "An angel has nothing" was a reference to what Nolan had told her after she'd performed Fleetwood Mac's "Landslide." He'd said, "An angel's voice has nothing on you."

After that, "An angel has nothing" had become a catchphrase for the Pipermints, something they used in lieu of "goodbye" after she'd signed a piece of memorabilia. The Fame Chat message *had* to be from a Pipermint. And a Pipermint wouldn't want to harm her... would they?

The weight of her indecision roiled queasily around her stomach. She couldn't run it by Firio. He'd only order her not to go meet anyone, and probably try to forbid her from even using Fame Chat anymore.

There was Hayden. But what could he do for her? He had a Broadway show to put on. She knew what it was to have the heavy burden of thousands of fan tickets and millions of dollars riding on the ability to put on a show, no matter your physical or mental state. There were many times she'd wanted to crawl into bed and curl into the fetal position rather than get on stage, but that was never an option.

Loverly looked physically and mentally taxing. And now Hayden had to perform knowing someone, perhaps even someone in the audience, wanted him dead. If the messenger had information that pertained to the letters, she'd let him know about it.

Besides, the Prospect Park skating rink was a heavily trafficked area. So long as she went during the day, she should be completely safe.

Piper clicked on the camera button inside of the site's software. In a blithe, all-is-well voice, she said, "Hi, Pipermint 278. It's so nice to hear from you. I can meet you tomorrow at the skating rink at noon. Looking forward."

Chapter Thirty-Nine

*A*t ten to noon, Piper arrived at the Bluestone Café at the Lakeside Center. Tucked under a starry blue dome was the ice skating rink and next door was a large splash pad being slathered with a droning ice machine for more winter skating.

The last dregs of autumn were quickly slipping away; the pristine, cool air livened her cheeks and smelled of impending snow. But the real cold hadn't hit yet, so she could get away with layering under winter leggings, a thermal top, and a cropped maternity puffer coat.

She went inside the café to get a cup of hot tea with the idea she could throw it into the face of the person she was about to meet if that became necessary. But it was Saturday and there was a snarling line of people. Back outside, she headed to the only free wooden picnic table.

Sitting on the end, facing outward to give her stomach ample space, she scanned the crowd, trusting that "PM #278" would find her, as she had no idea who she should be looking for.

Behind the glistening splash-now-ice pad and a ring of old-fashioned black lamp posts and a red emergency ladder set up to rescue those reckless enough to walk on the lake once it froze over, she watched the rippling pewter lake, dotted with white gulls and fringed with long stalks of wild wheat.

Piper remembered how when it was still warm, she'd been walking around the lake when she saw a twenty-something woman pestering a flock of geese, kicking at their paddled feet. She'd stopped, calling over in no fooling voice, "Leave them alone!" and glared until the woman walked stonily away.

How had she gone from protecting geese to trying to kill a man? Things had been normal, she'd been preparing to give birth, then everything had tumbled, tumbled, tumbled, faster and faster, like a row of dominoes that had been flicked over.

What kept niggling at her was the idea that the letter writer had hooked into a part of her that was already there, dormant, waiting to kill.

"Piper." A woman was standing before her, pulling down a blue scarf wrapped around her head and the lower part of her face. "It's me, Megan."

Startled, Piper pressed her chest. "I didn't recognize you, Megan." Piper couldn't tell if Megan was using the scarf as a barrier against the chilly air or was... disguising herself?

Megan sat on the bench opposite her. "That ten-year anniversary piece said you lived in Brooklyn, so I thought this would be convenient for you."

"Yes, it was."

Megan grimaced, the pale gray light illuminating the lines ribbed around her jaw. "Sorry to drag you out here," she said, looking absorbed in thought, not the excited fan-face Piper had seen in the subway.

"It's fine. I'm glad I got your message. You sounded… do you want anything to drink? The line is long."

"No, I'm okay. I thought I should…" She placed a big, bright red purse on the wooden bench table and stared disconsolately at it. "About six months ago, my husband was diagnosed with mouth cancer."

"Oh, I'm—I'm sorry to hear that," Piper said, tripping over her words as she tried to imagine why Megan felt this was something she needed to urgently convey in person. Piper had once heard a similar pronouncement from her mother, so her heart went out to Megan. But there was the old tug-of-war within herself—her desire to stay emotionally engaged with her fans while still maintaining personal boundaries.

"Thank you," Megan said. "The thing is, we have our own business, the toy business. You remember?"

"I'm sorry, I don't." In the past, she would have pretended she remembered this, but impatience was beginning to rake her stomach as it dawned on her why Megan had wanted to see her.

Money. She was going to ask for money.

"My point is, we're small business owners," Megan continued. "We have the cheapest health insurance we could find. So when Jack was diagnosed, we were under-insured. We're going to owe thousands."

"That's terrible," Piper said, but her voice was a monotone, her mouth curdling as she realized her guess had been correct. After happening to run into Piper in the subway, Megan must have decided Piper would be the perfect person to help out with medical bills.

"So I put up a fundraiser. We're trying for one hundred thousand to cover the bills and loss of work. The fund was going okay, not spectacular, but okay. We had about eight thousand."

Piper's attention roved to the skating rink. Teeny-bopper music spilled from speakers as at least a hundred people whizzed and wobbled around in a circle. Her mom's medical bills had almost broken her financially. She couldn't afford a fan's husband's treatment. How was she going to say this?

Well, she would donate something. But Megan probably thought she was filthy rich and could pay for it all. Like most people, Megan equated fame with money. All that free promotion this Pipermint had done for her over the years, without ever being asked, and now she wanted payback.

Piper's mind began to spin off in other directions. Could she do a future gig to help Megan out? Would enough people buy tickets to make it worthwhile? Could she even *sing* well enough anymore? Could she still memorize lyrics?

"Then one day I got a private message on the site. The messenger was willing to give me fifty thousand dollars," Megan said.

"Oh." Piper's rambling thoughts cut off at this unforeseen turn in the narrative.

"I thought it was probably some kind of scam, but couldn't ignore it, in case it wasn't. The person asked me to download an app to communicate with me. It's called Teleport. All the messages are encrypted. And they can be completely wiped out by the sender or receiver."

"All right," Piper said, quietly.

"The person would give me fifty thousand dollars towards my husband's fund, but I had to do something." She paused. Piper stared, wrestling with the urge to tell Megan to get to the point. "What I had to do," she continued, "was to come to New York. The person would pay for a flight and hotel and give me ten thousand for a down payment. I had to stand in the Broadway station on the platform by the north end of the Forty-Fourth Street side at a certain time every night for two weeks. I had to keep an eye out for you."

Her expression was searching, as if Piper would understand the meaning behind this.

Piper was too baffled to respond.

"The whole thing sounded bizarre," Megan went on. "But it didn't sound... *bad*. If it had sounded bad, I wouldn't have done it, even though I needed the money. And, of course, I wanted to see you. None of the Pipermints knew why you took down your social media. We were so worried until we saw the *Entertainment Daily* article, then thought you were taking a pregnancy break. Me, Carol, Lily, Mauricio, you know the San Fran crew. We were all at the *Hearts Afire* CD release party. Remember?"

"Sure," Piper said, wishing Megan had a fast-forward button. "So this person told you to look for me? In the subway?"

"Yes. To watch for Piper Dunner."

"That's the night you saw me, right?"

"Exactly. And the person said, when I see you, to take note of the day and time. And to truthfully tell anything I saw to anyone who asked. After that, I'd get the rest of the money. And *only* then." She kneaded her knuckles worriedly, mouth turned down. "I flew here and set up at the Comfort Inn in Times Square. I didn't see you for a few nights, but then... I did see you."

Piper said nothing for what felt like an eternity. When she spoke, her voice was a croak. "And you came over and spoke to me."

"Yes," Megan nodded.

"Did the person say to keep a lookout for Hayden Tower as well?"

"No. But I saw him too, or thought I saw him." She laughed nervously. "I'm a Pipermint for life, but always liked Hayden too. I split my votes until top three." She looked abashed. "Sorry, I don't think I ever told you that. I had to make a decision and there was no contest. But I always hoped you two would get together." She smiled shyly. "I wrote a few fan fics. In the most popular one, you and Hayden get married, but in the past."

"Then what happened?"

"Well, the two of you are stuck in 1829—"

"In the *subway*," Piper clarified, unable to control the irritation in her voice.

Megan darted her gaze around. "That's when it got

308

even stranger. At the hotel, I texted the person that I'd seen you and spoken to you. The person was very, very angry. Started using all caps." She deepened her voice in apparent imitation of an *all caps* text. "You weren't supposed to speak to her!" Her silver-shadowed eyes popped. "How was I supposed to know? I saw you, and naturally I wanted to say hello. I told the person it's their fault if they didn't give the instructions correctly."

"Who is this person?" Piper asked. "Their name?"

"I don't know. Goes by a number: 10-11."

"Then what happened? Not in 1829."

"The person—10-11—said I'd have to return the ten thousand dollars they'd already given me. How I got the money, that's another story."

"I'm listening."

"I was sent cash in the mail. Regular old mail. A thousand dollars in each envelope. No return address. Imagine sending all that through the mail."

"Where was it postmarked from?"

"I don't remember the zip code. I was so astonished to get that kind of money. I went out and bought a small thing with a hundred dollar bill, to see if it was real. I was terrified it would be counterfeit and I'd be arrested. But it wasn't. I put most of it in my bank."

"Did you keep the envelopes?"

"No. I worried Jack would get mad about the whole thing. So I tossed them, and would tell him the money came from donations."

"What about the rest of the money?"

"That was supposed to come after. But when 10-11 learned I spoke to you, it all broke down. But I kept arguing. What's the difference if I see Piper and speak to her or see Piper and *not* speak to her?" She shook her head. "I was told I have to give the money back or I'll regret it."

"And have you?"

"No, but…" She heaved a big, defeated sigh. "I decided I have to. I don't know who I'm dealing with. I have to put the money in a bag and bring it to a gym in Rockefeller Center. I have to get a day pass, go to the locker room, and use a combination lock, then text the locker and combination to 10-11."

"Men or women's locker room?"

"I think it's unisex. There's only one. But it's very, very annoying," she said, hands flailing. "I come all the way out to New York, after giving my husband a story about meetings with FAO Schwarz to carry our toys. Which I'm going to have to tell him didn't happen." Her bottom lip quivered. "I can't shake the feeling I got involved in something that could hurt you. Which I would never want, not ever. But I was desperate. And it seemed okay. I mean, just watch for you. What harm could that do? Then it dawned on me. I'm ashamed I hadn't thought about this before. Are you hiding from someone?"

Piper sat drawing her finger over and over on a tiny piece of wood that splintered up from a table plank. Her mind was spiraling downward into something terrible, a darkness closing in all around her.

"I was being set-up," she said.

"You were—what?"

"I was being set-up," she said, speaking more to

herself. "You were the witness. It would be credible that you'd recognize me—even nine months pregnant and not looking anything like I did on *Star*—because you were a superfan. And you'd recognize Hayden even wearing glasses and with that cap smashed over his head."

"Of *course* I'd recognize both of you," she said, proudly. "I could spot you two from the top of a mountain, pretty sure. But… what was I supposed to witness?"

Piper slowly raised her eyes to Megan. "Tell me what you saw that night."

"I saw you come down the stairs. You were looking around, seeming kind of nervous."

"And?"

"And you kind of—you went behind one of the subway map board thingies, and looked out towards the train. You kept looking up at the timetable. You moved towards the edge. That's when I went over to say hello. Then I saw Hayden—or someone who looked like him—get in the train. How strange you were both in the subway like that. Was that really a coincidence?"

Piper closed her eyes as heaviness and pressure around her temples intensified. The tinny cartoonish voice of a female singer emanating from the café's speakers rang in her ears. She thought she'd never heard a more grating voice in her lifetime.

Megan was the witness, all right. Surveillance cameras might not be working, or have poor quality, or be unable to see Piper from wherever they were positioned—and in the decrepit city subway system, any one of those scenarios was quite possible.

But there was superfan Megan Donnelly to obediently report to police that she saw Piper Dunner following Hayden Tower. That she saw Piper Dunner looking nervous, and hiding behind the map board, and keeping track of the train's arrival time. Saw Piper Dunner not *accidentally* tumble into Hayden Tower's back as she fainted, but in fact, saw her stalk him and plot his demise.

Only the "witness" had messed up big time. She'd unknowingly interrupted the impending crime.

Once Megan informed 10-11 that she'd spoken to Piper, 10-11 knew, as Piper had known, that the murder attempt couldn't be undertaken a second time, because Piper wasn't stupid enough to try it again in the same location. And there are only so many "accidental" murders one can plan for the same person.

Impulsively, Piper reached out and grabbed hold of one of Megan's pink, chaffed hands. "Megan, the person who sent you money is a danger to me and my family. And to Hayden Tower. They could also be part of a cult that's dangerous to many people." She paused to see if Megan was absorbing this, but Megan only looked stunned into speechlessness. "I have to find out who 10-11 is. And—and I have an idea how to do that. But I'm going to need your help."

Megan's face registered no real comprehension. Piper assumed she would have to say everything all over again. But Megan tugged her hand away.

"Cult?" She fluttered her clump of fake lashes. "I

don't want to do anything else to make this person angrier. What if they come after me and my husband?"

"All the more reason to find out who it is. So—so you don't have to worry about them ever again," Piper said, stumbling on her thin logic.

She watched as Megan made a fist over her purse strap, a discouraging indication she was getting ready to leave. But a sly, conspiratorial smile inched across her face.

"Well, I did say Pipermint for life, didn't I?"

Chapter Forty

On Sunday night, Piper lay on her bed in a pink-and-white striped cotton nightie, her legs hoisted over a pillow, thumbing through *The Ultimate Baby Name Book*, marking names with a pen. Firio came back in from his office and kissed her on the forehead.

"Any good ones?" he asked.

"How about Eve? I still like that. Elongated to Evie."

"Why not? Very Garden of Eden."

"Eden! That's pretty."

She jotted "Eve" and "Eden" down on a notebook resting next to her. There were about twenty names each for boys and girls, but only three or four for each were serious contenders. Piper preferred old-fashioned names or ones that were slightly androgynous, like her own.

Of course, a girl would get Penelope for a middle name, in honor of her mother. A boy would get Lorenzo, for Firio's father. She still hoped a name would strike her when she looked at the baby's face, that the baby would communicate who he or she was.

"What about Errol?" Firio asked, taking off his shirt.

"Errol?" She crinkled her brows. "For a boy or girl?"

"Boy, as in Errol Flynn, the old movie star. I've always liked him."

"Not sure about that, honey, he drank himself to death. Bad juju."

He smiled at her, slid out of his after-work sweatpants, dumped them on the floor, and disappeared into the bathroom. As soon as Piper heard the shower running, she put the baby name book aside and placed her tablet on her thighs.

Opening the BabyTrakker app, she watched a circle of vibrant blue as it hovered on top of The Comfort Inn in Times Square. If the app could have drilled down deeper, it would have shown the tracking device hidden beneath the cardboard cutout inside a flap of fabric on the floor of a travel bag.

Earlier in the afternoon, Piper had waited until Firio went for a run, which he did the same time each Sunday. Then she took a car service to Prospect Park, where she once again met up with Megan at the Bluestone Café. This time, Piper handed Megan a black paisley-patterned travel bag. Piper may no longer be famous, but she had been once, there was no forgetting that. And pop stars travel. A lot.

Over the years, she'd become a travel bag expert. She knew which ones fit all of her liquids (and there were plenty of them: sunscreen, face and body moisturizer, toner, hair gel, etc.), and what would fit underneath a plane chair so she could grab things in-flight. She liked bags with plenty of inside pockets, where she could store what she wanted to find quickly: Phone, book, sleep mask, hairband, toothbrush holder.

Which all led to her black paisley travel bag because it was one of her favorites. As the design was retired, it would pain her to give the bag away to some psycho, but it was the only one of hers she knew that had a flat fabric floor and, underneath that, a thick piece of cardboard which she slid in and out of the floor flap when she washed the bag.

Underneath this cutout, she'd secured the BabyTrakker. Inside the bag is where Megan would place ten thousand dollars for 10-11.

* * *

PIPER DIDN'T HAVE a solid plan for what would happen when she tracked where the travel bag went. All she hoped was that she would then know who was mentally torturing her, torturing her into murder.

What would she do then?

Could she get the authorities to question the person for trying to incite a murder that hadn't happened? Would police take her seriously unless she admitted she'd come so close to killing a man? And not any man but a very famous one? She could see the headlines now: *Failed American Star Plotted to Kill Once-Rival and Oscar-Winner Hayden Tower Due to 'Cult Curse.'*

After an admission like that, she'd never work again. Not to mention what Hayden, Firio, her friends, and fans would think. The headlines would last forever. Her child would grow up to read them.

But she saw no other way of punishing the instigator, the person going under the name 10-11 with Megan. And, with Piper, known as her "friend." If this person wanted Hayden Tower dead to the extent that he or she would plot such a wild plan, he or she wasn't going to stop now.

One thing seemed fairly certain—the moneybag wouldn't track to Mitch McCabe.

"Yep, he's in L.A.," Hayden had told her the day before on the phone. "A database has pap shots of him coming out of a juice shop in Silver Lake with some hot model chick."

"Hmm," Piper had said, staring out at her backyard from the kitchen sink window. "If it is him, he's not going to postmark a letter from L.A. and give himself away."

"Something else," said Hayden. "I was searching around last night after the show, to see if I could find anything to explain where Mitch was when he was supposedly in rehab. I couldn't find that, but what I did find could be the reason he left The True Way."

Piper said nothing then realized she was holding her breath.

"About eight months ago, this L.A. DJ called Demented Damien died in a skiing accident in Gstaad. There was no foul play. A group of people saw him go over the side of a mountain. Guess he'd had some kind of seizure."

"That's terrible," Piper said, having an eerie feeling of what was coming.

"Yeah, and I remember Mitch complaining about

the guy. He was competing with him for the same guests and first radio plays. Once, I heard him joke he'd like to see the guy fall off a cliff."

"Guess he wasn't joking. So does this mean The True Way can manifest death after all?"

"I suspect Demented Damien would have been gone long ago if the group could do it to make Mitch happy. More likely what you said—if something bad *does* happen, the Way takes credit for the 'manifestation' like it did with me and Anton Bishop." He paused. "Demented Damien had three young kids. Mitch disappeared from his radio show right after he died. I bet Mitch tried to manifest besting Damien in the ratings, and when he died instead, leaving three orphans, Mitch got completely freaked and split from the group."

"That's certainly one theory."

They went silent. As Piper listened to Hayden's breath in her ear, a memory floated to the surface: The contestants, worked like oxen, used to take cat naps in their rehearsal room. One time, Piper had fallen asleep on top of Hayden's beat-up, brown leather jacket, using it as a pillow. She'd woken up when he began gently scooting it out from under her head. Even with the chatter of the other contestants somewhere else in the room, she could hear Hayden's breathing, so knew he must be only inches from her face.

This was a few days after their hotel room make-out session. Too embarrassed to look directly at him, she'd kept her eyes closed, feigning sleep, while she'd felt him poised over her for at least a minute before he moved away, leaving the jacket under her head.

"Thanks for digging around, Hayden," she'd said on the phone.

"Thanks for not killing me."

She couldn't help but burst out with a morbid *Ha!* They'd said their goodbyes, promising to keep each other informed of any other developments.

But she didn't update Hayden on her plan with Megan and the moneybag, worried he might insist on getting his security involved. She didn't trust whoever his security was to not muck things up, and possibly put herself or Megan in danger.

She tried to brace herself for finding out the worst she could imagine—that the moneybag would track to Jojo's apartment. But there would be no bracing enough to withstand that.

* * *

"YOU OKAY?"

Firio sat at the kitchen island, finishing up his morning coffee and a banana. "You kept making noises all night like you were having a nightmare. Anything you're not telling me? A letter?"

"No, honey," she grumbled, padding to the fridge. "It's not that. I'm due next week. Things are very uncomfortable right now." After pouring some juice, she grimaced and rested her aching back against the sink, feeling too bulky and awkward to even function.

Within the past few weeks, her body had ceased to be anything she recognized as belonging to her. It was merely a skin-covered, blood-beating, oxygen-pumping safety deposit box for a not-so-small-anymore human being, one that gave her pains in places she didn't know it was possible to have pains.

"Did I keep you awake?" she asked.

"I finally took a sleeping pill." He grinned groggily at her, pushing the banana peel into the garbage disposal. "Hope I can make it through the day, those things wipe me out. But at least I got a good sleep."

She almost apologized for being the cause of him taking a sleeping pill, something he'd had to do fairly regularly because of her jostling around with restless leg syndrome, but couldn't bring herself to do it. Her discomfort was such that she had little sympathy left over for him.

He didn't walk like a duck on land, or feel like a burp was forever stuck in his chest, his tongue wasn't permanently chalky from the frequently-consumed Tums, nor did he have to go to the bathroom three hundred times a day. She'd give anything to be able to take a sleeping pill and jet off to dreamland.

She adjusted his diamond-patterned, golden-purple tie. It was a tie she'd given him for his birthday, and it still gave her a little charge when he wore it.

"What about Flynn?" she asked.

"Flynn?" He looked uncomprehending before the suggestion sunk in. "Ah, as in Errol? What happened to bad juju?"

"Flynn is a nice name for either a boy or girl."

"Add it to the list."

At the door, they kissed, and he squeezed her now-quite-ample bottom, saying, "See you tonight."

He walked down the paved walkway and took a right onto their street. They had a little car they used for occasional weekend getaways, but he mostly took the subway to work. When he passed out of sight behind a neighbor's hedgerow, Piper closed the door and locked it.

Chapter Forty-One

a t 9:30 a.m., she sat with a cup of tea and watched on her laptop as the blue dot exited The Comfort Inn and made its slow, glowing way up Seventh Avenue.

I see you, Piper texted to Megan. They were both using Teleport, Megan under the name she'd been using with 10-11: MRD. Piper was Minty1.

OK, Megan texted back.

The next hour was spent watching as Megan went to a branch of her bank, took out the funds, stopped at a hardware store to buy a lock, and walked to the Equinox in Rockefeller Center. In between the watching, Piper would eat and do light cleaning chores.

Done, Megan texted at 10:48 a.m.

Don't tell 10-11 until you're safe at JFK.

About ten minutes later, Megan replied: *In a cab.*

Let me know when you arrive.

Yeppers!

Piper watched as three gray bubbles appeared,

showing that Megan was typing. But the bubbles disappeared. Then reappeared. Megan was trying to decide what to type. Finally, the words came:

One day you'll tell me the whole story?

Piper's finger hovered over the keypad for several seconds. She typed:

Yeppers.

* * *

WHEN PIPER'S PHONE RANG an hour later and she saw Jojo's number, she sat staring at it, hesitant to pick up.

Soon, she could find out that Jojo had been trying to set her up for murder, and her feelings about her friend were still too unsettled to want to make chit-chat. But habit made her pick up anyway.

"Piper, did you hear?" Jojo said, sounding miserable and incredulous. "It's all over the news."

"I haven't heard anything. What's going on?"

"They found the guy who hit me."

"They *did*?" Piper cried. "Who was it?"

She feared Jojo was about to say Hayden. Piper would have regretted not plunging that knife into him after all.

"It—it was Nolan."

"What?" Piper shrieked.

"I mean, not him directly. It was a guy who washes dishes in a restaurant he owns. He'd heard Nolan bitching about the idea of me being on the reboot, and took it upon himself to run me over, thinking he'd get in good with his boss. He and his friend found out where I lived and watched my routine. He took some dishwater from the restaurant's kitchen. He's saying he didn't mean to hit me, but… Piper, he's only *sixteen*. A kid!"

"Oh my God. What does Nolan say about everything?"

"He released this big statement saying he knew nothing about it. Plus, he went straight to the cops when the little shit fessed up. But I wonder. Could—could Nolan hate me?"

"That asshole!" Piper fumed. Despite still not knowing if Jojo was secretly her enemy, the distress in her friend's voice made Piper want to soothe her. "I'm sure he doesn't hate you. He was being Nolan, probably said something nasty about all of us but you're the one the kid overheard."

"I can't even *believe* I defended him over the years. I have a call with Oliver Corbyn today. I guess he wants to know how I feel about being on a panel with Nolan. I'm going to tell him the truth, that I'm not comfortable with it. It could get ugly. They're not going to pick me over him. Nolan *is American Star*."

"Ugh, Jo."

"Listen, I have to go down to the precinct. But I had another thought. Hold on." She blew her nose, then got back on the phone. "Could Nolan be behind the letters? If he didn't want me being on the show, that would explain my letter."

"But what about mine?" Piper asked, her fingers poised over her lips as she contemplated this new turn of events.

"Maybe he didn't want you on either. Who knows why."

"But… why would he pretend he did? He could tell Oliver and the network he didn't want me. I'm sure they'd listen to him. Why try to get rid of us this weird way?"

"I don't know, Piper. I'm only saying, I don't think we know half of what there is to know about Nolan. I'm going to ask the detective to make sure that he isn't let off the hook so easily, that they look into him. He could have ratted on the dishwasher to look like a good guy when he's the one who told the kid to do it."

Great, Piper thought, just what she needed: Yet another suspect in this fiasco.

The pair wrapped up their conversation. Piper searched for stories about Jojo's hit-and-run and Nolan's involvement. Seeing that it was indeed all over the news and social media, she felt guilty about her suspicion that Jojo had plotted her own hate crime. What kind of friend was Piper anyway?

But she knew she couldn't fully relax about Jojo until she traced where the moneybag went.

Piper saw that both Nolan and Jojo had been trending online all morning. An old video snippet of Nolan's insult at Jojo's audition had been dug up and was making the rounds.

"I emphatically and categorically deny I had anything to do with Jojo Barr's attack," Nolan said on social media. "As soon as I learned information I thought might be helpful to the investigation, I called my solicitor and we went straight to the nearest police station.

As for a very rude comment I made to Jojo about her weight a decade ago on *American Star*, what can I say except I'm a terrific arsehole sometimes. Sorry! (My memoir, *No, You Can't Sing*, is out this summer. Be sure to peruse all the other awful things I've said.)"

So much for Nolan's assertion that he would never apologize for past transgressions, though Piper had to give his *mea culpa* some credit for retaining that special Nolan "pizzazz."

Chapter Forty-Two

*A*round four p.m., Megan was well on her way to the opposite side of the country, and Piper was getting nervous.

Firio would likely be home in a couple of hours. As her pregnancy advanced, he'd come home earlier. Once he was here, she wouldn't be able to keep an eagle eye on the BabyTrakker. She could tell him she was responding to Fame Chat requests in her office. That way, he'd leave her alone. But that would only buy her an hour or so.

The moneybag was sitting in a locker at the Equinox in Rockefeller Center. The gym's website said it was open until midnight, and Piper worried 10-11 wouldn't pick up the bag until then.

Unsure what to do, she waddled around the house, for these days it truly felt like she was waddling. She kept an eye on the blue dot alternately through her phone and laptop and was too distracted to do much of anything else but look out the windows, sip hot tea, stretch, practice her labor breathing, and stare at the sitting blue dot. Her entire life felt suspended, waiting.

Finally, at 5:48 p.m., she saw the blue dot move. Her heart lurched into her throat. "Here we go," she murmured. For a few moments, she wondered if her eyes were playing tricks, until the dot most definitely inched west on Forty-Eighth Avenue. "Where are you going, fucker?" she whispered hotly.

A minute later, the dot disappeared right where the map showed the Forty-Ninth Street subway station. Her heart was hammering and her lungs felt compressed. This couldn't be good for the baby and she worried about her blood pressure.

"Breathe," she whispered, caressing her stomach. "It's okay, Flynn," she said, a jolt of recognition going through her. The name had come unbidden out of her mouth, and it sounded so right and natural.

She paced with her phone in her palm, unable to look away. Ten-eleven could be taking the subway anywhere—a couple of stops away, or to the Bronx, or to Far Rockaway, Queens. It could take minutes to see the blue dot again; it could take an hour or more.

The wait for the blue dot to reappear was agonizing, the tension unbearable, thick and surly. The only thing that helped alleviate it was talking out loud.

"Who are you?" she demanded of the unseen blue dot. "Why are you doing this? Where are you going? Show me! Show me, damn you," she said, knowing she sounded like she'd lost it, but not caring.

Panting, she placed her phone on the kitchen island

and paced before it, keeping one eye on the app's map. She groaned as an aching sensation spread through her uterus, an intense spasm, more like a period cramp than the pain that had started about a month ago, the sharp needle jabs behind her pelvic bone called "pelvic girdle."

It couldn't be the baby, no, not this early. She had another week. Only two days ago, Dr. Malhotra told her she was on track to deliver on her due date, that her cervix hadn't dilated. "Not now, don't come now," she begged, walking back and forth and, like magic, the cramp dissipated.

Must have been a Braxton Hicks contraction. She wouldn't open her contraction-timing app unless the cramp happened again, but vowed to calm down. This stress could bring on contractions or even trigger an early birth.

Sitting at the kitchen table, she stared at the map, biting her lip, her hands shoved tightly under her knees. The blue dot reappeared. "There you are," she gasped, forgetting all about her resolve to stay calm.

The blue dot was on West Broadway. She watched as it floated slowly down Chambers Street, towards the Hudson River.

"What is this?" she said, lowly. Her bowels liquified and she shook her head. "What is this?" she said again, her whole body going numb.

The blue dot hovered at a building called The Skyhorse. The name of the building was right there on the app's map.

"This isn't right," she muttered, furiously shaking

her head, as if that would reverse what she was seeing. "No."

There had to be some mistake. Something had to be wrong.

"I don't believe it!" she called out. But she did believe it. Her hands were trembling so badly she couldn't pick up her phone.

Why would Firio want her to kill Hayden Tower?

Chapter Forty-Three

*S*he sat in a cataclysmic state of shock, watching the blue dot as it hovered at the building where Firio worked, The Skyhorse. It was a large building, perhaps twenty stories tall.

She'd met him there several times for lunch, usually outside. But a couple of times, she'd ridden up to the eighth floor, where his firm was located. His small office overlooked the Hudson River.

She pressed her palm into her erratically jerking heart, worried she could faint or have a heart attack. None of this made any sense. What motive could Firio have to want her to kill Hayden? Or anyone for that matter?

Had—had he ever loved her?

A disturbing wailing noise came from somewhere outside and she startled, but within a moment, realized the noise had come from her mouth. She buried her head in her hands, her mouth contorting, the wailing still coming. How frightening, how alien the noise sounded. Not like her at all.

This couldn't be. It made no sense, none.

The Skyhorse was a big building. Thousands of people worked there. This could be an abhorrent coincidence. Or it could be someone who knew her through Firio because the person worked with him. But who and why?

It eventually grew quiet and unsure of how much time had passed, she realized if she was going to look for answers, she needed to do so now.

Somehow, she got up the stairs and into their bedroom and started for his closet. It was open; she could smell his familiar odor, the molecules of him gliding off the hanging suit jackets and work shirts—the smell of safety, of love, of sex, of baby.

She swept her hands into one jacket pocket after another. Found a receipt and looked at it. Dry cleaning. Found a business card. Someone named Dan Pritzkier from Manhattan Capital Group. Found a squashed ten-dollar bill and a half-packet of cinnamon gum.

She glanced up to a shelf where more shirts were folded and stacked. There was a black box. What was in it?

Grabbing the chair from his desk, she rolled it over to the closet, but because of its wheels, she realized she couldn't stand on it while ballooned with pregnancy. She rolled it back, wanting everything to appear as it was when Firio left that morning.

Why would he want her to kill Hayden Tower? Why would he want her in prison?

"Why, Flynn, why?" she cried out in raw anguish, then listened, as if the baby would respond. She sensed the answer all around her, but it remained agonizingly out of reach.

The True Way. The name charged through her mind, handed to her.

Firio must belong to the cult. It wanted Hayden dead for some reason—perhaps because he'd left it— and deduced Piper would be the perfect person to make that happen. With her history of tragedies and failure, she was the ideal dupe. The cult figured she'd be resentful of Hayden Tower and all his success. Easy to talk into killing him.

She stood with one hand clutching her neck as it all frighteningly, chillingly, fell into place.

The True Way had sent Firio to her. It had been watching her, knew where she used to live in the West Village. The cult had instructed him to come out of the bookstore and bump into her, start a conversation, begin dating her and…

Her eyes roved down to her stomach, the beach-ball roundness of it, and the most terrible thought imaginable took soul-searing, grotesque shape.

The cult didn't only want Hayden dead. It wanted a *baby*.

"Oh my God," she whispered.

A baby. Like that witches coven had wanted one in *Rosemary's Baby*. It wanted a baby for who knows what reason—to brainwash, to spread its twisted message about manifestations.

Her legs went rubbery. Using the side of Firio's desk

as a crutch, she carefully lowered herself into his work chair—fearful she might fall and not be able to propel herself up off the floor.

How could the cult guarantee she would get pregnant?

Her mind rewound to the weekend she had most likely conceived, when she and Firio jaunted off to the fishing village of Mystic, Connecticut for their first romantic getaway.

The first morning there, she realized she'd forgotten her birth control pills. Then it slipped her mind. Late that night, back at the inn, wined up and horny as hell for each other, they didn't even feel they could wait to go out to get condoms, as they didn't know the area and weren't sure anything would be open anyway. So they'd decided he would use the pull out method, but... that hadn't happened. Nor did it happen twenty minutes later, nor the next morning.

At the time, Piper had thought, *If I get pregnant, I get pregnant. He's the one.* She was more buoyant about the prospect than was wise given they'd only been dating a few months. But she was thirty-four. Ripe and ready. And she'd never felt as comfortable with a man as she did with Firio, felt she could be herself around him.

He must have been keeping track of her menstrual cycle. She'd had her period twice while they were dating, and both times she'd informed him so it wouldn't be a surprise. She hadn't *forgotten* the pills. Knowing she would likely be ovulating that weekend, he'd taken them from her travel bag, got her mildly drunk, and seduced her.

His initial unenthusiastic response to her pregnancy —to cement the fiction that it had caught him off-guard. How else should a young man who'd been dating a woman for so little time have reacted?

He'd only married her so he wouldn't have any issues with legal rights to the baby, the one he would have full custody of as soon as she went to prison for killing Hayden. He'd even gotten a cheap house out of it, as she'd paid for half the down payment.

"Jesus, God," she moaned. Could any of this be true? Had her hormones invented the most nightmarish story she could think of?

Realizing she was losing track of time, she twisted her bulk around and glanced out of the windows. It was already dead-dark outside. He could be home any minute.

Something occurred to her. Something so ghastly, she covered her mouth with both hands in horror.

What if Firio recognized her travel bag, the one he had right now? If he recognized it as hers, he'd know that she and Megan were working together. He could come back here and try to…

She pushed herself up and teetered her way downstairs, clutching the banister, her mind frantically toggling between wanting to get out of the house and wanting to stay and confront him. How dare you! How DARE you! You will NEVER get my child, you freak! YOU DEMON!

"God," she groaned, and clasped her abdomen. She hadn't felt another contraction, but her gut was nauseous, her skin feverish. She stumbled to the half-bath, grasped the toilet, and barely managed to maneuver to the floor before the contents of her stomach heaved out of her.

* * *

AFTER ABOUT FIFTEEN MINUTES, her stomach settled, and she plodded shakily out to the kitchen and located her phone. She went to her photos and clicked into the section labeled "Mystic."

There it was: A picture Firio had taken of her in front of their mid-nineteenth century country inn. Thin and newly impregnated Piper had on black jeans and knee-high boots, a slim-cut burgundy pleather jacket, and a black wool cloche with a pleated crown.

In her hand was her matching burgundy travel bag, *not* the black paisley travel bag. As she had retrieved the black bag from a large plastic storage container in her closet, she became almost certain that he'd never seen that travel bag before.

Which gave her more time. Time she needed. She needed to search for evidence that he was behind everything, because he would, of course, deny it if she accused him. And if she took off tonight, right now, went to a friend's house or even got a train to her father's place in New Hampshire, he'd hire a lawyer, no doubt paid for by The True Way, and come after her.

She'd read of cases where mothers had been desperate enough to grab their own children and run from abusers, only to be considered kidnappers and lose custodial rights.

If she could dig around more, she'd find something that would incriminate him enough that she could get full custody of the baby. Otherwise, there was a chance Flynn would fall into the clutches of The True Way. If possible, she would find enough to guarantee that Firio never even got visitation rights, at least not without her present.

She had to be smart and methodical, ruled by her intellect and cunning, not by her frenzy and panic.

Then she remembered something else.

The Christmas lights she'd wanted him to put up on the porch roof that he never did. The ones she'd strung on the wall herself. The fact that when she'd showed him the tinsel-and-red-bow wreath she'd bought for the front door, he'd evinced little interest in that too.

He had no intention of spending Christmas with her.

Once the baby was born, he would take it to the cult.

And when he realized Piper wasn't going to kill Hayden and go to prison, he and the cult would have to get rid of her.

Just as she had that thought, she heard the front door open.

In the movies, when danger closes in, people can run. They can scream. But she couldn't do either. She couldn't move her legs or arms or mouth as fear fastened every fiber of her being.

Firio appeared in the kitchen. The only thing in his hands was his usual briefcase.

"Honey?" he asked with a quizzical half-smile. "You feeling all right?"

Chapter Forty-Four

She couldn't speak. Her mouth gulped like a guppy, but nothing came out. Then gibberish passed through her lips, sounding like no known language, like toddler-warble.

Firio rushed over and led her to a chair, carefully lowering her into it. "All right, Piper," he announced loudly, as if she might have trouble hearing him. "I'm calling 911."

She shook her head, her gaze fixed on his briefcase, which he'd placed on the table. She had to see if the money was in it. This could be her one chance to know for certain.

"No, it's okay," she said, weakly regaining her speech. "It was a Braxton Hicks. Happened right before you came in. This could go on for days."

He sat next to her, holding her hand, his dark eyes glowing with what in the past she would have read as true concern, but now she didn't know what to read as. "Are you sure?" he asked.

"I'm pretty sure. I'll turn on my contraction app. If I get to ten minutes, we'll go in."

"Okay," he said, still staring at her intensely. "If you're sure."

They sat longer, Firio holding her hand, and her limply letting it happen. It was as if something inanimate, plastic, was pressed over her hand, yet she wanted to reclaim it and vigorously rub her skin on her leg to slough off his atoms.

Finally convinced she was not going to have another contraction, he went upstairs to change and shower.

First, she checked the BabyTrakker app, saw the blue dot still hovering at The Skyhorse building. Then she went to their bedroom, listening for the soft rain of the shower before going to his office and finding his briefcase on his desk. With trembling hands, she unzipped it and peered inside, thankful he didn't have one with a combination lock.

She slid out some folders and documents, finding no money. Zipping his briefcase and putting it back exactly where she'd found it, her mind inexorably began to turn away from the worst, back towards the possibility that someone else who worked at The Skyhorse had the money and was behind everything.

But as much as she wanted to wind the clock back, back before she saw the blue dot float to Firio's building, as much as she wanted her husband to be the man she'd fallen in love with, some deeper intuition refused to allow it.

Chapter Forty-Five

She listened to his rhythmic breathing, louder and raspier than usual, thanks to the sleeping pill. Before bed, she'd brought the pill right to him, saying, "I'm very uncomfortable now. It won't be a pleasant night for you."

An hour into his light snoring, she gingerly unwrapped the covers. Lately, he'd had to grasp her hand and haul to get her out of bed, but using the headboard, she was able to pull and lever herself up, holding her breath as the mattress depressed under her. She padded to his side of the bed.

His left arm was stretched behind his head on the pillow, his right arm draped over his bare chest, his mouth half-open. She touched his hand, prepared to tell him she didn't feel well if he woke up.

He didn't move.

She held his warm, flaccid fingers. "Firio?" she whispered. Nothing. "Honey?" she said in a non-whisper, lightly shaking his dead-limp fingers. Nothing.

The pill had done its job.

She lifted his phone off the bedside table and slowly, slowly lowered his thumbprint on the circular home button, using her index finger to push down once, gently but firmly.

The phone lit up.

Heel to toe, she pressed one foot down flat after the other, sharply aware of every creak in the floorboards, and made her way to the bathroom.

She locked the door, tensing with the click of metal into the frame, and sat on the toilet lid. Her fingers shook as she looked over his apps, expecting any second to hear banging on the door. She hadn't settled on what story she would tell to explain having his phone in a locked bathroom.

On the third page of apps, she saw it: A gray icon with "T" in the middle, and below that: Teleport. Her thumb twitched so badly that it took her three tries to stay on the app. But when it opened, it was password protected. There was no guessing at it, the row of blank circles wanted a long string of characters. She'd never figure it out.

But she didn't need to, did she? He had Teleport. How many people had that? She'd never even heard of the damn thing until Megan mentioned it.

She swiped back and tried to open his email account, but that too was password protected. "Bastard," she mouthed silently.

He would take his phone to work tomorrow and there would be no going through it then. Her eyes went up and down the colorful rows of apps, but none of them looked like anything unusual. She spent minutes opening contacts, notes, and photos apps, not seeing anything that would indicate he belonged to a cult or wasn't who he said he was.

She swiped to another page and hit a dead end. Her eyes darted up and down the last rows of apps, trying to take in what each of them was labeled.

She saw a small orange square that looked like a calculator, with plus, minus, multiply and divide symbols. Something about it struck her, and she stared at it, wondering why a calculator app would insist on drawing her attention. She did a quick calculation—two plus two. Four appeared. Then, something told her to hold her finger down on the app. She did and up came six empty circles.

It wanted a passcode.

Now she knew why the app had pulled her attention. Last year, she'd narrated a book where a character having an affair had used a fake calculator app to hide nude photos of another character. She'd thought the idea was so clever that she'd done a search and discovered the app wasn't fiction. It existed.

And here it was on her husband's phone.

She put in Firio's birthdate and the app shook a little. Wrong code. She tried her own birthday. Nothing. The baby's due date. Nope.

Worried the app would lock and he'd see that the next time he tried to open it, she decided to try one last time before giving up.

Her finger pushed *one two three four five six*.

The app opened, and her heart was pumping so

thickly she could hear the *thump thump thump* of it pulsing in her ears.

She saw a blue folder labeled "P." Inside were various PDFs. She opened one, and it took her a few moments to register that it was the performance review she'd found on his desk about six weeks ago, the one that showed his tanked stock picks.

Eyes wide and mouth frozen open, she scrolled through it. It was the same document. She suddenly realized what this meant—the performance review she'd read was faked. He hadn't picked any bad stocks. He'd merely found bad stocks and pretended he'd picked them.

He'd left the document out for her to find, knowing his uncommunicative behavior during those weeks and his continual blaming it on "work stuff" would make her start to snoop around his work materials. And the desperate-sounding Post-It note to his friend Michael would lead her straight to what he wanted her to see. How the hell did he know her so well?

She closed out the PDF and opened a JPEG labeled "H&M."

It was the picture of Hayden and Mitch that "For-merTruther" had emailed to her. The picture of them staring at an older man with white hair, presumably the leader of The True Way, the man Hayden called "President."

Her gut was so cold and sick, and her hands so unsteady, that she lay the phone on her knees. Her stomach was too big to place the phone on her lap, so she kept her knees angled upwards so it wouldn't slide off and hit the hard tile.

With her face in her closed fists, she sat pulling long funnels of air through her nose, thinking she would probably wet herself or throw up any moment.

Firio had emailed her the photo. The original post on the "Cults Exposed" site from FormerTruther was a few years old, so that must have been legitimate. But she remembered that after reading the post, she'd left her laptop on the kitchen island. Firio must have seen her email, later set up an account and sent her the photo. There was no other way he could have a photo like that unless he was part of the cult.

But she suspected Firio hadn't taken the photo himself. If he had, he probably wouldn't have risked going backstage and meeting Hayden at *Loverly*.

She didn't think she could handle any more information, but found herself picking up the phone and searching for more. Seeing a PDF labeled "Favorites," she opened it.

This was a scan of a Q&A she'd given to a magazine years ago. One of the thousands of interviews she'd given over the years.

Q: Favorite drink?

Piper: Coffee in the morning. Licorice tea at night.

Q: Favorite animal?

Piper: My dog, Marvin. He makes me laugh.

Q: Favorite vacation spot?
Piper: Venice.

Q: Favorite food?
Piper: Pizza. I love everything Italian, what can
I say?

Q: Favorite book?
Piper: I couldn't possibly pick a favorite. But
right now I'm reading *Ancient Surprises* by Lilith
Odemay. Highly recommended. My favorite line
is when she says that the world had been leaning
like the Tower of Pisa until she met her one true
love.

That last answer had been highlighted with a yellow
marker.

* * *

BACK IN BED, she was consumed with horror, listening to
the deep, rhythmic breathing of the *thing* next to her.

It was the deliberateness, the calculating, she
couldn't grasp. What she'd almost done to Hayden, that
had been planned, but in a blur of madness. It wasn't
this. To study her and stalk her, to deliberately impregnate her, to manipulate her into murder, this was the
work of a cold-blooded psychopath.

She felt emotionally ravaged, invaded. He must have
analyzed every interview she'd ever given, then spliced

together the driving forces of her personality so astutely that he was able to control her.

Clutching the comforter up around her neck, mute and disoriented, her brain felt shut down, shut down to fend off some of the shock.

She didn't feel competent enough to get anywhere. Her spatial awareness was eroded, she could hardly tell left from right, up from down, and it had taken monumental concentration to unlock the bathroom door and navigate her way to the bed. There was no way she could put on clothes and shoes, get down the dark, creaky stairs, out the locked front door, into the cold, dark front yard, and summon some kind of help. That capacity had simply abandoned her.

Tomorrow, she thought. *In the daylight. When he's gone. I'll pack and find my passport and Social Security card and birth certificate and doctors' files and grab as much baby stuff as I can. I'll go to Jojo's and call police. I can't do it tonight. Please, God, forgive me for not being strong enough to do it tonight. Mom, give me strength.*

There was an ominous chill in the room, an abnormal hush beyond the window drapes, and the old radiator across the room clattered violently, as if being whipped with a chain.

She sensed that a giant force was gathering power outside, but was too incapacitated to get up and try to see what it was.

Chapter Forty-Six

She didn't know when she fell asleep, or how, but the next thing she knew, she awoke out of a dream of peeing herself and felt a dreadful wetness gushing out of her. Sitting up, she reached down to confirm the worst.

Then she said, loudly, "Firio?" and for a long, treasured moment, she was calling for the husband she knew and loved. He still existed. He would flutter his eyes open and take charge. But she remembered: the blue dot at his building, his phone on her lap as she hunched on the toilet, but none of it seemed real. All that was real was the liquid between her legs and needing help.

"Firio!" she said, louder, and he grunted and stirred. "I have to call the doctor," she said, pushing her hand down on his chest.

"Whah?" he slurred.

"My water broke."

He drowsily sat up and turned on the bedside lamp.

Tufts of his hair stuck straight up, the skin on his face was slack, the effects of the sleeping pill.

"My water broke," she repeated, authoritatively, so the announcement would get through to him. "I'm soaked."

"Okay," he said, shaking off his lethargy, and jumping from the bed. "Let's do this."

Downstairs, she stood dressed in a long sweatshirt and thick leggings, a pad between her legs, the birth bag at her feet, and stared with awe through the frosted outside glass door. The world was white. The sun hadn't completely risen yet, but the world was a colorless blanket, and the snow was still falling, so heavily she could barely make out the silhouettes of houses across the street.

"Firio!" she called. "They haven't plowed yet!"

He came and stood next to her. "The Bomb Cyclone. They were warning about it all day yesterday."

Bomb Cyclone. When the hell did they start calling a snowstorm that? "What do we do?" she asked.

"They must have plowed on Church. That's a major street."

"What good does that do us?" Their Mini-Cooper, a mouse of a car, wouldn't even make it out of the driveway.

He looked at her, and it was almost impossible to believe he was evil. His face registered every bit of care that she would want a husband to have. Was it possible he'd used her and loved her at the same time?

He'd done so many things he didn't have to do: His nickname for her. The way he'd hold her hand when they'd fall asleep. The way he'd comfort her after a nightmare. The way he'd rub her sore feet and thick ankles. The later stages of pregnancy were no joke, and he'd practically had to help dress her like a child, even down to putting on her shoes as she could no longer bend over far enough to do it on her own. Could it all have been an act?

He looked at his phone, scrolling and reading, with that slight lip movement thing he did, which was no longer endearing to her, but a grotesque affectation.

"Okay," he said. "There are no cars allowed on the road except emergency vehicles."

"Oh my God!" she wailed and started to cry.

Soon, she would be in the most intense physical pain of her life. Then, she'd be so vulnerable, with a newborn suckling on her breasts and screaming in the night.

How was she going to do this all alone? Who could help her? Sure, friends, her father, would do what they could. But who could be there all the way, all the time, as she and the baby needed?

Pure terror clawed her, to the point where she thought she could rationalize everything she'd seen, everything she knew. He could have been sent to impregnate her, but had fallen in love with her anyway. He could be a victim of the cult too.

He placed one hand on her shoulder, still reading. "Calm down, honey. This is an emergency. We can call 911."

"There's a foot of snow on the road!" she said, thrusting her palm on the frosty glass. "I doubt even an ambulance can get to us."

He ignored her and, in a second, had his phone up to his ear, saying, "Ambulance. Yes, hello, my wife is pregnant and her water broke. She could go into labor any minute. The street isn't plowed, we can't get out." He gave their address then looked over at her, clearly asking for the dispatcher. "Are you having contractions?"

"Not yet."

"No, not yet. Uh-uh." His face went pensive in a way that made her even more afraid. "Hmm. Okay, um. That… hm."

She pawed the phone away from his ear until she had it at her own, wanting to make sure there was a voice there.

"Hello? I'm not contracting. Not yet."

"Ambulances are delayed because of the storm," said a woman with a tinny Brooklyn accent. "I can send one out, but this would be low priority."

"Do you know when they'll plow?"

"Plows are out, ma'am, but when they'll get to your street, I couldn't say."

"Oh. Okay. We'll call you back if need be." She hung up and handed him his phone, painfully aware of everything that was inside of it. "Is the subway running?" she asked.

He tapped at his phone, staring at it for several moments. "According to the MTA it is. Limited service."

"The hospital is only five stops away. That would probably be the quickest."

"Then let's put on your boots."

Chapter Forty-Seven

The neighborhood was empty. They were in a white dystopian world, where everyone but them had disappeared under a nuclear bomb of snow.

Car-shaped mounds of snow lined the street, Christmas lights feebly glowed, and the sidewalk hadn't been shoveled. The white was monolithic, the big, swirling wet flakes needled Piper's lower lids, forcing her to squint.

Her boots went deep into the freshly dumped powder, right up to the fake fur rim around her calves. She clung to her husband's bicep, clung to it as she had on nights when they'd gone out to dinner and had a little too much wine.

At this rate, they wouldn't get to the subway for an hour. After a couple of blocks of difficult and sticky slogging, Firio turned to her. "I'm going to carry you."

"You can't. I'm too heavy."

He ignored her and hefted her into his arms. She

hid her face in his neck as tears silently tried to roll down her face, but the cold was so sharp they froze in the corners of her eyes.

Two blocks later, he lowered her with a grunt, shifting the birth bag back to his shoulder. "We're almost at Church," he said, not making eye contact, as if embarrassed that he couldn't carry her one more foot.

Church Avenue looked recently plowed, with two or three inches of packed snow on the street. A truck barreled towards them, two white-hazy headlights flashing through the veil of swirly snowflakes. Firio stuck out his arm and tried to wave the truck down, but it rumbled by them, kicking up a spray of dirty slush.

Firio hung one glove in his teeth and stared at his phone. Then he pulled it out and said, "I don't see one damn car lift."

"They're not supposed to be on the road."

"Neither was that truck. We should try 911 again."

"No." She shook her head. "I'm not contracting. If ambulances are delayed that means there's people who need them more than I do right now. Let's keep going. If the trains aren't running, we'll call."

She trudged ahead and he had no choice but to follow. A few minutes later, she spotted the green glass globe capped with snow that marked the subway stop.

He firmly held her arm as they navigated the snow-drifted steps down into the subway. They had reached the slushy floor when her uterus seized with pain, causing her to grab Firio's arm and double over moaning. She stood bent in half with eyes clenched shut and cheeks puffed out until the pain drew away. The contraction felt like it had gone on forever, though she knew it was only about thirty seconds.

"Fuck this," she said, breathless from the sharpness of the pain, the realness of it, no longer a distant fear or curiosity. "Fuck this shit!"

"Oh, Bella." Him using his pet name for her sent a waft of disgust through her, a rancid odor she could smell. Lying faker. How had he done this to her? Why had he done this to her?

"Make sure the train is running," she ordered as he looked at his phone again.

"According to the MTA it is."

"Fucking MTA, you better not fail me now!" she shouted. "I'm in no mood!"

Firio looked scared and that gave her a momentary pleasure. Her belly pressed through the turnstile, and they inched down the stairs to the westbound platform. When she spotted a speckle of people waiting at the other end, relief poured through her. The subway was running. And, like a voice from the heavens, came an announcement.

"There is a local westbound train three stops away," intoned the slightly inhuman female voice. Piper glanced at the subway timetable: A train would arrive in seven minutes.

Her anxiety ebbed away, the antiquated subway system coming to her rescue. Knowing that a train was on the way, and she would soon be safe in the hospital, her primal reliance on Firio abated.

With that came a bigger opening for her anger. It boiled up as she stared at his chiseled face, that chin dimple, those lips she'd kissed so many times. That face she'd loved looking at, but now appeared hard, aloof, and shark-like, with no human spark. A smashable face.

"I'm not your breeder, *friend*," she said in a low voice.

He looked down at her, eyes flapping wide in astonishment. "Excuse me?"

"I said I'm not your *breeder*."

"Piper, are you—"

"Don't touch me," she said, pushing away his hands.

"Breeder? Are you—?" An indulgent smile. "Oh, I get it. It's all my fault. The pain. I'm sorry you're going through this, honey. Lean on me."

"Don't touch me!" she exploded.

"Bella, you've got to—"

"Don't call me 'Bella,' you piece of shit." Something had taken over. There was no controlling it, not with trying to manage her pain too. "I know you got me pregnant on purpose. I know you've been trying to make me kill Hayden, so I'd go to prison. I know *everything*."

She watched as his face marveled at her, wondrous with unadulterated shock. Then slowly, very, very slowly, like gear wheels turning, his dark eyes grew even darker, until they were flat and black as onyx. A look she'd never seen on him before. That was when she knew beyond any doubt that her worst fears were true.

"Where's your phone?" he asked, his voice low.

She said nothing, and he glanced down at the birth

bag at his feet. The implication was clear—he wanted to make sure he wasn't being recorded. But her phone was in her coat pocket. Taking it out, her pulse pumped wildly as she held the off button until it chimed and showed him the black screen. He looked around, checking to see if anyone was near them.

"I didn't get you pregnant on purpose," he hissed out. "Ava wasn't happy about it at first, either."

Her mouth dropped. She had a sudden vision of how stupid and cartoonish she must look, her jaw hanging wide open. She wanted to shout, *Ava?!!!* It was right on her tongue. But her brain was working faster than her impulse. She had to let him think she knew everything, though it was abundantly clear she didn't know half of it.

The stirrings of another cramp grumbled deep within her uterus, and before she'd have to double over, she snarled, "So you got lucky."

"Not exactly. But after it happened, what could we do? Now Ava likes the idea of a kid for us. Can't say I'm too thrilled at the prospect, but she controls the purse strings."

"Your whore isn't coming anywhere near my child," she seethed.

"Listen, getting a divorce and having your new girl-friend help raise the kid isn't illegal. Any chance you'll tell me how you figured this all out?"

"Guess I'm not as gullible as you thought, asshole. So Hayden dead, that would…" She tried for a confi-dent, neutral tone that would lure him into confirming her suspicions. "Get both of us out of the picture. Then you and Ava have a child for The True Way. A little True Way robot."

"Robot?" He scowled at her. "You've got some disturbing ideas. We don't belong to that stupid thing. But Ava knew all about it."

Her throat went dry as she realized the main theory she'd been hanging everything on was apparently wrong. But she had to keep talking so that he would keep talking.

"The picture of Mitch and Hayden with the cult leader. Ava took that?"

"Far as I know. She'd gone to some meetings before he quit."

Realizing the plan hadn't been about breeding for The True Way, she could only think of one other reason that people generally wanted other people dead. He'd mentioned "purse strings."

"It's about the money," she threw out. "Hayden's money."

"He hasn't written a good song in ages, can't tour because of health problems, the Broadway thing is ending," he said, sounding like this was all patently obvious. "The judge thing came up, but she knew there was no chance there, not with Ferrari wanting to be the only stud on the panel." His eyes roamed over her head, checking on the train's arrival, then back to her. "She's got all kinds of insurance on him. He changed his will to leave her everything. He's worth far more dead than alive. If he got killed by his *American Star* rival? Ava figured his back catalog would skyrocket in value. Now guess which lowly stock analyst would help manage those copyrights?"

Poor Hayden. He was either oblivious or in total denial that his fiancée had so many financial reasons to want him dead. He was as naïve as Piper realized she too had been. The man she used to love was looking down at her, a revolting smear of self-satisfaction on his face.

"So you didn't figure it all out, eh?" he asked.

"I know everything except how long—" A cramp began to take hold, and she clenched her eyes shut, huffing air in and out of her cheeks. *Whoo whoo whoo.* But it wasn't a full contraction, just the threat of one. When it mercifully drew away, she swallowed hard and continued, "—how long you and Ava have been together."

"Oh," he said, looking reminiscent. "Year and a half ago? She came to my firm to invest Tower's money. I had to research him, and that led me to you, and your ex, and how much I looked like him. Ava joked about it one night, whether I could get you to kill Tower, given how much you probably hated him. Imagine my surprise when you began saying you felt like you'd been cursed after you won the show. Bingo. It became a game. One with a big payoff if it worked."

"All those late work nights. You were with her. Hayden was clueless because he was doing *Loverly*."

His only reaction was a barely perceptible shrug.

"So you never loved me. Do you even love her?"

"What is love?" he asked, philosophically.

"How can you do this?" she asked, despising how needy she sounded. "What did I ever do to you? I loved you! Do you think money will fill up your soul? I've had money. It won't!"

"I didn't mean… It's not like I don't…" He sighed almost apologetically. "You weren't supposed to get pregnant."

Piper could read his thoughts with chilling clarity. Stranger he may be, but she'd spent enough time with him to know something of him. It's not that he didn't feel *something* for her. He just didn't feel the way others, others not like him, would have felt. There was no point in trying to appeal to his feelings, because he didn't have those kinds of feelings.

Now she only wanted answers to parts of the plot and had an intuition that even though she was supposed to have figured everything out, he'd want to boast.

"How did you know Crystal would tell me about The True Way?"

"We didn't. We planned to spell it out for you, but once she did that, we didn't have to."

"Hayden smoking a cigarette by the Broadway station. How'd you keep tabs on that?"

"Ava paid the driver to keep an eye on him."

"You knew I'd follow him. Did you have a tracker on me?"

"Tracker?" he snorted. "I knew the more I'd tell you not to follow him, the more you would. The more I'd tell you not to open the letters, the more you would. Pretty much every interview you'd say, 'Tell me I can't do something, and that's a sure-fire way to get me to do it.'" He paused and eyed her with what looked like admiration. "You put a tracker in with the money, didn't you?

That fan ran her mouth. I told Ava to forget the ten grand, but she doesn't take losses well."

"Why would you tie yourself to the money? It's sitting in your office."

He looked as if he might laugh at her. "Not anymore. I'm sure Ava's picked it up by now. She's greedy, that one." The way he said *greedy* made Piper realize he was *attracted* to that trait of hers.

"The letters—which of you wrote those gems?"

"I'd call it a joint venture. She thought we should wait until the second trimester to start sending them, until the pregnancy was safe."

Piper remembered how he'd suggested Ava as the letter writer and realized that must have been part of the fun for him, skirting so close to the truth while still evading detection.

"Thank your piece of trash for that," Piper said, acidly. "Do you understand the danger you put us in? You didn't give a shit about my high blood pressure or that I could have gone over the platform with him, or that I could have fallen and hurt the baby that is yours too."

His eyes glazed over, as if he didn't quite understand everything she was saying. "It's not like that," he mumbled, an answer that made no sense because it *was* like that. The hint of regret in his voice infuriated her even more because it meant he'd had enough feeling, enough morality, to understand he should reverse course, but hadn't.

"Now I'll be telling your fucked up story to the cops," she said.

He slowly shook his head. The look on his face was one Piper recognized—it always preceded him calling her "Bella" and saying something condescending.

"I don't think you'll have much success there. There's no proof of anything and I'll tell them how you've been acting. Would you like to hear something?"

She watched as he drew his phone out of his coat pocket. He tapped at it. She heard her own voice, choking with sobs. The voice she'd had the night of her nightmare about Marvin blackened with fire, and her stabbing Hayden.

I'll kill him. Hayden. I'll kill him. I hate him. I hate him so much.

He cursed me!

Firio pressed his phone. Her nightmare voice disappeared.

It took her a moment to realize what had happened. When she'd awoken Firio with her nightmare cries, he'd turned to look at his phone for the time. He'd also activated a recording app.

"You want child protective services to hear that?" he asked. "You're determined to kill a man you think cursed you. My baby isn't safe around you."

In a flash, her arm jerked up and knocked his phone from his hand. It went clattering to the platform.

"Bitch," he growled, eyes storming.

He moved towards the phone and bent over. She heard the grumble of the approaching train and saw a cone of light splash onto the grimy wall of the tunnel.

The full contraction slammed her, and she staggered forward as he began to stand.

There was a moment, she would always know it, when she could have twisted off to one side. But in that moment, she continued mission-like ahead, throwing all her baby weight and rage-force at his back, her animal cry of pain melding with the boom of the arriving train.

Chapter Forty-Eight

American Star's Piper Dunner is Still Standing

An *Entertainment Daily* Exclusive

By Amy Baldash

*S*he was our *American Star*. Millions of us power-dialed for her win like our lives depended on it.

With the voice of a feisty angel, the look of the girl next door, and the ambition of a Fortune 500 CEO, Piper Dunner won not only the iconic talent show but our hearts and wallets, making her debut album, *There's Nothing Between Piper and Her Dream*, go platinum.

But the ensuing years were rife with calamity—Piper's mother, a proud fixture in the show's audience, died of uterine cancer at 57. A paralyzed vocal cord left Piper's post-*Star* career on life support. And her beloved rescue dog, Marvin, perished in a Los Angeles apartment fire that also claimed years' worth of precious songwriting.

Then, like in an *American Star* coronation song, Piper rose from the ashes with marriage, pregnancy, and newfound happiness.

Only the cruel fates descended once more, sending the seventh *American Star* champion headlong into a hellish nightmare from which, a year after her husband's death, she is only beginning to emerge.

For the first time since her life took such an unfathomable turn, Piper Dunner is speaking in our cover story about that life-altering day.

"It's been surreal," she says, curled up in a mauve cardigan on a plush white sofa inside of her candle-lit alcove sitting room in the bucolic Brooklyn neighborhood of Ditmas Park. A small Christmas tree twinkles in the corner. "I never thought I'd have the most horrible and most euphoric experiences of my life on the same day."

As the country knows, Piper went into labor during the New York City-paralyzing Bomb Cyclone of last December. She and her husband, financial analyst Porfirio Romano, tried making their way to the hospital by subway. On the platform, Piper fainted, falling onto her husband and sending him into the path of an oncoming train.

"That was the worst, and yet the best day of my life, meeting my baby girl and saying goodbye to my husband at the same time. And knowing that I—" She takes a sharp breath as her face collapses. "What they told me had happened. What the people on the platform saw."

Her hands flutter on her cheeks, wiping away tears.

"I wish—I wish our last time together had been a better one. I was in a lot of pain, and kind of took it out on him. At one point, I even told him not to touch me." She appears so sad it's unclear if she'll be able to finish the interview. But she bravely continues, "Those hormones were rushing through my body like a raging river. I remember having a contraction so hard I knocked my husband's phone from his hand. Then I… blanked out. When I came to, people were looking down at me." She heaves a sigh of relief. "Thank God Flynn was okay."

On cue, a smiling, hearty-looking older man, Piper's father, enters the sitting room. Eleven-month-old Flynn is fast asleep in the carrier strapped to her grandfather's chest.

The baby has Piper's flawless skin and rosy cheeks. But, Piper asserts, Flynn's eyes are the spitting image of her father's. Seeing her baby, Piper's tears instantly dry and she stands, kissing Flynn's light auburn curls. "Let's not wake her," she whispers to her father, who nods and disappears into another room.

"Firio had the most beautiful eyes—deep, dark, and tender. Every time I look at Flynn I see him. It's a comfort."

What will she tell Flynn about how her father died?

Piper's face is an anguished mosaic of emotion. "I'm committed to telling her the truth when she's old enough," she finally says, taking an unsteady sip of tea. "Very bad things, tragic accidents happen, and unfortunately, she'll grow up knowing this truth much earlier than she should. But she'll have all the love in the world, and that's more than a lot of children have.

Of course, no marriage is perfect. Firio and I had our disagreements. But as far as Flynn is concerned, she'll grow up knowing her father was a loving man who already adored her." She twists her fingers in her lap, staring at them. "The last thing he said to me was, 'Hold on, honey, we're almost there. I'll be with you.'" Looking back up, her eyes are glistening with tears, and she touches her heart. "I feel that. He's with us."

After a month-long investigation, the district attorney declined to bring charges against Piper. "To be investigated, it was…" Unable to continue, she grabs a nearby tissue and hides her eyes behind it for several moments. But once again she finds the strength to go on. "I understand they had to do their jobs."

It was shortly after the tragedy that *American Star* announced that the Season 7 winner would be returning to her talent show roots, this time as a judge on the competition's reboot.

"I didn't know if I should reach out to her, given everything," says executive producer Oliver Corbyn. "But I was assured by Jojo [Barr] that Piper needed something positive in her life. And we wanted her. We wanted her before all of this happened. She and Jojo make a great team and the audience agrees. This season's ratings have been beyond our expectations."

As the country also knows, at the same time Piper was suffering unspeakable catastrophe, Nolan Ferrari, who had been slated to take up his mantle as the nopunches-pulled judge on the panel, fell under suspicion for his role in a hit-and-run on Jojo Barr.

A sixteen-year-old male, whose name is being withheld due to his age, pled guilty to charges of misdemeanor vehicular assault for hitting Barr with an SUV last fall, breaking her wrist. Reportedly, the teen committed the crime to please Ferrari, who is part owner of The Ginger Moggy bistro, where the teen worked as a dishwasher.

Ferrari has not been charged with any crime, and he vehemently denies any part in what authorities called a hate crime against the popular singer, but the network and producers made the decision to release him from his contract.

"I don't have anything to say other than what I've already released," Ferrari emailed through his publicist. "I'm happy for the success of the new *American Star* and am celebrating my memoir's twenty straight weeks on the *New York Times* bestseller list."

"It was difficult," says Corbyn. "I've known Nolan half my life. I don't believe he had anything to do with what happened with Jojo. But we wanted to start on a clean slate. The show is about talented kids reaching for their dreams. We didn't want to distract from that. Nor did we want Jojo in an uncomfortable position."

Corbyn says the desire to add Piper to the judges' panel was a natural one, but he wasn't sure she would accept it. But she did, and along with Crystal Pell, the panel became an all-female crew.

Piper says joining *American Star* in the wake of her husband's death saved her from a debilitating depression that kept her a recluse in her house, fending off paparazzi camped on the sidewalk trying to get snapshots of her baby.

"I'll always be grateful to Oliver," she says. "Work was what I needed to pull myself together for Flynn's sake. Returning to the *American Star* family was like coming home."

She has her true fans too, the ones who've been with her since the original *Star* days, her "Pipermints." Pointing at a three-foot-high white teddy bear with a red bow around its neck propped in a corner rocking chair, she says, "That's from my friend Megan in San Francisco. My fans mean everything to me."

"She's one hell of a trouper," says Jojo Barr, who remained friends with Piper from the time they were roommates during Season 7. "I can't imagine going through everything she's been through and still being able to get up in the morning. But she wants her daughter to have a mother who can function emotionally, who can be stable, even joyous. That's very important to her."

Flynn wasn't the only family member Piper gained in the past year. According to tabloid reports, her late husband's parents, whom Piper believed to be dead, were alive and well and living in Italy, along with a large extended family.

Piper refuses to get into the details, only saying, "This is the one time I'll address this. Yes, it's true. Flynn had grandparents that I hadn't met. We have since met them, and so long as everything goes well, they're welcome to a relationship with her." A flinty look crosses her face and it's clear the topic is closed.

Piper also has some news that she hasn't shared with anyone until now.

"You'll be the first to know that Hayden Tower will be returning to *Star*, as a special mentor. He's got quite a nurturing side that the public hasn't seen yet."

While there have been tabloid reports that the pair are dating, Piper has not yet responded to the rumors.

Is there anything else she'd like to tell us?

"Hayden has been so supportive of Flynn and me. I don't know what we'd do without him. He even came over last week and cleaned out my chimney flue." She giggles, the sound of undiluted happiness. "Or tried. He got all sooty and we called in a professional."

Millions of women would be thrilled to see Hayden Tower covered in soot and—more to the point—in need of a shower. Is Piper one of them? Is "Hayder" finally a reality?

Piper sips at her tea, as if trying to hide her flaming cheeks. "We're friends. It's been a rough year for both of us."

Indeed, if there wasn't already enough drama on the *American Star* front, Hayden Tower had his share of it, firing his longtime manager, Ava Smythson, and ending their engagement.

It's unclear what sparked the break, but an anonymous item in *The Hollywood Buzz* claims that Smythson was having an affair with a man who worked on Wall Street. (Reached on her phone, Smythson said, "How did you get this number? No comment!" before hanging up.)

"Karma is an interesting thing. Sometimes people get what they deserve." Piper smiles cryptically, then says, "Hayden needs someone genuine."

Could Piper be that person?

She waves, the color in her cheeks still burning bright. "We're taking things as they come." She then appears mortified at having revealed more than she intended.

"I'll always be there for Piper," says Hayden Tower on the phone. "She's become one of my best friends. I can't wait to nurture fresh talent with her, Jojo, and Crystal. The show needs a shot of testosterone, don't you think?" He laughs. "I mean, besides Mitch."

Perhaps the biggest talent to come out of the new *American Star* will be Piper herself. Her six-song EP, *Survivor*, drops next week. [Also: Check out our next issue, where Piper Dunner will reveal the secrets of her fabulously toned post-baby bod!]

Some early reviews are in, and the album sounds like it has the potential to be a smash hit. The most special song, Piper says, is "My Christmas Angel."

"Written for Firio. It happened so close to Christmas, and it was... not having him here... but he's like an angel around Flynn and me." She takes a deep breath that seems to renew her, and says with a flash of the perky, steel-willed smile we know from *American Star*, "Christmas songs, if they hit, it's royalties forever."

"It may seem odd that I was recording during this time," she continues. "But the show was only filming two days a week. I didn't want to fall into depression. There was so much emotion—despair, guilt, and happiness because of Flynn. I had to get it all out or I'd go insane. I kept writing and writing. Hayden helped set up a studio in my garage. We got producer Carlotta Graves, which was a huge coup, and banged out the songs in a few months. I was fortunate to get signed by Oliver's new label."

Is Piper truly ready for superstardom again? The paparazzi, the tabloids, and the social media outrage?

Piper shrugs, folding her hands in her lap. "I only concentrate on the good aspects of fame. The fans, the *Star* contestants I can help, and my charities. Please check out my website [www.pipersdream.com] for more information on the Run for Cancer, which I'll be participating in this spring, in honor of my mother. Otherwise, I don't pay attention to mean people. I choose positivity."

At the door, there's a flare of resolute hope in Piper's eyes. Her house is warmly lit up, her baby is fast asleep, and her peaceful neighborhood is serene in the gloaming.

"Life has a funny way of working itself out," she says, inhaling the fresh, crisp air. "With family, friends, and fans, anything is possible."

She smiles again, this time it's the smile of a woman who, against all the odds, has achieved her dream.

"I'm still here," she says, "and I'm still standing."

There's Nothing Between Me and My Dream

I was in darkness
Trying to find my way out
Waiting on life
To begin

But all at once
I realized
It came down to me
To turn on the light
So I could see

There's nothing between me and my dream

Won't stop myself anymore
It's right here in front of me
I can touch it, taste it
I'm mellow like Jell-O
Sweet as marshmallow

There's nothing between me and my dream
Here is my moment, my time in the sun
Just reach for it
The dream has begun

There's nothing between me and my dream
Me and my dream
Me and my dream

Everything is in you

Nothing will pass you by
If you trust in the stars
And open your own heart

Forever is here, now is the time
The horizon is in you
The sun and the moon
Kick that mountain over, yeah, another too
The dream has begun
For me and for you

Me and my dream
Me and my dream
There's nothing between me and my dream

More Thrillers by C.G. Twiles

Please see CGTwiles.com or my Instagram page for all books and retailers.

Please request my books at your **local library** or **bookstore**.

Brooklyn Gothic*: A Modern Gothic Romantic Thriller*

While working in a Gothic mansion, an idealistic young reporter begins to suspect her multimillionaire boss—and lover—is keeping dark secrets.

The Neighbors in Apartment 3D*: A Domestic Suspense Novel*

Cintra suspects her new neighbors have kidnapped a child. But who will believe a compulsive liar?

The Little Girl in the Window*: A Psychological Thriller*

When a little blonde girl with eerily blue eyes appears in Romy's window hurling insults, she knows her buried secret has caught up with her. But how does the little girl know about it? And how to stop her before she reveals it?

About the Author

C.G. Twiles is the pseudonym for a longtime writer and reporter who has written for some of the world's largest magazines and newspapers.

She enjoys traveling, animals, old houses, ancient history, and cemeteries. She lives in Brooklyn.

Please find her on social media, she'd love to connect!

facebook.com/cgtwiles

instagram.com/cgtwiles

goodreads.com/cgtwiles

bookbub.com/profile/c-g-twiles

Acknowledgments

Thank you first of all to my readers, who make everything possible.

I'd like to thank those who took the time to read earlier drafts of *The Last Star Standing* and offer feedback and support: Liz Alterman, Megan Easley-Walsh, Kim Brittingham, Amna Naseer, Megan Monaghan, Jean Erbesfeld, Heather Teixeira and Sally Neiman. Eternal thanks to Mary Cain for being a design savant and to Shannon Bennett for being the voice of reason.

A debt of gratitude to the obvious muse for this project: *American Idol* and its Idolsphere, including the old forums reached via Wayback Machine and the Mjsbigblog. Special thanks to the man who will always be my Idol baby, Season 7 winner David Cook.